Sally Patricia

The Sweetest Empire

By

Sally Patricia Gardner

Henry May Publications
Copyright © 2007 by Sally Patricia Gardner
All Rights Reserved

Also by Sally Patricia Gardner:

Lillian's Story,
One Woman's Journey through the 20th Century

Painting by Numbers

Finding Cordelia

To a Lady, with some painted flowers.

Flowers to the fair: to you these flowers I bring,
And strive to greet you with an earlier spring.
Flowers sweet, and gay, and delicate like you:
Emblems of innocence, and beauty too.
With flowers the Graces bind their yellow hair,
And flowery wreaths consenting lovers wear.
Flowers, the sole luxury which nature knew,
In Eden's pure and guiltless garden grew.
To loftier forms are rougher tasks assign'd:
The sheltering oak resists the stormy wind,
The tougher yew repels invading foes,
And the tall pine for future navies grows:
But this soft family, to cares unknown,
Were born for pleasure and delight alone.
Gay without toil, and lovely without art,
They spring to cheer the sense, and glad the heart.
Nor blush, my fair, to own you copy these:
Your best, your sweetest empire is – to please.'

Mrs. Anna Letitia Barbauld.

This is the story of successive generations of women
who refused to know their place.
And a heartfelt 'thank you' to their real life
counterparts.

Table of Contents

Prologue.

Part One: Mary, born 1850

Part Two: Elizabeth, born 1878

Part Three: Kitty, born 1894

Part Four: Hyacinth, born 1907

Part Five: Charlotte, born 1922

Part Six: Esther, born 1938

Epilogue.

Prologue

She had always been frightened of horses, so that made it all the more ironic. But deep down she knew that her very fear had to be part of the sacrifice if it was going to mean anything at all. This time she was not going to fail.

It was a mellow, warm June day. Odd to be thinking so carefully about what to wear. As if it had ever mattered. Though as she chose a scarlet hat and gloves, the colour her one nod to both the gaiety and the defiance she was feeling, her mind flew back to that other red hat, so long ago. If she closed her eyes tightly she could still see her mother's delighted expression as she tried it on in front of the large, gilt-framed mirror over the dining-room fireplace and the look of pride on her father's face…

Part One: Mary

1868

"New hats for both my girls," declared her father, gently pushing Mary to stand by her mother. Mother and daughter's reflections beamed back at him together. Mother with the frivolous hat perched on her dark curls. Mary in her shiny new mortar-board. Wide smiles on both faces.

"This is going to be a year to remember for the Morrison family, thanks to my two talented women," he pronounced.

So like him to celebrate her achievement as a triumph for the whole family, thought Mary. As indeed it was. Mary knew how fortunate she was that her parents believed in education for women and were happy to let her accept the scholarship to the college. Most of her school friends would not have been given the time or the encouragement to study, let alone take the exams. Even the Queen seemed to think that educating women was a waste of time. But Richard Morrison had married Dora at least partly because her intelligent conversation delighted him, not in spite of it. The news of Mary's academic success afforded him the kind of pride that most fathers reserved for their sons.

Putting his face between them so that all three were posed in the mirror he announced, "And tomorrow I have a treat for us all. We are going to the Derby. A chance for your mother to show off her new hat, and for me to show off my clever daughter."

They all rose early the following day. Richard had been to the Derby a couple of times before with some colleagues from the bank, but neither of the two women had ever been near a racecourse. It was quite a long ride on the tram, but, with their picnic basket stowed at their feet, their excitement helped it to pass quickly. When they finally arrived at Epsom, Mary was taken aback by the noise and bustle of the large crowd, but thrilled by the feeling that she was part of something exciting and special.

They did not manage to get near to the rail for the first race and so were only able to see the flash of the jockeys' colours through the cheering figures in front of them. Mary was startled by the noise of the horses' hooves on the turf and the way the ground seemed to shake as they pounded past on their way to the finishing post. The winner of the race received an enormous cheer, though for most people it must have been merely a reaction to the tension, as all around them betting tickets were being thrown away with grimaces of disgust.

"Would you like to choose a horse for the next race?" asked Richard.

Mary and her mother looked at him in disbelief. From virtually every pulpit in the land sermons were preached against gambling, which apparently went hand in hand with the demon drink as the shortest road to hell. Richard laughed at them.

"Come along now, choose a name from the board and I will place a bet for us all. It will add to the fun, I promise you."

And so it did. They chose a horse called Nightingale and found they were shouting for him in a quite abandoned way, to Richard's amusement. But, as he pointed out, the aristocratic ladies in the stands were behaving in a similar boisterous fashion, so after that Dora relaxed. Nightingale trailed in somewhere at the back, to their disappointment, but Richard insisted that they try again. This time they chose a horse called Blue Gown, because Mary was wearing just such a dress. Richard said it had quite long odds and was unlikely to win, but they had glimpsed him in the paddocks and had seen that he was a splendid horse so they told Richard that they would stay with their choice. They had secured a place at the rail by now and their excitement knew no bounds when their horse came in first.

Richard went off to collect their winnings. "Enough for several hats," he chortled.

The two women decided to walk round the course to try and catch another glimpse of their favourite. As they moved toward the paddocks a sudden commotion broke out in front of them and a scream rent the air. Startled, the two women were torn apart by a rush of people and before they had time to realise what was happening, a large black horse came surging toward Dora, who was powerless to move out of its path. Mary heard herself scream as she saw her mother thrown to the ground. The next moment someone had grabbed the reins of the panicked horse and was holding on for dear life as it reared and foamed at the mouth. Several men came running up, and as the horse was finally calmed down and moved away, Mary pushed her way toward her mother's lifeless figure.

"Let me through, oh please, let me through," she sobbed, and people fell back to make a path for her.

As she reached her mother she heard a masculine voice saying, "Make way, please, I'm a doctor."

She looked up to see an elderly gentleman emerge from the crowd. He fell on his knees beside her and took her mother's wrist in his hand.

"Thank God," he said, "There is a pulse. She is still alive. We must get her home. Is she your mother?"

Mary nodded.

"Bear up, my dear," he said, "I think she hit her head when she fell, but I don't believe there is any other damage. Do you have a carriage here?"

Mary shook her head, suddenly unable to speak. With relief she heard her father's voice and the next moment she was in his arms.

"Sir, is this lady your wife?" asked the doctor, as Richard knelt beside the motionless figure.

Holding his wife tenderly, he replied, "Indeed, she is, Sir."

"Tell me where you live and I will take you all home in my carriage, then you can send for your own physician."

Back in their Norwood home, Dora was still lying unconscious on the sofa. Mary, recovering some of her usual composure and trying to stop her hands shaking, carefully removed Dora's hat. She was shocked to see that it had been concealing a mass of dried blood. Richard sent their maidservant, Alice, for Dr White, who came straight away.

Dr White examined the wound on Dora's head and sent Alice for some warm water. Between them, he and Mary cleaned the wound and while they were doing this a long, soft sigh escaped from Dora's lips. Almost immediately her fluttering eyelids showed that she was coming back to life.

"Mrs Morrison, this is Dr White. Can you hear me?"

After a moment's blank look, Dora focused her eyes on the doctor and nodded weakly.

"Mary," she murmured, "Where is Mary?"

Mary moved forward to take her mother's hand, as Richard, who had fallen back to allow for the doctor's ministrations, came into his wife's line of vision.

All he was able to say was, "Oh, Dora, my love," before a sob stopped his voice.

Dora struggled into a sitting position and, with a touch of her usual perkiness, asked, "Just how did I get home? No, never mind, tell me later. Are we all going to have a cup of tea now? As I remember we never did eat our picnic."

Everyone realised that, pale and shaken though Dora was, she was trying to restore some normality to the situation, and Alice was dispatched to make the tea.

Having prescribed a dose of laudanum for Dora in order to calm her nerves, Dr White departed, promising to call again the next day. Richard went to the apothecary in the next street with the prescription while Mary summoned Alice to help her take Dora upstairs to bed. Mary was alarmed to see how unsteady her mother was and relieved when Richard returned with the medicine. Unused to dealing with drugs, they measured it carefully into a tumbler of water, and Richard took it up to his wife.

Mary and her father picked at the supper of cold ham that Alice had prepared for them before deciding to retire to bed themselves. Richard, still almost as pale as his wife, kissed Mary goodnight, saying ruefully, "Sorry, my darling, not quite the celebration I had in mind."

Mary decided she was too worried and overwrought to sleep so she lit the oil lamp, and, sitting in the chair by the fire, picked up her much-thumbed copy of John Milton's *Paradise Lost*. She was to read literature at Holloway College and already had her reading list. She had been delighted to find that she already possessed most of the books on it. Tonight, though, the words and images were superseded by the events of the day.

At last, she drifted into an uneasy sleep, waking in a panic at the noise of horses' hooves. She discovered the volume of poetry had slipped off her lap, knocking the brass companion set onto the tiled hearth. Wearily, she set everything to rights, doused the lamp, and finally prepared for bed. Her last conscious thought, as the dawn started to colour the sky, was to wonder what the morning would bring.

1870

Mary let herself into the darkened house with her usual slight trepidation. The silence felt like a physical presence. She was relieved to hear Alice bustling along the hall toward her.

"Oh, Alice, how is Mother?" she asked, removing her hatpins and laying her hat and satchel of books on the side table, "Has she had a good day?"

"Passing good, Miss," replied Alice. Mary knew what that meant. It meant that Dora had slept a lot, eaten a little and spoken hardly at all. "I gave her the medicine about half an hour ago. She's asleep again now."

"Thank you, Alice," Mary said. "Look, I'll get the supper tonight. You go out with that young man of yours."

"Well, if you are sure, Miss," said Alice, already loosening the strings on her apron.

"Of course I am," replied Mary. "Go on. Let yourself in quietly when you come home though, in case Father retires early."

Going through into the drawing room she collapsed onto the sofa under the window. She was conscious of familiar and recurring pangs of guilt because when she was at college she felt young and motivated and full of life and fun, but the minute she arrived home depression descended on her like a dark veil. Her father would be home soon. Always coming through the door anticipating some miracle. That Dora would be dressed and animated, or at very least bearing some relation to the woman he had loved and married.

In her heart of hearts, Mary knew this was never going to happen. The woman Dora had been died on that fateful day at Epsom. The querulous, sometimes demanding, but most often frighteningly fragile and passive invalid upstairs was the remnant of that intelligent and active person. Richard had consulted various physicians who talked vaguely of 'nervous disorders' and 'pressure on the brain' but offered no remedies that might release Dora from her twilight prison.

Mary went through to the kitchen to prepare a meal for herself and her father. If they ate as soon as he came home she would have time to study. As she chopped vegetables and filled saucepans her mind was occupied with the day's lectures. She could no longer discuss her lessons with her parents as she had when at school. Dora was not well enough and Richard was too distracted. But her longing for the stimulation of intelligent conversation was now being filled by her college friends.

She had become especially intimate with Violet, who, like herself, was on a scholarship and reading literature. Mary greatly admired the sharp mind of her friend and they had fallen into the habit of eating their lunchtime sandwiches together. The two girls had many lively and enjoyable debates concerning the merits of their favourite writers. Each had visited the other's house to meet their families and had encountered mutual approval.

Mary had felt able to confide in Violet how distressed she was at seeing her mother's gradual deterioration. Just being able to admit to another person that she had little hope of improvement in Dora's condition helped to ease the burden of the constant optimism she showed to her father.

"Though he probably does the same for me," she admitted ruefully.

"Yes," replied Violet, "but I expect he has friends at the bank to talk to, whereas until you started college you did not have anyone."

Mary did not like to admit even to Violet that caring for her mother was becoming so demanding that she was beginning to think that she might have to forego her studies for a time. She was planning to talk to her tutors soon, as she was finding it more and more difficult to manage. She thought that they would keep her place as she knew she was an above average student. Though when she might be in a position to resume was quite another matter.

She was startled by the sound of the door bell. Drying her hands as she went into the hall, she made out two figures through the frosted glass on the door and she suddenly felt a wave of apprehension. Hesitating, she took a deep breath before opening the door. The two men looked vaguely familiar.

"Miss Morrison," said the younger of the two, a man in his twenties. "You may remember me. I am a colleague of your father's. I brought some accounts round to him one evening and he introduced us. My name is Daniel Parson, and this is another colleague of your father's, Mr Robbins. We have some difficult news for you and your mother. May we come in?"

"What has happened? Where is my father? Why are you here?" Mary could hear the mounting hysteria in her voice but was helpless to do anything about it.

"Please, Miss Morrison," and Daniel took Mary by the elbow and guided her along the hall and in through the open door to the drawing room. Seating her in the large armchair by the fire – her father's armchair, thought Mary – he stood with his back to the hearth in front of her and waited for his colleague to speak.

"Miss Morrison," Mr Robbins began hesitantly, then, "Oh, dear Miss Morrison, there is no easy way to tell you this. Your father had a seizure at work early this afternoon. It was not immediately realised as he was working alone in the inner office. By the time we found him and sent for the physician I am afraid it was too late. As I am sure you are aware, he has been complaining of chest pains for some time. He refused to see his doctor although several of us had urged him to do so. We believe his heart may have been under too much strain lately, and ultimately was unable to cope."

Daniel dropped to his knees and began to rub Mary's hands, which had begun to tremble uncontrollably. Spotting a decanter on the sideboard, Mr Robbins poured some of the golden liquid into a glass for Mary, and Daniel put it into her hand and urged her to drink. The sip of whisky coursed through her like fire, enabling Mary to stop the shaking that was suffusing her entire body.

"Where is my father now?"

"The bank has already made some arrangements and his body…" Mr Robbins broke off abruptly, then, clearing his throat, he began again. "Your father is with Mr Perrin, the undertaker. I hope that is acceptable. Would you like to see him tomorrow? If so I will inform them."

"Please." She seemed incapable of saying more.

"Miss Morrison, have you someone who can stay with you? How is your mother? How will she cope with this terrible news?"

How indeed, thought Mary, trying, through her shock and grief, to confront the logistics of the situation.

"Gentlemen," she said, gathering up the remnants of her strength, "I have no-one I can send for, but I shall tell my mother after she has had her medication so that she is the stronger to bear it. Forgive me, and please do not think that I do not appreciate your concern and what you have already done for us, but I think I must be alone now."

Rising unsteadily but with determination, she shook

hands with each man in turn, before ushering them into the hallway.

"May I call in the morning and see how you are?" asked Daniel.

"Thank you. That would be most thoughtful," replied Mary as she let them out.

She was surprised to see that the evening sun was still shining and that life in the road was going on as normal. It was as if time was standing still and she was acting in a dream. Her father had never mentioned chest pains to her, though she had been aware that he had grown thin and for some time had little appetite. She had put it down to the strain of her mother's illness.

Which brought her back to the moment. How to tell her mother. She went back into the kitchen to resume the supper preparations. Her mind felt numb. As she bent over the sink she was suddenly aware of the tears pouring down her face and dripping onto the half-peeled potato that was shaking uncontrollably in her hands.

Her mind was suddenly flooded with memories. Her father arriving home from the bank and hoisting her four-year-old self on to his shoulder with loud shouts of, "How tall you've grown today," as she gripped his hair and gurgled with laughter. A picture of him sitting at her school desk, much too small for his long legs, as her teacher charted her progress, and winking slyly at her as her lack of talent for, and application to, drawing and painting was bemoaned. Him waiting for her at the bottom of the stairs until she appeared in her first grown-up gown to attend her first adult dance, his face suffused in proud smiles. Always there. A rock in her life. Gone. Forever. Her sight misted over and she sank to the floor and gave way to a paroxysm of weeping.

"Oh, Father, Father, please don't let this be happening," she wept. "Please let it be some awful dream and let me wake up." But she knew that her plea was the fantasy and the nightmare was the truth.

When her storm of crying was finally exhausted she rose to her feet and straightened her clothes. Rinsing her face at the sink, she measured out Dora's laudanum into a small glass as the kettle boiled on the range. Squaring her shoulders, she ascended the stairs with the freshly made tea and her mother's medicine on a tray.

Dora was half sitting up in bed. "Mary, darling, I thought I heard voices. Isn't Father home yet?"

There was the slight slurring of her words which Mary had become used to, even while telling herself she was imagining it.

"Yes, we have had some visitors," she agreed. "Here, Mother, take your medicine while I pour the tea."

She watched surreptitiously, making sure that her mother drank it all. Dora lay back on the pillow, exhausted by even this small effort. Bracing herself once more, Mary began to tell her mother, as gently as possible, the dreadful news.

1877

Mary was deep in Jane Austen's *Mansfield Park* when Alice's head popped round the door. "Miss," she whispered, "The Master's coming."

With muttered thanks Mary stowed the book under the cushion on her chair and picked up her embroidery. Even as she did this she silently berated herself for her cowardice. It was ridiculous that she should be pretending to Daniel that she was not studying. She just couldn't face another evening of the silence that felt like a tangible, disapproving presence every time she raised the subject of going back to college.

"You are much cleverer than I am," Violet had said on one of her clandestine visits, "surely you don't need Daniel's permission to take up your place again and get qualified?"

But it seemed that she did. It was humiliating but true. She sometimes couldn't believe that she now found herself in the situation that her parents had deemed completely unacceptable for her contemporaries. Richard had always been such an advocate of education for all. After Dora's gradual fading away, though, Mary felt so alone, so rudderless. Dora's had been such a quiet, such an undramatic death, as if all the drama had taken place on the Epsom racecourse that day and left no room for any other. Mary was sure her real wish had been to join Richard and what little will to live she had left died with his death.

So Daniel's constant attention, which gradually turned to courtship, had been such a balm, such a lifeline. She had talked about going back to college but she now realised how easily he had diverted her. As soon as she was out of mourning, they had married, with Violet and her parents their entire wedding party. Violet had never been entirely sanguine about the marriage but was won over by Daniel's undoubted charm.

At first, Mary had taken some pleasure in rearranging the house to suit them, and with Alice's help she had spring-cleaned the big front bedroom which had been Richard and Dora's. Together she and Alice had moved the big dark furniture about until it all looked quite different and she and Daniel had moved into it after their marriage. Daniel had been in lodgings near the bank so he brought little in the way of appurtenances with him. His parents lived in Scotland, he said, and his mother's ill health precluded them from coming to the wedding. Mary was disappointed, as she had looked forward to meeting her new relations. She had hoped that with her marriage she might gain another family, having so tragically lost her own. Daniel promised that they would visit his parents one day, but it had become one more subject that she was reticent to raise, due to his taciturn rebuffs.

With memories of her own happy childhood, she had hoped that they might soon have children of their own, so coyly referred to as 'the patter of little feet' by Alice, but the monthly bloodstained cloths in the bucket had finally silenced Alice's optimism on the subject. Much of an age, the two young women had lived in the same house for a decade, and had few secrets from each other. Alice's young man, Anthony, was in the army, but they were planning to be married on his next leave. They had been betrothed for two years, and his mother, a widow, had told Alice that they would be welcome to share her home. Mary was pleased for Alice, but knew how much she was going to miss her.

However, Anthony was one of the many British soldiers who had been sent to India the previous year to prepare for the forthcoming visit of the Prince of Wales. The Queen, of course, was now Empress of India, and whilst appreciating the importance of the Prince's visit, which was constantly discussed in the newspapers, Mary was occasionally irritated to hear Alice talking as if Anthony was personally responsible for the success of this event. But Mary was guiltily relieved that he would not be home for some time and did not really begrudge Alice this consolation. She was conscious of how much Alice's loyalty and support had come to mean to her.

She looked up with a smile as Daniel entered the room. "Hello, darling, how were things at the bank today?"

"Much the same as every other day," replied her husband tersely, crossing the room and standing with his back to her looking out of the window.

Mary's heart sank. Something was wrong. She tried to think what could possibly have upset Daniel. A knock at the door, and the moment of revelation was delayed by Alice's entrance with a tea tray. Supper in the Parson household was served later than was currently fashionable, so Daniel liked to have tea as soon as he arrived home. Husband and wife waited in silence as Alice poured the delicate Earl Grey beverage that Daniel insisted upon. She handed them each a cup and then threw an anxious glance at Mary before exiting.

"So," said Daniel. "And what has my clever wife been up to today?"

Mary remembered the same phrase in her father's mouth, spoken with such love and pride to her mother, and wondered fleetingly how the same words could sound so contemptuous. "Oh, nothing much," she answered with a laugh that sounded false even to her own ears. "I went shopping in the town this morning, but nothing unusual, really."

"Yes," replied Daniel. "I was told that you had been seen in the town. Talking to your spinster friend, the school teacher."

Indignation welled up in Mary, feeling like a pressure in her chest. "I had no idea that my movements were being monitored, Daniel. I did indeed meet Violet and we did take refreshment together."

Finally turning to face her, Daniel said icily, "I will not have you being seen talking to such a person. You are my wife now, and a woman who disregards her obligations to her sex such as this teacher person is not a suitable friend for you."

Mary could barely believe her ears. "Daniel, Violet is my closest friend. My parents were as fond of her as I am, and in any case I am certainly not having you dictate to me who I can see or not see."

She turned to leave the room and was startled as he grasped her by the upper arm and turned her to face him, pushing his face close to hers.

"On the contrary, my dear wife, you will do exactly as I tell you. I forbid you to see this woman again, and if you do not agree I shall not allow you to leave this house except in my company."

"Don't be absurd," gasped Mary, trying and failing to pull away from him. "What are you going to do – keep me prisoner in my own house?"

"I think you mean *my* house," replied her husband.

"Let me go," Mary ordered. "You are hurting me, and you know perfectly well that Father left this house to me. I really cannot believe that you are behaving in this loutish fashion."

Wresting herself from his grasp she tried once more

to leave the room, only to reel back clutching her cheek as he hit her across the face.

"Understand this, Mary," he snarled, backing her against the closed door. "Whether you like it or not, you are my wife. Which means that this is now my house, as much my property as you are. You will not ask that woman, or indeed anyone, into the house without my permission. You will not leave the house without my permission. If you disobey me I will inform the police and have you brought back like a common vagrant. And as for this," he picked up her copy of *Mansfield Park*, which had fallen to the floor in the scuffle, "the only place for it is there."

He threw the book on the fire and stood back watching the pages curl and catch light. "I am going out. I will be back at seven-thirty. Tell Alice supper will be served then. And please tidy yourself. I do not like to see my wife so disheveled."

Mary sank back into her chair, holding her breath until she heard the front door slam. As she rose shakily to her feet, Alice came hurtling through the door.

"Oh, Miss Mary, I heard, I heard it all. What are you going to do? It was dreadful. I was so frightened. I thought he was going to murder you."

Mary reached out to hold her hand, wondering whether it was to give or receive comfort. "Alice," she whispered, "Alice. What have I done? Is this a temporary insanity or have I married a monster? Did he only marry me for gain? I thought he loved me. But how could he..?"

Overcome with despair she wept in Alice's arms, her servant and friend crying with her. Eventually straightening up, she took Alice by the shoulders and wiped their mutual tears away, trying to laugh.

"What a couple of frights we look. Come, Alice, let's get His Lordship's supper. We don't need another scene tonight."

Or indeed ever, she thought, as they went into the kitchen. Shaken and hurt though she was, she realised that her main emotions were indignation and pure rage. If there was one thing she was certain of it was that she had never been anybody's chattel, and it was not a role she was about to undertake now. Perhaps in her loneliness she had been deceived into mistaking avarice for love, and charm for sincerity, but it had just been made crystal clear to her what the position was and she was not going to hanker after what might have been. For better or for worse, she thought grimly, she would find a way out of this. Somehow, Daniel was going to find out that Mary had not been brought up to be anyone's property, and she was not going to start now. Chopping parsley with angry vigour, she began to plan.

"Alice, I shall need your help tomorrow. As soon as Mr Parson has gone to the bank, I must take the tram into town and go to speak to Mr Dyson, Father's solicitor. He will tell me what I must do. It was he who explained to me that Father had left this house to Mother, and eventually to me. But I need to make quite sure that what Daniel said was nonsense. Then I shall enrol at college again, whatever he says. I swear that I will never let him hit me again. I have perhaps not exerted myself enough or he would surely have never spoken or acted toward me in such a fashion."

"You know I'll do anything to help, Miss, but do go and tidy up now," urged Alice. "He'll be back soon. I'll carry on here."

Seeing the sense of this, Mary ran upstairs and quickly straightened her dress and combed back her hair, which had fallen out of the heavy plait she habitually wore round her head. Pinching her cheeks to restore the colour she glanced down at the street and saw Daniel on the other side of the road, talking to a young girl. They were laughing together in an unquestionably familiar way. The girl looked across at the house, and Mary drew back into the shadows. As she watched, she saw Daniel hand what appeared to be money to the girl, who nodded and walked off. Daniel turned and made for the house.

Mary ran rapidly down the stairs, calling to alert Alice, and began to lay the dining room table for supper. As she struggled to control the pounding of her heart she came face to face with a truth that she had hitherto not acknowledged. She was afraid of her husband. And with that realisation came a determination that she would not be cowed.

"I am," she told herself firmly, "an educated, independent woman, living in England in the nineteenth century. It would be absurd to let Daniel or any other man think he can subjugate me. Tomorrow I shall put an end to this. Tonight, however, I must play the submissive wife."

Hearing his key in the lock, she forced a smile on to her face, and went into the hall to greet him.

1878

The room was so dark. She had drawn the curtains back, which enabled a chink of light to peep through, but she didn't want to risk waking Elizabeth. Quietly, she crossed the room and looked down at the sleeping baby, thumb contentedly tucked into her mouth, her little lace cap framing her face. Mary crept back to the chair by the window, careful to make no noise.

A roar of laughter rose from downstairs, making her jump. She knew Daniel had asked some of his friends round to the house this evening. She had watched them arrive from her window, and guessed it was another gaming party. No doubt Evangeline was holding court, in her dual role as hostess and servant. Mary sometimes wondered which the woman enjoyed most – taking Mary's place both in Daniel's bed and at his table, or acting as Mary's jailer.

Elizabeth started awake as one of the men burst into a drunken song, his voice joined almost immediately by Evangeline's. Mary quickly picked up her daughter and buried her face in Elizabeth's chubby neck, pacifying them both. As she rocked the baby gently back and forth she wondered how soon she would hear from Alice. Dear Alice. How would she have managed these last months without her? Alice was her only real link with the outside world now.

She remembered so well her shock and disbelief when she returned on that fateful morning from Mr Dyson's office to find Daniel waiting for her with the news that he had dismissed Alice, "And, as you have so blatantly disobeyed my orders, you shall now go to your room until I call you."

With this he had literally forced her up the stairs and pushed her into the bedroom that had been hers when a child, at the back of the house. She had listened to the key turning in the lock with growing horror. Her mind was still reeling from what Mr Dyson had told her. That her property now belonged absolutely to Daniel. That by her marriage she had lost her right to own anything. She had stared at her father's lawyer with incredulity.

"But why," she stammered, "why did I not know any of this?"

Mr Dyson shrugged noncommittally. "I can only imagine that your father had no presentiment of such a situation occurring, Mrs Parson. He could hardly have envisaged his own unfortunate early death. The house was, of course, entailed to your dear mother, with instructions that it should pass to you on her demise. Both these events happened much sooner than anyone could have imagined. I hesitate to seem critical, but your father did have some slightly odd ideas regarding the ability of your sex to manage financial affairs and suchlike. I would suggest that you return home and concentrate on pleasing your husband, my dear, which is, after all, your duty. Your husband is quite within his rights to forbid you to leave his house. I fear your father was remiss in not explaining to you the obligations and responsibilities that a wife has to her husband."

Rising to her feet, Mary held Mr Dyson's gaze for a long moment. "And does my husband have no such obligations to me, Sir?"

Mr Dyson also stood. "Mrs Parson, as far as I can tell, you are fed and clothed and housed. Those are your husband's obligations, and these he has obviously fulfilled. Forgive me, I have other appointments."

Thus dismissed, Mary arrived home stunned and totally unprepared for the terrible events that awaited her. She had little memory of those first days, locked in her room, her only visitor the ubiquitous Evangeline, insolent and surly, who she recognised as the woman she had seen talking to Daniel in the street. It was as if she had entered into a black space and was unable, physically or emotionally, to pull herself out. Then, one evening, lying on her bed, she had heard a noise under the window. Crossing to see what had caused it, she found Alice below.

"Oh, Miss," came the whispered voice, "Am I pleased to see you! I thought he'd murdered you."

Alice. Her path back into the sane world. Under her window every evening whispering, planning, bringing her hope. A promise of escape, somehow. Then the shock of realising that her constant nausea was not solely due to her unhealthy imprisonment, that her tender breasts and thickening body heralded something quite different. How glad she would have been three months earlier. How ironic that this should happen now. Evangeline must have noticed the signs and told Daniel.

He finally appeared at the door of her prison. "So I believe that I am finally going to have a son? I had thought you incapable even of that. I want your word that you will not leave the house without my permission."

She gave it. What else could she have done? For a time a semblance of normality resumed. In spite of the ever watchful Evangeline, Elizabeth, now released from her room, was able to pass notes to Alice via various tradesmen and endeavour to assure her friend that she thought all might eventually turn out well. That Daniel might become a better father than he was a husband had been her fantasy.

Then one long day and night of pain. At some point Evangeline was sent to fetch the midwife, then Dr

White. Finally, through the mists of exhaustion, the baby crying, Dr White's triumphant voice, "It's a beautiful, healthy little girl."

The feel of Elizabeth at her breast. A joy she had not imagined. "I shall never be alone again," she thought as she drifted into sleep.

Waking to hear Daniel's voice, "A girl. A snivelling brat. You couldn't even manage to give me a son."

And so the nightmare began again. But now she had someone to live for.

1879

Mary sometimes wondered what sixth sense had made her keep Dora's jewellery hidden away in the box at the back of her wardrobe. She had simply not wanted to wear any of her mother's pretty things. It was too soon, too raw, such a potent reminder of the effervescent personality that had once been her mother. Richard had been such a generous and loving husband. Every anniversary, great and small, had been remembered with a ring, or a bracelet, or a brooch, usually set with her mother's favourite rubies or garnets. Their glittering colours now represented Mary's path to freedom.

So she made her plans. While Daniel was at the bank and Evangeline at the shops, Mary penned and passed notes to Alice through the kitchen window, thrusting her head and shoulders as far out as possible so as to breathe in the friendly fresh air. She often thought that only her concentration on the future stopped her incarceration in the house from driving her insane. That and her baby daughter.

She knew that she and Elizabeth must have money to live on while she finished at college. She also knew that Dora would have entirely approved of her jewellery being sold for this purpose. She had already transferred most of it into Alice's trusty care, along with some of her father's books and a couple of miniatures she was reasonably certain Daniel would not miss. She was aware that Evangeline pilfered from the house regularly and that he never noticed. Thankfully, only Mary, the rightful owner, was familiar with every item in this house where she had grown up.

Alice and her Anthony had been married for several months and Alice was expecting a child of her own. She was waiting daily for news of Anthony. Her young husband's regiment was in South Africa and some of the stories filtering back were very worrying. Her widowed mother-in-law, in whose house they now lived, was the only person, apart from Violet, who knew Mary's story. Alice had rightly believed she would be sympathetic. Anthony had told Alice about his father's penchant for ale and his treatment of his mother. She knew that one of the reasons he had enlisted was to flee a domestic scene that he found totally unpalatable while his father lived. Her mother-in-law had assured Alice that Mary and Elizabeth would be welcome to stay with them. So a date for their escape was set.

Evangeline's daily habit, as Mary knew well, was to partake of a large glass of gin in the afternoon and then doze off on the bed she shared with Daniel. Listening at the door, Mary waited until Evangeline's heavy breathing indicated her unconscious state, and then she slipped into the drawing room. In a paper in her pocket she had the four doses of laudanum that were left after Dora's death. Hands shaking and heart pumping she poured them into the decanter of brandy from which Daniel and Evangeline habitually drank from after supper. Quickly shaking the decanter so the powder was absorbed she ran back up to her room.

That evening she left the house that had once been such a happy home to her. Creeping away like a thief in the night she knew that she was unlikely ever to be able to return. And she understood that in the eyes of the law she was now a criminal. As she was a runaway and disobedient wife, Daniel had every right to set the police to look for her. But she did not think he would. Bitterly, she thought that now he possessed everything that rightly belonged to her, he would be glad to be rid of her and his daughter.

The following day Mary enrolled again at college, uplifted by the welcome some of her old tutors gave her. At last a new and better life began for her and her child. Alice cared for Elizabeth during the day and when her own son, John, was born, the house became full of love and laughter. Anthony wrote to say he was well and how pleased he was that Alice and his son had such company, which removed Mary's last doubt about the arrangement. Alice, Granny (as Alice's mother-in-law was always affectionately called) and the children formed Mary's new family.

Her only worry was that when she qualified and began to teach, as was her intention, she would see even less of her daughter. Violet was typically pragmatic when told of Mary's concerns.

"Such a worrier! You are doing the very best that you can. The most important thing you can do for

Elizabeth is to make sure that she never falls into the same trap that you did."

"At least no-one's going to marry her for her property," replied Mary ruefully.

Violet fixed Mary with a stern gaze. "That is not what I meant, as you well know. Mary, you and I have better brains than most of the men in our lives. Yet we exercise our intelligence only by permission of our fathers or brothers or husbands. They can lock us up like animals, as Daniel did to you, on nothing more than a whim. I have just read this." She handed Mary a rather battered book. "Someone gave me a copy when I was at college and told me not to let my parents see it. Mary, to my shame I forgot all about it until recently. You *must* read it. It just ..." She paused, searching for words, "It makes you realise how wrong everything is. I mean, you, of all people, are aware of that. But instead of trying to alter things, most women just go on hoping that their masters will take care of them. It doesn't even occur to them that it might be possible to change anything. Read it, Mary. It's important. For you and for Elizabeth."

Moved by her friend's passion, Mary took the book and placed it in her reticule. The following evening, Elizabeth in bed and her duties done, she began to read the book, published 90 years earlier, that was to revolutionise her life once more.

1882

Mary let herself into the house and stood listening quietly for a moment, a smile curving her mouth. She loved hearing the children's chatter as they helped

Alice and Granny in the kitchen. And the wonderful smells! Granny had a copy of Mrs Beeton's *Book of Household Management* that had belonged to her mother, and she and her daughter-in-law enthusiastically tried out many of the recipes, "Though on a rather smaller scale," laughed Granny.

Granny remembered her mother helping Mrs Beeton when she started the soup kitchen from her own house in Pinner in a desperate attempt to try to ameliorate the poverty she saw around her. "I had moved here by then and Anthony was just a baby but I know my mother thought she was a wonderful person and that it was tragic when she died so young. Only twenty eight years old. Mr Beeton gave Mother the book as a 'thank you' for her help when his wife died and I shall give it to Alice when I go."

Sniffing appreciatively, Mary was just putting her hat on the hall stand when Elizabeth and John came bursting out of the kitchen door and she was engulfed in hugs.

"Well," said Alice, coming up behind them as she wiped her hands on her capacious apron, "You can't complain at that welcome. So how did it go today? Are they coming round tonight?"

"Yes, they certainly are!" replied Mary, her face alight with eagerness, "I talked to the two new teachers today and they will be here at seven o'clock. It is getting easier, you know. I don't know if that is because women are becoming more aware or whether I am getting better at explaining what we are trying to do."

"Bit of each, probably. Is Violet coming?"

"Indeed she is."

"Right, then, children," said Alice, "Off you go to

set the table. We'll be eating early tonight."

The children bustled off importantly.

"And are we going out when we've talked to our guests?" asked Alice.

"I am," said Mary "but, oh, Alice, you don't have to come."

The sound of Granny's voice made both women turn. "Of course she doesn't have to. Any more than you do. Or Violet. But of course she will. As I would if I was a bit younger. Anyway, someone has to stay with the children. So don't be daft, Mary. We all believe in this, not just you, my dear. Come along, supper is ready."

Helping to carry through the dishes Mary reflected, not for the first time, how important Granny had become to her. Born into a middle class family, daughter of a successful coal merchant, Granny had grown up, as she had herself, in a liberal and caring home. Her marriage to Henry, a clerk in her father's office, had been approved by everyone and to begin with was happy enough. Granny wasn't even sure when the marriage started to 'go downhill', to use her own phrase. But Henry had increasingly come home late smelling of drink and behaving in an aggressive fashion toward her.

It was only when the marriage had deteriorated alarmingly and she had begun to dread his arriving home that she told her father of the situation. Anthony was nearly ten by this time, and Granny had begun to be frightened for them both. Henry was still the person she had loved and married when he was sober but those periods were becoming increasingly rare. Granny's father had bought their house as a wedding present and he still owned it. He gave Henry an ultimatum, "Stop drinking or leave my house."

Granny said that she believed Henry had tried. Until the night he got himself into a fight in the East End. The police found his body. A knife through his heart. Granny said it was through hers, too. But she was free of the fear. And so was Anthony. Alice had known Granny's story. Known that she would help Mary. Known a natural ally. She had been so right. Mary thanked heaven every day of her life for these two women.

The three of them, together with Violet, had so much to talk about nowadays. Mary Wollstonecraft's book had galvanised Mary as it had Violet. Alice laughingly declared she had been unable to get beyond the first page, but Granny's interest, coupled with the enthusiasm and teaching skills of Mary and Violet, had ensured that she had absorbed a lot of Mrs Wollstonecraft's ideas. Many long periods of discussion had finally been summed up by Alice.

"It's quite a long book with quite a long title, really, just to say that we're as good as any man in the land, isn't it?"

Stopped in their tracks, the other three women looked at each other and then at Alice. Simultaneously they burst into laughter, making Elizabeth and John, happily playing with building bricks at their feet join in with great gurgles of joy.

"Alice," said Violet, "You have just summed up *The Vindication of the Rights of Women* in a most succinct and enviable way."

"But," reflected Alice thoughtfully, "if my Anthony ever comes out of the army and comes home to live, what's he going to think about all this? Because though it all seemed quite obvious to me once I started to think about it, most men treat their women reasonably well and would think that this is a lot of fuss about nothing."

Granny looked at her daughter-in-law sternly. "Alice, I promise you that Anthony will not think that. I have never said anything detrimental about his father to him. But he knows how different our story might have been. And I am quite sure he is aware how easily what happened to Mary could have happened to us."

"And," added Mary firmly, "if anyone, whatever their sex, feels like that, then we must change their thinking. No woman should have to be reliant on goodwill instead of proper rights. I am beginning to realise that we have to take a stand. The only thing that is going to make a difference to the position of women is to get the law of our land changed. Fifteen years ago John Stuart Mill tried to get parliament to give women the vote. Hardly any of his fellow MPs supported him. I was only sixteen at the time and simply didn't understand how important it was. Alice, of course we know that your Anthony is a lovely, generous man, but all your rights depend on him, even down to your liberty, as you and I well know. That is not as it should be – at the moment a pet dog has about as much legal standing as we do!"

Mary was starting to recognise that although society might well condemn her for what it would deem revolutionary thoughts, she was buoyed up by knowing with absolute certainty that her parents would have wholeheartedly agreed and approved.

Supper was finished, the cooks praised, the table cleared, the dishes dealt with and the children bedded just before Violet arrived. Their guests were due soon after.

"My turn tonight," she declared. The others nodded. That they had developed an effective strategy was proved by their growing circle of converts. Converts from both Violet and Mary's schools. Educated, thinking, single women.

They took it in turns to tell their visitors Mary's story. Keeping it both as simple and as horrendous as it was. Not ever revealing that the victim was in the room with them. They were all conscious that Daniel could appear and legally march Mary and Elizabeth back to their imprisonment in his house, so they were careful to hide her identity whilst highlighting the dreadful injustices of a system that most of their listeners had never questioned.

Then they sent them away with a copy of Mary Wollstonecraft's book and an outline of the progress that was currently being made. And waited for the carefully chosen women to come back to them. Which they nearly always did.

As a result of these efforts they now had a group of fifteen like-minded women who were constantly bombarding parliament as well as every well-known person in the country with letters decrying their 'inferior' status and insisting that the law must be changed. They were beginning to get answers, even though many of them amounted to 'know your place'. But there were stirrings of interest.

The evening proved to be interesting. The two young teachers were receptive and asked a number of discerning questions. One had been forced to work as a governess for several years before resuming her college course. The death of her father had left her unable to afford to continue, as, although on a scholarship, she still had to find the virtually impossible sum of twenty pounds a term. There was almost no way that she could earn enough to save so large a sum except in such a post. And only then, as she confided to her new friends, by never going home to see her mother or spending anything on herself at all.

Mary greatly admired the girl's single-minded determination and felt that she would be a definite asset to their cause. At the end of the evening they were reasonably certain that they had two more converts.

As soon as their visitors had left, Alice, Violet and Mary donned their outdoor clothes and picked up the baskets that Granny had ready in the kitchen. "Be careful," she warned, "stay together. Promise me."

Stepping out into the London fog they were only too happy to make such a promise. Granny knew that it was her memories of Mrs Beeton's soup kitchens that had inspired them to look at the hardship that was still everywhere around them. And to try and help to improve things in some small way. So she felt a measure of responsibility for their safety on their nightly missions, even though they assured her that they were grown women and made their own decisions.

It was not long before they saw a shadowy figure beckoning to them.

"Cathy," Mary called softly.

The child motioned them into an alleyway. Silently they followed her. Through a doorway into a deserted warehouse. They had been here before. Like little ghosts the children appeared.

Without a word the women distributed the contents

of the baskets. The children devoured the food hungrily, eyes darting back and forth over the crusts of bread. A small boy dropped a piece of bread and expertly kicked aside the rat that swooped on it. The women stoically refused to shudder. They were getting used to it.

"Where is Anna?" asked Alice in a whisper.

The boy gave a non-committal shrug. Gradually, without noise, the children began to dissolve back into the night. As the women turned to go, Mary felt a tug at her skirt. Cathy put a finger to her lips and pulled her over to the corner of the building. She pointed to a bundle of rags.

"I fink she's bad, Miss. It was the gent wot comes in the carriage. Mr Fred took the money and brought 'er in here when 'e'd finished."

With a stifled cry, Mary dropped to her knees and pulled back the rough covering. The child's face was chalk white but her skirt was red with the blood that had seeped through the rags from the lower part of her body. A large figure loomed out of the fog.

"What's going on 'ere? You leave my girl alone." The man pushed Mary aside.

"Please, let me help her," she gasped.

"She don't need no 'elp. She's my daughter. Get out of 'ere." With that he hoisted the child over his shoulder. "And before you think of making even bigger fools of yourselves, let's be clear. She's thirteen years old. What she does is what I tell her to do. And it's legal. Now get out of my way."

As he exited with the child, Cathy emerged from the shadows and ran after him. Mary became conscious that Alice was crying quietly. She put her arm round her and looked over her head into Violet's eyes.

"How are we ever going to make a difference? How can we fight all this?"

Violet was on the verge of tears herself. "Anna is never thirteen. Probably not even ten. But she'll lie for him or he'll kill her. Come on. We won't make a difference by giving up."

Together they went back out into the night. Under the light of the street lamp they examined the remnants of food left in Granny's baskets.

"I'm not sure there is enough left to warrant going further," said Mary, turning toward home.

"Please," came a voice through the fog, "please don't throw it away."

The three women turned in consternation as an incongruous figure loomed in front of them. Instinctively they moved closer to each other. They were able to make out a tall woman wearing a bright red dress, still sparkling with jewels although it had obviously seen better days. Her face was gaunt, accentuated by garishly flamboyant make-up. She was frighteningly thin and unsteady on her feet.

"Forgive me," a surprisingly educated voice issued from her lips, "I was…" but the rest of her sentence was lost forever as she seemed to fold up before them. Alice and Violet moved to catch her before she collapsed onto the ground.

Almost at the same moment they saw a policeman approaching. Mary quickly took off her cloak and wrapped it round the unconscious woman, standing in front of her so she was not visible.

"What are you ladies doing out on a night like this?" asked the policeman. Then, spying the baskets, "Oh, I see. Well, on your way, ladies. I know you think you're helping, but if you ask me these people don't deserve your charity. Drunk most of the time and the women no better than they should be. Go home, now. Stop wasting your time."

"You're right, of course, Officer," said Mary. "We're just on our way. My friend has hurt her ankle and we were hoping a cab might come by," and she smiled at him without moving.

The policeman took out his whistle and gave the two short blasts that habitually conjured a cabbie out of the night and Mary smiled her thanks. As soon as they heard the rumble of the approaching vehicle and the accompanying clatter of hooves the policeman doffed his helmet and moved off, wishing them "God speed."

Between them the three women lifted their burden into the cab, assiduously keeping her covered with Mary's cloak so the cabbie should not see her. It only took a few minutes to arrive home but she was starting to recover consciousness.

"Not a word," Mary whispered to her as they disembarked.

They let themselves quickly into the house, calling for Granny. Summing up the situation at a glance she soon had the stranger ensconced in the armchair by the fire with a glass of her own special brandy and hot water.

"Alice," Granny ordered, "Soup. On the range. Get a cup immediately for our guest. Then you all come and sit down and get warm. Mary, you look frozen, too."

"She probably is," came shakily from the armchair, "As I seem to be wearing her cloak."

"And most welcome you are to it," replied Mary, turning to face the owner of the voice. "Please don't speak unless you feel able, but can you tell us your name?"

"My name is Valerie."

At that moment Alice returned with the soup but Valerie's hands were shaking too much for her to hold it so Granny sat in front of her holding the cup and gently encouraging her to drink. Alice and Violet went back into the kitchen and returned with soup for all of them and they sat silently, relishing the warmth that was seeping into their bones.

Presently, Valerie sat upright and looked properly at them all, as if for the first time. "My good Samaritans. Thank you. I am most grateful to you. I was very hungry. I will not presume on your hospitality any longer, however. It is time for me to go."

With this she began to rise from the chair.

Granny was before her, however. "I never heard such nonsense. You are not fit to go anywhere. Sit down this minute."

Startled, Valerie sank back into the chair. Mary began to laugh.

"Oh, Valerie. You don't know anything about us yet, but I should warn you that Granny is a formidable woman. I don't know what your story is, but I can tell you that she has kept me safe for quite a time, and, probably even more importantly, anonymous. Trust her. Trust us. We will not pry if you don't want to confide in us. But we will not betray you."

Valerie's make-up and dress were so at odds with her cultured voice that Mary was all too aware that her story was going to be a desperate one. She also knew that under the law any woman who was even suspected of being a prostitute could be forcibly taken from the streets and subjected to a brutal, humiliating and painful physical examination, ostensibly to make sure she was not suffering from venereal disease. Presumably in case she passed this to some poor innocent and unsuspecting man.

Although the officer who had spoken to them appeared to be conscientious and responsible, their mission on the streets of London had taught Mary and her friends to take nothing and no-one for granted. They had realised instantly that Valerie must be hidden from the law.

"You can sleep here, by the fire," said Granny. "There are two small children upstairs who will rise at the crack of dawn, no doubt, but we will try to keep them from disturbing you. Tomorrow, whatever you want to do will not be questioned. But will you give me your word that you will stay with us long enough to eat some breakfast?"

Valerie's haggard face was transformed by a smile. "That is an amazingly easy promise to give."

"Then," said Granny "as we all have work to do tomorrow I think that it is time for bed. Come along, everyone, or we shall be too tired to do what must be done."

With a gasp as she noticed the lateness of the hour, Violet rose and gave her friends a quick hug. She touched Valerie lightly on her shoulder as she wished her goodnight. Mary was relieved to see that the fog had abated slightly as she let her friend out.

"See you in the morning," she whispered to her fellow teacher.

Within minutes the house was cloaked in darkness.

The morning dawned unexpectedly bright. Mary wasn't sure whether she was woken by the sun streaming through the windows or Elizabeth's chubby face being pushed against hers.

"Come on, Mummy. Wake up. Time for a cuddle." With a laugh Mary drew her daughter to her. "There's a pretty lady asleep by the fire, Mummy".

The events of the previous evening came rushing back to Mary. "Well, then, my sweetheart, perhaps we'd better get dressed and go to say 'good morning' to her."

When they arrived downstairs Valerie had already stirred and Granny had brought her a bowl of hot water to wash in. Without her make-up, for all her thinness, Mary could see that Valerie was indeed a 'pretty lady'. "Did you sleep well?" she asked.

"Better than I would have believed possible," came the reply.

"I have to be at the college soon," explained Mary. "Violet and I are teachers there. But Alice and Granny will be here with the children. Please stay with us a little longer."

Valerie treated her to one of her rare but wonderful smiles. "I have already been persuaded by Granny to stay for today. You were right. She is formidable."

Laughing, Mary agreed. "Good. Then I'll see you this evening."

On her return home several hours later, Mary was amused to find Elizabeth and John building an enormous edifice in the sitting room with Valerie's help. As she crossed the room a great shout went up as the building bricks collapsed with an all too familiar crash.

"Oh, Mummy," said Elizabeth, noticing Mary in the doorway, "we were building St Paul's for you."

"But obviously we have not quite perfected Mr Wren's skills," said Valerie, picking up the bricks from the floor with little John's help.

Granny was heard calling the children to their nightly task of table laying, leaving the two women alone.

"I can tell you are fond of children," said Mary with a smile.

"Indeed." There was a pause. Valerie looked up at her and Mary saw that her eyes were full of tears. "I think perhaps I should like to tell you about myself." She paused, obviously searching for words. "It has been so long since I spoke to anyone at any length. But it seems it could be right to do so now. And from what you said yesterday, I gather that you also have things to hide?"

Mary nodded.

"Then," said this enigmatic woman, "I believe that I can trust you. You have shown me already that you would not easily betray me."

Mary reached over and took Valerie's long, thin hand in her own. "If you can bear to, it might be better to share your confidences with Granny and Alice too."

After a brief moment Valerie nodded.

"After supper, then?" said Mary. "Granny will put the children to bed. Alice and I will go out with the food baskets straight away so we will not be late back. Violet can't come with us tonight as she has promised to escort her parents to the opera. They are going to see the new one by Mr Gilbert and Mr Sullivan at the Savoy Theatre, and are very excited about it. Poor

Violet doesn't like opera much, but it will be good for her to have an evening off."

Valerie treated Mary to an enormous smile. "I cannot tell you how much it means to me to be back in a world where people go to the opera and speak of civilised things. I will try to have my thoughts in order for when you return from the streets. I would come with you but I fear I may not be strong enough yet and would merely hinder you."

Elizabeth's head came round the door. "Granny says you're to come into supper *now*," she announced importantly.

"Well, then, we'd better not disobey," laughed her mother as they followed the child into the hallway.

Later that evening, the children in bed and the baskets emptied, the four women sat round the fire in companionable silence. With the firelight flickering on her face Valerie gave a long sigh, and began her story.

"My mother died giving birth to me, so I never knew her. My father was a kind enough man, I think, but remote. He was away a great deal. I was left in the care of a series of housekeepers, and then later a governess. When I was sixteen years old, my father came home with a new wife. He had given me no warning and I was very shocked, but hoped to like my new stepmother. She seemed very young, even to me. My father doted on her and when she fell pregnant he was like a boy – radiant with anticipation. I wanted so much to be part of his happiness, but it was as if I didn't exist for him. I constantly offered to fetch and carry, indeed to do any errand, from filling his pipe to calling his carriage, anything at all that might make him notice me. But he would merely thank me vaguely without ever really looking at me. His new wife was his whole life and I felt that I was both a stranger and an intruder in the only home I knew."

Valerie paused, staring into the flames.

"Then their son, Oliver, was born. My father's joy knew no bounds. A son! For the first time I realised that I had always been a disappointment to him. I think my stepmother was not a bad woman, but she did not know how to include me in the family circle, given my father's indifference to me. And perhaps I made her feel a little uneasy by my very presence. After all, we were very close in age, but had little in common. She was very small and pretty and her favourite occupation was sending for materials and choosing dress patterns for the social occasions she loved and had taught my father to enjoy. I, on the other hand, was tall and thin and probably seemed somewhat austere, spending my allowance on books and drawing materials, loving nothing better than to stride around the fields with only our dogs for company. She undoubtedly thought my very lack of frivolity boring and unnatural, and she may well have been right. But I had been party to no other stimulus. It was all I knew."

The three women were listening intently. Valerie gave them a fleeting smile.

"Oliver was a delightful baby, but I was not allowed to have much to do with him. However, his bubbly charm inspired me to ask my father if I could help at the local church school and he agreed. I enjoyed the school more than I had ever enjoyed anything. To my surprise I found that I was a good teacher, able to impart knowledge with ease and enthusiasm. Mr Samuels, the schoolmaster, a widower, ran the establishment well and they were happy days.

"One afternoon, just after my eighteenth birthday, I came home to find Father waiting for me. He seemed so pleased to see me that my heart lifted. Then the blow fell. 'Valerie,' he announced, 'Mr Samuels has asked for your hand in marriage. I have given my consent.'

"I looked at him in consternation. Mr Samuels and I had always worked well together, but he was the same age as father and rather stout and not, well, just not someone I would ever want to marry."

Valerie sat looking down at her hands for a moment. When she looked up the women could see that the memory of what happened next still had the power to upset her.

"It was dreadful," she confided, with a sob in her voice. "Father could not believe that I was refusing to marry Mr Samuels. Finally he sent me to my room and said that I must stay there until I changed my mind."

A shudder ran through Mary. She recalled, all too vividly, her recent experience of incarceration in her own home. Her heart went out to this fellow sufferer.

Valerie continued with her story, "After four dreadful weeks, in which I was not allowed out of my room, and only saw Mrs Reynolds, the housekeeper, who brought me food and washing water, Father called me downstairs. The most terrible quarrel ensued but I was adamant in my rejection of Mr Samuel's proposal. Finally Father sent me back to my room. A week later he appeared at my doorway and told me that I was no longer to be thought of as his daughter. He was washing his hands of me. He had arranged a post for me as a governess in Hampshire and I was to leave the next day. That was the last time I saw him.

"The coach took me to the largest house I had ever been in. I quickly found that my two charges were most agreeable and, rather to my surprise, I settled into a kind of contented harmony with my lot. I had virtually no money, but access to a splendid library and I was well housed and fed. I had been used to my own company and found myself happily tramping round the countryside when I was not required. There were even some friendly dogs who were allowed to explore with me. It seemed to me that it was all infinitely preferable to marrying Mr Samuels. I had been there about six months when the son of the house, who had been away at college, came home."

Valerie paused again, obviously gathering strength to continue. Her hands, still elegant in spite of their broken nails and sore, chapped skin, twisted against each other in her lap.

"It is very hard for me to talk of this, but if I am to explain how I came to be where you found me, then I must. Charles was just a little older than me. He was very personable. A kind of intimacy grew up between us. He began to sit in on my lessons with his young siblings. Then he would catch up with me on my walks and ask permission to accompany me, which I willingly gave. He had a ready sense of humour and made me realise how little laughter there had been in my life. We discussed with animation everything from the novels of Miss Austen to the campaigning works of Mr Dickens. I felt as if I had been reborn.

"When Charles asked me to marry him I was ecstatic. He explained that he would need to break the news with some care to his family, who were expecting him to marry an heiress who would help with the expenses of living in such a grand old house. I told him, truthfully, that I would happily wait forever.

"My friends, my only excuse for what happened next is that I was very young and very innocent. I found myself with child. My naivety was such that my confinement was virtually upon me before I realised what was happening. I gave birth to a daughter. Charles was distraught and insisted that he would marry me immediately. I do believe that he loved me. But his family were too strong for him. He was sent away and I was dismissed without a reference. I came to London with my baby. I was weakened from my confinement but knew I had to find work to keep us both. I quickly found that there was only one kind of work open to me."

Looking up with tears running down her cheeks, Valerie said, "So I did what it took to keep my baby from starving. But it was not enough. Like many other women, I fell into the hands of the man, Bramwell, who controls everything that happens on the streets of London. I kept my baby secret from him. I had to leave her in the rooming house while I worked but there was always one of the other girls willing to keep an eye. This went on for several years. In spite of everything, my little Rosalie and I had some happy times. As she got older, I tried to put money aside so she could escape the streets. When she was seven, I arranged with the mother of one of the other girls for her to live with them in Hastings and go to school there. It was very hard to part with her but I knew it was the best thing. I had to keep her from getting trapped as I had been. I promised to come and see her as soon as I was able."

There was a long silence. Mary went and stood behind the bowed figure of her new friend, placing her hands lightly on her shoulders.

"I was tricked," said Valerie. "For three months I sent the money, and then I went down to Hastings to see her. She was not there. They laughed in my face. Bramwell had her. That was three years ago. Every night I roam the streets looking for her. They call me the mad woman. Perhaps I am. But if I do not find my Rosalie, I shall die looking for her."

At this, she finally broke into sobs which racked her entire body. Alice and Mary folded her into their arms while Granny disappeared into the kitchen. Coming back with a tray of tea a few minutes later, she stood with her back to the fire surveying the younger women.

"Well, my dear," she finally announced, "We shall just have to help you find her then, won't we?"

1884

Mary saw the advertisement in the newspaper straight away, which was odd in itself as she didn't usually look at the personal column, but her own married name, though never used now, leapt out at her: '*Will Mrs Daniel Parson please contact the firm of Dyson, Dyson and Mortimer at her earliest convenience.*"

The shock and fear she felt were quite physical, and a wave of nausea swept over her. For a minute she thought she was going to lose consciousness but then her courage asserted itself and she began to think rationally. If Daniel knew her whereabouts then he would have no need to advertise for her. She was still safe. But why, why was he trying to find her? There could be no other motive for such an advertisement. Whatever the reason she was certainly not going to respond. And why did he think she would be stupid enough to do such a thing? Her head whirled with it all.

Alice and Granny were busy in the kitchen.

"Look," said Mary, "Do come and look at this. I don't know what to make of it."

The two women turned from chopping vegetables at the sink and dried their hands as Mary spread the paper on the table. When Alice realised what she was looking at she gave a gasp of horror.

"Oh, Mary, what can it mean? Why on earth is he trying to find you after all this time?"

"I wish I knew," answered Mary grimly. "But it's not likely to be anything good, is it?"

"Hold on a minute, you two." Granny was reading the advertisement again. "It asks you to contact these solicitors, not your husband. We need to find out why, without revealing your whereabouts. How about if you write a letter to them? I'll deliver it by hand and say I'll wait for a reply. That will mean they will have no need to know your address."

"But," pointed out Alice, "if this is Daniel's work, then he knows who you are and he will guess that Mary and Elizabeth are here."

"Then we need to find someone to represent you who won't be recognised," replied Granny.

At that moment they heard the front door open and a voice call, "Hallo, where are you all?"

With one accord the three women said, "Valerie!"

as they turned to greet her. The woman they embraced was barely identifiable as the Valerie they had first met. Slim now, rather than thin, dressed in a simple grey dress which complemented her dark good looks, her height and bearing gave her an air of authority.

"I thought you were at college today," smiled Mary.

"No, I've been working on a portrait at home. I am quite excited. It's the one of Mrs Gamage, my history tutor, and she is so pleased with it that she says it will be worth £40 to her, and that will be my last two terms fees paid."

"Oh, Valerie, that is wonderful. You must be the only student there to have painted her way through college," Mary laughed, her delight for her friend temporarily outweighing her unease at the advertisement.

"I couldn't have done any of it without all of you," replied Valerie. "Finding me lodgings where I have been able to work my keep, and letting me treat your home as my own. And helping me to search..."

A shadow passed over her face and Granny said briskly, "None of that, now. We *shall* find your girl. And in the meantime we need your help. Read this." And she pushed the paper over to Valerie.

It took a surprising amount of time to get the letter right. "Not too much and not too little," was their declared aim. In the end they settled for:

'Dear Mr Dyson
With reference to your advertisement, I have asked my friend to deliver this letter to you. I trust her absolutely and should be grateful if you would place your response into her hands. I would like you to

clarify your reasons for wishing to contact me.
This lady will forward your reply directly to me.
I am, Sir, your obedient servant,
Mary Parson.

"That should do it," said Granny, as they sealed the envelope. "If they know you're going to post it they won't bother to follow you. Thank you, Valerie, my dear."

"Yes, indeed," said Mary, hugging her friend. "We'll meet at the usual place tonight and then you can tell me what happened."

Alice and Mary left the house after dark as usual, with their baskets. They were joined by four other women, all with baskets of food and they quickly deployed them to different areas, but always in couples.

"Are you all carrying whistles?" Alice checked. The women nodded. As they were quietly going their separate ways Violet came running up accompanied by her sister.

"Primrose," said Mary, "How nice to see you. I didn't know you were planning to join our mobile soup kitchen."

Alice's husband, Anthony, had come up with this description of their nightly journeys, half laughingly, and it had stuck. Mary suggested that they proceed together to the warehouse area, where they had arranged to meet Valerie with another volunteer. The four women walked briskly on, greeting the neighbourhood policeman on their way.

"He may not approve," commented Mary ruefully, "but at least he's given up trying to stop us."

When they reached the warehouses, as always the

children silently materialised from the shadowed alleyways. Violet kept Primrose close to her. She knew how unnerving this absolute lack of noise could be to the uninitiated.

Valerie and her companion were waiting in the alleyway as planned and the women exchanged hushed greetings as they entered the vast and chill expanse that was now so familiar to them. Working quickly the women distributed the food, a softly spoken word occasionally addressed to a familiar face. Mary noticed a girl hanging behind one of the larger boys and gently called her forward. The boy glanced behind him and pushed the child in front of him.

"She's new," he declared. "Won't tell us 'er name or nuffink."

"Never mind," said Mary. "Here, please take this," and she handed the girl a large chunk of bread. The child ate ravenously.

There was a slight movement behind Mary and she looked over to see Valerie anxiously searching the girl's face. Mary stifled a sigh. So many years searching. Sometimes she found it hard to share Granny's faith.

Valerie came past Mary and went up to the newcomer. Mary realised she was moving almost like a sleepwalker. Watching the girl's face she felt a surge of hope as the child moved to meet Valerie. They stood in silence, inches apart but not touching. Then, with one fluid movement, they were in each other's arms.

A whisper. "Rosalie. My daughter. Rosalie. Rosalie."

Even the street children were smiling.

It was not until the following morning that Mary remembered the advertisement and almost before she had formed the thought, Elizabeth came running in waving a letter.

"Mummy," said the child, bubbling with excitement, "It's a letter and it's for you!"

Mary allowed herself a wry smile. Most of the letters received in this household were from Anthony, still stationed most of the time in far flung parts of the Empire, and Elizabeth's animation reflected the uniqueness of a communication to her mother.

Recognising Valerie's handwriting, Mary discarded the outer envelope, and then found she was almost too nervous to go further. Finally, deliberately putting all thoughts of Daniel and his treachery aside, she tore open the solicitor's letter. It took a moment to digest what she was reading:

'Dear Mrs Parson,
'It is my sad duty to inform you of the death of your husband, Mr Daniel Parson, some months ago. Mr Parson died intestate. It is therefore my
understanding that you stand to inherit his estate. I should be grateful if you would contact my office at your earliest convenience to enable me to undertake the necessary formalities regarding this matter.
I remain, etc, etc,
Obadiah Dyson.'

Mary sat in silence for a moment. Then, "Elizabeth, would you go and ask Granny and Alice if they could spare a minute? I have some news for them. When you have done that you may go and play with John while we talk."

Appearing in the doorway the two women found Mary doubled over, the letter having fallen to the floor. Rushing to her aid, they were startled to find that she was rendered helpless by laughter.

"Look," she said, handing them the letter. "After all, there is some justice in the world. It seems I have inherited back what was rightfully mine anyway."

"But how..?" asked Alice.

"Heaven only knows," replied Mary briskly, "but I am not going to be such a hypocrite as to pretend that it is anything other than an enormous relief."

"Good for you, my dear." Granny was wreathed in smiles. "No more living in fear of him finding you or Elizabeth. And your house back! My goodness, though, we shall miss you."

"You are my family now. Regaining my own home will not make any difference to that," said Mary, giving Granny a hug. "I shall go round to see how Valerie is, and then I will attend to Mr Dyson. Do you know, what with finding Rosalie last night, and now this today, I'm beginning to be afraid that I shall wake up and find it is all a dream!"

Some time later Valerie's landlady opened the door to Mary, greeting her with, "I'm so glad you are here, Miss. I'm a bit worried. No-one's been downstairs yet, and I can't hear any noise at all."

Mary climbed the stairs to Valerie's room. Valerie was usually an early riser and helped Mrs Brown in the house as part of her rent so the pall of silence was beginning to seem slightly ominous. As she raised her hand to knock on the door it swung open and Valerie was revealed, one finger pressed to her lips. Silently,

Mary slipped past her into the room.

Rosalie was asleep on the bed wearing one of Valerie's nightdresses, which was enormous on her. Valerie beckoned Mary toward her sleeping daughter. Where the nightdress had slipped from the child's shoulders her flesh was black with bruises. Her skeletal frame reminded Mary forcibly of her first encounter with Valerie herself.

Valerie's eyes were full of tears. "She hasn't spoken yet," she whispered, "Just clings to my hand. Her whole body is a mass of bruises like these. And her back looks as if she's been whipped. Oh, Mary, I think Bramwell must have given her to that monster who nearly killed little Anna."

Mary put her arms round her friend. "We can protect her now. Her body will heal. And if she has half her mother's courage, so will her spirit. I have news for you which will benefit us all." And she handed Valerie the letter. "You and Rosalie are coming to live with me. As soon as everything is arranged. Take heart, Valerie. She is young enough to put all the horror behind her. Here, I've brought you some of Granny's special broth, which, of course, she swears will put you both back on your feet in no time."

Placing the covered basin on the table, Mary was relieved to see Valerie's lips curl in a tentative smile. "If anyone has magical restorative powers, then it's certainly Granny," she agreed.

Going back down the stairs leaving Valerie sitting by her unmoving daughter, Mary reflected grimly that Granny was going to need all her healing powers to aid this bruised and beaten child and her distraught mother. As were they all.

Mr Dyson ushered Mary into his office with what seemed a measure of embarrassment. Presumably, thought Mary, he also was recollecting their last meeting. Seating herself, she waited politely for him to begin.

"Mrs Parson," he began.

It gave Mary a degree of pleasure to interrupt. She wanted him to be aware that she would not be bullied by him a second time.

"I prefer to be known by my own name, Mr Dyson. Please be good enough to address me as Mrs Morrison."

After a slight hesitation, Mr Dyson resumed, "Mrs Morrison, I am sure you will be grieved to hear that your husband, Mr Daniel Parson, died as a result of a fall down the stairs, in his home. It was late at night, and apparently he was," Mr Dyson paused delicately, "I believe 'in his cups', was the term the coroner used. He appears to have hit his head upon the newel post and his body was not found until the next morning, when a colleague from the bank called to see why he was not at his desk."

Mary wondered briefly what had happened to Evangeline. "I understand," she replied, thinking that she probably understood a great deal better than Mr Dyson. "However, *you* must understand that I have had no contact with my husband for some considerable time and I am only interested in the consequences of his death as they apply to me and my daughter."

I am not, she thought, going to play the grieving widow for you, Mr Dyson. She realised how changed she was since she had last sat in this office, when he had seemed such a formidable personage to her.

"I should like to arrange to go back to live in my home immediately. Perhaps you would be kind enough to hand me the keys. I would also like to know how much of my father's money is left. I will return tomorrow for those figures, Mr Dyson, if you would be good enough to investigate. I know that my father believed that, as his executor, you would always be vigilant in guarding my interests."

Taking the keys that an obviously shaken Mr Dyson produced from his office drawer Mary turned to leave.

"Until tomorrow, then," were her parting words to him. As he hurriedly rose to open the door of the office for her, she reflected that sometimes life's little victories could be very sweet.

1887

"Look what we've got, oh, do come and look!" The three children burst through the door, their elated exhortations echoing round the house. Mary laughed out loud at the expressions of pure joy on their faces, such merriment was contagious. The children thrust their booty in front of them. Alice and Mary dutifully admired the colourful Jubilee mugs that were being displayed with such pride.

A somewhat bedraggled figure came through the door. "Tea, hot and strong, please," croaked Valerie, and with a giggle Alice departed to the kitchen followed by John, words tumbling out as he tried to describe the whole thrilling day to his mother.

Elizabeth and Rosalie were skipping around the room. "We had buns, and milk, and we had to sing this song that Prince Albert wrote *ages* ago, and there were millions of other children in the park and we very nearly saw the Queen! Oh, it was all very, very, very exciting! You should have been there, Mummy." And Elizabeth joined hands with Rosalie and whirled her round the room again.

Groaning theatrically, Valerie eased off her shoes, and as Alice returned with the tea, she remarked, "I must have been mad, volunteering to take them up to Hyde Park for the Jubilee celebrations. I'm absolutely exhausted."

But the three women sat smiling at each other, knowing that watching Rosalie dancing round the room like any other fourteen-year-old schoolgirl was all the reward Valerie needed.

"The others will be back soon," remarked Alice. "And I've promised Anthony not to be too late home tonight. He says that John needs some male company, apart from his little brother."

The women laughed companionably, aware that Anthony worshipped both his young sons. They also knew that, since his discharge from the services, Anthony was both grateful and astonished at the education that John and the other children were receiving at the hands of Mary and her fellow teachers.

"You know, he's convinced that John will eventually be Prime Minister, at very least," remarked Alice with amusement.

"Well, we could certainly do with a politician with a bit of sense, and John has plenty of that," replied Valerie. "Your Edward will soon be old enough to join the classes as well, and you can see that he's as bright as a little button already."

Alice was putting her hat on, "Talking of Edward, I

think I'd better get home and take him off Granny's hands, he leads her merry dance, he's into everything! Come on, John. I'll see you in the morning," and addressing this last remark over her shoulder to Mary, she gathered up her elder son and let herself into the street.

"What would we do without her?" mused Mary.

"Work even harder, I imagine," replied Valerie, wiggling her toes luxuriously.

"Here comes Cathy," called Rosalie, running to the window, "and she looks very happy so they must have done well today."

"I should hope so," said her mother, "if people haven't bought every sprig of the heather and the red, white and blue posies on this day, to say nothing of Cathy's lovely buttonholes, they never will! Goodness knows, they took us all enough time to make."

But what a labour of love, reflected Mary, watching Cathy come into the room chattering animatedly to Rosalie and Elizabeth. She scattered her day's takings on to the rug so that they could count the money together. Mary's house was now a home, if only a temporary one, for many of the street girls. She and her group of like-minded friends strived constantly to find them employment that would enable them to become independent, but their initial time in the house enabled them to heal and to grow in confidence. The Jubilee had been a godsend, and a little gold mine. Although Mary still had considerable doubts about a Queen who believed that her female subjects were inferior to their men folk, the surge of patriotism had meant that for several weeks anything in the national colours could be easily sold.

Mr Dyson's investigations had revealed that Dora's dowry, untouched by Richard, was still intact and indeed had grown quite considerably. Mr Dyson was hinting that he had withheld information regarding it from Daniel, but Mary suspected that it was more likely to be an act of negligence rather than benevolence on his part. Nonetheless, she blessed her father for leaving it with the bank that Dora's parents had always used rather than transferring it to their own bank. This had rendered it invisible to Daniel, and had subsequently helped her to turn her home into a place of refuge for the children.

She had always loved the tall terraced house where she had grown up, built in the reign of King George the Third, with its high ceilings and the bright and spacious drawing room occupying most of the ground floor. This was usually divided by exotically panelled folding doors, but when there were visitors to be entertained her parents had thrown them open to reveal the large bowed windows at each end of the room. Even the basement, where the kitchen and laundry rooms were situated, was usually flooded with light due to the south-facing position of the garden, which rose up above the windows.

Keeping the largest bedroom with its small balcony outside the floor-length windows for herself and Elizabeth, and the one on the opposite side of the landing for Valerie and her daughter, it had not been difficult to utilise the other two upper floors into suitable accommodation for the street girls. Four small dormitories were created there, with the two tiny attic rooms at the top of the house reserved for those needing more privacy when they arrived. These girls were

61

usually absorbed quite quickly into the little community, but Mary was very aware that sometimes the sheer effort required to seek refuge in the house had temporarily drained them of their last vestige of courage. She knew better than to rush them.

With the aid of an increasing number of sympathisers to her cause, Mary had been able to set up a charitable fund to help with the rescue work. This helped them to educate some girls and find occupations for others. Donations were regular, although some of their wealthier benefactresses preferred to contribute in secret, unsure of the reaction of their husbands. But the new law allowing married women to own property had brought an unprecedented level of independence to some middle-class women, who could now legally manage their affairs.

Two of 'Mary's girls', as they were affectionately named, were now in their second year at college, training to be teachers, and two more were apprenticed to a milliner in the West End. But Bramwell's shadow loomed large over the streets and many of the girls were too frightened to accept the proffered help. However, the women continued their nightly patrols in the town and word of their activities was spreading and bearing fruit. The police had become, if not protective, at least no longer cynical.

"I expect it's because I'm respectable again," Mary commented wryly to Granny.

"Nothing like money to achieve that, my dear," agreed Granny.

Violet's father had died the previous year, and her mother, much younger than him, had surprised them all by becoming interested in their work. To Violet's amazement, Mrs White had bought the little florist's shop that she had patronised for years and set up some of the girls there. She proved to be a vigilant and knowledgeable employer, confiding in Mary that flowers had always been her passion and that this was the fulfilment of a life-long dream. Four of the girls, of whom Cathy was one, worked happily under her instructions and took turns in serving in the little shop.

The Jubilee party had promised to be such a festive occasion and, to everyone's surprise, it was Cathy who had suggested that they set up a little stall outside Hyde Park to sell patriotically coloured buttonholes and posies. Everybody in the house had helped the girls, as they had worked well into the previous evening tying together the little red, white and blue flowers. Then they had risen before dawn that morning so they could set their wares out on their flag bedecked table before the crowds arrived.

Looking at their vivacious faces now, as Elizabeth and Rosalie helped Cathy to count the day's takings, Mary guessed the venture had been a success. Removing the girls from prostitution had sometimes seemed easier than finding them employment that would help them regain their self-esteem. Most working class women had to help support their families financially so there was no lack of jobs. But so many of them were almost as demeaning and debilitating as prostitution.

When she first began the process of rehabilitating some of her charges Mary had found Jenny, one of the older girls, employment in an underwear factory. A small local firm, it had seemed ideal. Jenny had already proved to be a competent seamstress under Valerie's tuition and was enthusiastic about going to work there.

The girl returned home on the first day looking white and exhausted. Mary thought it was just the strain of being in a strange environment. But two days later she noticed that Jenny's hands were covered in scratches and bruises. Questioning the girl gently she gradually elicited the information that Jenny had been designated a stay-maker.

Mary was not sure what this involved but on investigation found that the girl was required to haul around heavy and tough whale bones, and on getting them in position, cut them into the required shape for corsets and bustles with a large and cumbersome knife. Not a task that had been mentioned to Mary when she visited the factory owner. Nothing that a woman would normally be given to do unaided either. But Mary realised her inexperience in this field had been exploited, and Jenny was the victim of this. Jenny was happily apprenticed to a lace maker now, but Mary never forgot that first lesson.

Valerie's expertise as an artist had not only furthered her teaching career, but had helped her to start a small business as a miniaturist. She had been hoping to find a girl with enough talent to help her as the demand for her work outstripped her capacity to produce it. Only one girl had so far shown both the inclination and the ability, and that was the small figure who had rung the door bell late one night before collapsing onto the steps.

Anna. Anna whose father had disappeared into the fog with his bleeding bundle all that time ago. Anna who never spoke. Anna who never smiled. Anna who ran and hid the first time she saw Anthony come into the house. Mary and Valerie had brought the unconscious girl inside that night and wrapped her in blankets by the fire. When she had slept and eaten a little they bathed her carefully. Her back was scarred with whip tracks. Her head tilted to one side and her mouth drooped slightly. Her eyes were blank. They dare not send for a doctor as the girl would have been terrified of him, but Violet's older sister, Primrose, was a nurse.

"I think she must have had some kind of a seizure. Probably not for the first time. It's affected her wits, and her body." Primrose regarded her patient compassionately. "She's just had more than she can bear. Just feed her and clean her and keep her warm. I doubt she even knows what's happening."

"She knew enough to find us," Mary said.

And so she and Valerie did everything Primrose said, and a bit more beside. Mary made sure that Anna was rarely on her own and, when she was, there were always some of Valerie's drawings and paintings near, and books with pretty pictures to look at, and the abacus standing near to her chair so she could move the beads around.

Granny came often to sit with the poor, deformed mute, and in typical Granny fashion announced one day, "There's more to that one than meets the eye. Give her something more to do."

So they let her sit near to Valerie, who was doing a miniature of one of the actresses from the nearby playhouse, and after a while Valerie saw how closely Anna was watching. She put a pen by the girl's hand and pushed a sheet of paper in front of her. One momentous day the pen was picked up, almost furtively, and Anna began to draw. Valerie watched whilst trying to appear not to, lest she intimidate this frail creature. An hour passed silently except for the ticking clock and the scratching of the two pens.

Anna was the first to put her pen down. A pause. Head hunched between her thin shoulders, looking at the table, she pushed her paper over to Valerie. Valerie picked it up and instinctively gasped in pleasure. The sketch was of her, bent over her work. It was astonishing. Anna not only had an extraordinary gift, she also had remarkable powers of observation. Even the way Valerie's jaw dropped open when she was concentrating was captured. Crossing to the girl, she put her arms round her. For the first time since she had been with them, Anna did not flinch.

"Will you help me, Anna? This drawing is wonderful."

Anna looked up. She nodded slowly and reached for her pen. Under the picture of Valerie she wrote in an uneven hand, *'THANK YOU'*. Until then, they had not suspected that she could read and write.

By the end of the month Valerie had her helper. Anna learned fast and although she still did not speak, her basic literacy skills enabled them to communicate. Valerie never tired of showing Anna's efforts to everyone and the rest of the girls seemed to regard her as a sort of mascot and treated her with affection. Granny and Mary were diligent in keeping a watch on her, as they still had no inkling of how she had come to be on their door step that night. But Anna prospered. Eating regular meals and keeping warm and busy had filled out her little frame. She would always be stunted in her growth, but now looked more like the young woman she was, instead of appearing to be a child. Rosalie had also taken Anna under her wing. Fifteen years old now, she was beginning to show her mother's talent for drawing and frequently the three women would be closeted together all afternoon. To everyone's delight, some clients were beginning to ask for Anna's work specifically.

At least her home was a cheerful environment, Mary sometimes reflected, but even though much had been achieved she felt it was like dropping a pebble into the ocean. The nightly patrols continued but the prostitution of young girls seemed to be accelerating. Everywhere could be seen the exploitation of her sex, women doing menial and often degrading jobs for a pittance if they were working class, and required to pretend they were brainless, passive dolls if they were middle class. Often, their very existence still depending on the whim of their husbands or fathers.

Dozens of women throughout the country were now writing almost daily to their MPs demanding more changes in the law. There was a growing awareness among thinking women that if their status was ever going to rise above the level of slavery then the whole structure of Government must alter. As Granny had remarked on more than one occasion: "We need the vote".

It was a measure of her own conditioning, thought Mary, that she was only now understanding that Granny was not exaggerating. They did indeed need to confront the inconceivable. They needed the vote. Violet had accepted this first. Just as she had discovered and absorbed the ideas of Mary Wollstonecraft and insisted that Mary read them, so she had been saying for some time that only the enfranchisement of women would bring about real change.

"Sometimes we get so involved with doing what we can here, we lose sight of the bigger picture," she told her friend, and Mary was aware that this was a constant danger.

Violet had recently become engaged to Harold, a fellow teacher at the school, who was an ardent believer in what he called the 'emancipation of women'. Mary had been worried when Violet announced that she was being courted by Harold, but Violet reminded her of Richard, her father, and Anthony, Alice's husband.

"Not all men are like Daniel and Bramwell, Mary. Remember it was John Stuart Mill who first tried to get us the vote. There are a great many good and thoughtful men who are only too anxious to see things changed."

Mary knew she was right, but how to further the momentous task of enfranchising women continued to elude them completely. The writing of letters seemed woefully inadequate, but it was still their most powerful weapon. There had to be something more. But meanwhile Mary tried to find the time to compose at least one letter daily, describing the poverty and despair she constantly encountered that would remain unchecked if the present discrimination continued. One morning she was so engrossed in penning such a letter to one of the younger MPs in the House of Commons that she barely heard the front door bell, only registering it when Alice's head popped round the door.

"Mary, I think you'd better come."

"Who is it?" asked Mary, rising from her desk.

"Well," said Alice slowly, "She's greatly changed, but unless I'm much mistaken, it's that woman that

Daniel moved in here."

Mary felt her whole body go rigid with shock. "Evangeline? It can't be... why should she come back here? You must be mistaken, Alice."

She pushed past her friend and went into the hall. She knew instantly that the woman standing on the doorstep, her face shielded by her bonnet and turned slightly away from Mary, was indeed Evangeline. All the anger and fear and contempt that she had felt nine years ago came rushing back to her.

"How dare you? How dare you come to my house? Please leave immediately and..."

But the words faded on her lips as Evangeline turned toward her. Lifting her cloak she revealed a child of indeterminate age. One side of the child's face was wasted, and a strange green colour, and her skull showed through her hair, which was sparse and tufted. As for Evangeline, her once buxom figure was reduced to a stick-like thinness. But it was the desolation, the sheer hopelessness of her expression, that made Mary realise that, however much she despised this creature, she could not arbitrarily turn her and the child away. At very least, she must know how and why they had come here. Indisputably, the child was dying. She drew back from the door and silently motioned them both inside.

Alice, startled but always compassionate, took the child by the hand and seated her on a stool by the fire. Then Mary and Alice turned together and studied Evangeline in silence.

"Why have you come here? Who is this child?" asked Mary.

Evangeline hesitated, then, "She's your Elizabeth's half sister. She was born to Daniel and me before he married you. He only married you for this house. But once he got it, and your money, he changed. He stopped being loving to me and Chrissie. He made me send Chrissie to my mother when I came to live here. Said Chrissie wasn't really his, though he knew she was. Then my mother died, and Chrissie went to live with my sister, who works in the match factory. So Chrissie went to work there with her as soon as she was old enough. Then when Daniel threw me out I went and worked there with them too. Sis and me was OK but Chrissie's face started to go funny. The foreman said it would get better, that it was nothing to do with the matches. But then this lady came to see us, and she said it's a kind of poison, phossy something or other, and my Chrissie won't ever get better."

Alice made a quick gesture toward the child, who was sitting, unmoving, gazing into the fire, but Evangeline shook her head.

"She can't hear you. She can't hear anything. She can't see much either. I thought, if I came back here, her father might help us. I didn't expect to see you."

Mary felt her legs give way under her. Sitting abruptly on the sofa, she indicated that Evangeline sit by her. "So, you were his victim too? But you helped to keep me a prisoner here. You seemed to enjoy persecuting me."

"Yes," agreed Evangeline, "I suppose I did. But I'm being punished now, aren't I? So where is His Nibs, then?"

When Mary told her of Daniel's death, Evangeline's emaciated frame seemed to become even frailer. "Right, well, I suppose that's it, then," she said, getting to her feet. "No help here, I see. We'll be off." And crossing the room, she touched Chrissie lightly on the shoulder.

Mary saw both mother and daughter's faces transformed as the girl smiled up at Evangeline. "No," she said. "No. Please stay. Let us find some food for you both and then I will call Dr White and see if anything can be done for Chrissie."

But even as she spoke, her eyes met Alice's and they both knew that nothing could save Chrissie. The conditions in the match factories were a scandal, but too few people realised how appalling they were. Women and girls worked for as many as sixteen hours a day for a wage that would barely keep them in bread. Tyrannical rules, enforced by foremen, imposed a system of fines that meant even this was not always received. If a woman was two minutes late, she could lose half a day's pay. Bryant and May, the owners of the factories, scoffed at the law that had reduced factory workers hours to ten a day.

Chrissie gripped her mother's hand and began to cough. The dry retching racked her body and Evangeline took her daughter in her arms and held her loosely. When the attack was over she began to gently rub Chrissie's hands, soothing the girl. Her anguished eyes met Mary's over the child's head.

Mary was almost overcome by pity and frustration. What choice for so many of her sex – prostitution or what amounted to white slavery? And a society that was largely ignorant and uncaring of these vile practices.

"I swear," she told herself, "to make the rest of the world understand how these women and their children are forced to live. If it means I have to give my life to do it, then so be it."

1888

Valerie left Anna drawing at her little desk and wandered into the kitchen. Alice and Evangeline were washing up the breakfast things. They looked up as Valerie entered and Evangeline asked, "Is Anna alright?"

"Yes, happy as a little sand-boy. Give her a pen and ink and she's in her element. I think she's got more staying power than me, only ten o'clock and I'm dying for a break and a cup of tea."

"Oh yes?" said Alice. "Come on, Valerie, you've got more stamina than any of us. I'll make the tea, and then you can tell us what is on your mind."

Valerie laughed ruefully. "No secrets in this house, are there? Well, I'm a bit concerned about Mary. Does anyone know what she is up to?"

Alice looked at her thoughtfully. "So you've noticed too? No, she hasn't said anything to me. I don't suppose she's talked to you, has she, Evangeline?"

Evangeline shook her head. They all knew that Chrissie's death had drawn the two women close enough to heal the wounds of the past but the scars still lay between them, making Evangeline an unlikely confidante for Mary.

"Do you know if she has spoken to Granny?" Valerie asked.

"No," replied Alice. "Or if she has Granny hasn't told me. But you're right. She is very preoccupied and spends a great deal of time out at the moment and then doesn't tell us where she's been."

"Which is not a bit like her," said Valerie. "She has something on her mind – and I think she doesn't want to involve us in it. Which is a bit worrying. I should be more comfortable knowing that she wasn't putting herself in danger on the streets. We all know that Bramwell is still out there, and that Mary is hardly his favourite person."

"Perhaps," said Alice, "We should stop guessing and just ask her."

Valerie smiled at her. "Always straight to the point, our Alice. Yes, I agree. Tonight we'll corner her. Can you get Granny to come round? We may be making something out of nothing, but I don't think so."

Mary was late returning home that evening. There were so many helpers for the 'travelling soup kitchen' that no-one had to go more than twice weekly now, so as Mary slipped into the drawing room, she found a reception committee awaiting her. Granny, Alice, Violet and Valerie were obviously not indulging in light banter and she was instantly alarmed.

"What's the matter? Where's Elizabeth? Is everyone alright?"

Granny quickly intercepted with, "Nothing is wrong, my dear. But we do want to talk to you. Have you eaten yet?"

Mary shook her head, and the next few minutes were a bustle of activity as the women prepared a tray for her. She sank back thankfully onto the sofa, obviously tired by the day's exertions. Eventually, partially revived by Granny's increasingly renowned soup, Mary examined her friends quizzically.

"Well?" she demanded, "Talk away, then."

Granny regarded her affectionately. "Where have you been, Mary? You are obviously exhausted. We need to know what is going on. Even Elizabeth is asking where you go so often. We are beginning to be worried about you, my dear."

"Ah," said Mary, her face clouding. "I am so sorry. I hadn't realised... it is just that everyone has so much to do, is so busy, and I suppose I didn't want to expose the children to more than is necessary. Also, to be honest," glancing across at Evangeline, "perhaps it was something I didn't want to talk about too much, for fear of upsetting anyone. But you are right. I should have told you what is going on."

Squaring her shoulders, she continued, "I have been trying to help Annie Besant, down in the East End. She is a journalist, a friend of Violet and Harold, which is how I met her."

Violet nodded approvingly, "She is a splendid person. I didn't realise that you were working with her, Mary."

Mary smiled at her, then glanced quickly at Evangeline before continuing. "She is rallying the women who work in the match factory. They desperately need support. Most of them are barely women at all, just young girls. You've probably seen that article Annie wrote for the paper about the appalling conditions in the factories. She has really managed to stir things up. So we need to move now, before public interest wanes. We are planning to take fifty of the girls and march on Parliament this week. Some of the Members of Parliament are going to come outside and listen to what the girls have to say, and then we are all going to link arms and march along the embankment. We would have liked to have gone to Trafalgar Square, but that is still banned."

She paused, knowing they were all remembering the reason for the ban. There had been many demonstrations by the poor and the unemployed from London's East End over the past few years, but last November's brutal dispersal of the demonstrators had resulted in what the papers had dubbed 'Bloody Sunday'. The Government was determined to be seen giving no quarter to the poverty-stricken people of London's East End, and had deployed two thousand police and four hundred troops with orders to stop the marchers at all costs. No-one knew for sure how many casualties had resulted from their actions as the injured could not afford medical treatment, but it was believed to have run into many hundreds.

Aware that she must reassure her friends that she would be safe, Mary continued, "Some of the girls will carry banners, and all of them have loud voices and, of course, a just cause. But, don't worry, this will be a peaceful demonstration, and I am proud that I shall be with them."

Evangeline sat unmoving, but Mary could see her eyes were full of tears. "I know you are doing this at least partly for my Chrissie. Thank you. Thank you from the bottom of my heart. I would come with you, but I have come to realise that I have not yet your strength. I might be more of a burden than a help." Looking round the room, she added: "You are all amazing women. I wish I had known you sooner. My life might have been very different."

"Come on, Evangeline," Valerie exclaimed, "We're not extraordinary at all, just women, like you, who have had some bad times and are trying to change a few things for the better. You are one of us now. And, Mary, I think we are all pleased at what you are planning to do. I can appreciate why you thought it might upset Evangeline, but I do think we should tell the children where you are going and why. They usually understand more than we give them credit for. And, please, please do be very careful."

Mary was to recall that admonition a few days later. She knew that there had been previous marches by the match workers which had ended in vicious brawls, with many of the girls being badly beaten. This was why Annie had so carefully orchestrated the demonstration. In spite of this, Mary was unprepared for the sheer frightening vigour of the mounted police as they swirled round. Holding her own banner high, she tried to shield her face, blocking out the sight of the horses. When the women reached the House of Commons the police dropped back, sitting quietly on their mounts. Lowering her banner, Mary realised that her whole body was shaking. Being at the back of the procession, she heard very little of the proceedings, but the women's voices that floated back to her sounded confident and articulate. Too young and too angry to be nervous, she reflected.

Finally the sound of voices ceased, and the women began to prepare for the march back. Mary hoisted her banner once more, conscious of the ache that its weight had caused across her shoulders. Startled by the proximity of a passing horse she dropped the banner, which struck the animal across the rump. Caught unawares, it reared, its hooves blocking the sky from

Mary's view. Her mind leapt back twenty years. Before anyone could catch her, she slid to the ground in a dead faint.

Several hours later, back home, she lay on the couch surrounded by anxious faces. Elizabeth was stroking her hand.

"Honestly, darling," said Mary, "I am alright. I just feel very stupid. I was supposed to be helping and two of those poor girls had to carry me to the cab."

"It was the horses," proclaimed Violet, who had been sent for by Valerie. "If we had thought about it we should have expected the mounted police to be there, and you would have been better prepared. After what happened with your mother, it's not surprising that you fainted today. Annie saw the whole thing. But she said to tell you that the day went well, and the campaign continues."

"Oh, Mummy," said the ten-year-old Elizabeth, "I wish you didn't have go to these places."

Mary sat up carefully and wrapped her daughter's hands in hers. "Elizabeth, darling, so do I. It would be lovely if everyone in the world could feel happy and secure, and go to school and have plenty to eat. But they don't, as you know."

Elizabeth nodded soberly. Her closest friends were the girls who sought refuge in the house, and Mary was always as honest with her as delicacy permitted.

"Until they do, then some of us who are lucky enough to have all those things feel that it is our duty to try to help, in any way we can." She paused, and then burst out laughing. "Oh dear, I sound like Mr Collins!"

They joined in her mirth, Elizabeth included. The

women had been taking it in turns to read *Pride and Prejudice* aloud in the evenings whilst they sewed or repaired their clothes, and Valerie had surprised them all with her talent for acting, her *piece de resistance* being her portrayal of the unctuous clergyman. Their laughter broke the tension, as Mary had intended, and soon Elizabeth was happily playing out in the garden and could be heard welcoming her dearest friend, Alice's son, John. Seconds after, Alice burst through the door, followed by Anthony.

"Mary, one of the girls came round and said you were hurt. What has happened?"

Her obvious concern was so intense that Mary was suddenly suffused with such a feeling of gratitude for her many friends that for a moment she was quite overcome. Then, rising off the sofa, she said, "Look, my dear friend, I am well. It was a silly weakness on my part and I shall guard against it happening again."

Alice studied her carefully. "You do look better than I had expected. So I'll believe you. But I must know everything, if only to report back to Granny."

Anthony stepped forward holding a familiar covered bowl, a large smile on his face. "We are all mightily relieved, Mary. Granny insisted on the inevitable basin of soup, however. Woe betide you if it is not drunk immediately."

Giggling weakly, Mary obeyed, while Violet and Valerie outlined the events of the day to Alice and her husband. Granny's curative beverage warmed her as was the intention. Mary lay back and closed her eyes. Heartened though she was, a plan was already forming in her mind to help the cause of the match workers. And also, she admitted, to redeem herself in her own eyes.

Whatever excuses were made for her, she had been a futile encumbrance instead of a support to the cause. She was determined to put that right.

That was her last conscious thought before she drifted into sleep, falling immediately into the dream that had haunted her for so many years. The terrible thunder of hooves had so long accompanied her slumbers that her unconscious mind now reached out to embrace it. Seeing her sleeping, her friends quietly left the room, unaware of the tumult within her.

Several days later, a much restored Mary announced to Valerie that she had some news that she wanted to discuss with everyone. Consequently, that evening found Valerie, Granny, Violet and Alice enjoying the summer warmth in Mary's small garden. Mary and Evangeline came out with tall glasses of home-made lemonade and some gingerbread still warm from the oven. Evangeline was proving to be a wonderful cook, much to her own surprise.

"Well?" said Granny, when they had all expressed their appreciation of this treat, "Pleasant though this is, my dear, what is it you want to discuss?"

"I wanted to tell you what I intend to do next week." Mary's friends waited in silence for her to continue. Mary took a deep breath. "I am going to Epsom. To the Derby."

There was a shocked gasp. They all knew Mary's history. How could they not?

Before anyone could interrupt, Mary continued, "The Duke of Portland, who is the Master of the Queen's Horses, has a horse running. It is called Ayrshire, and it is the favourite. My plan is to get as near the winners' enclosure as possible and at the moment when all eyes are on the owner, to raise this high in the air." Reaching behind her, she raised a banner with the words: *Stop White Slavery in Britain* and a sketch of a burning match with the Bryant & May trade mark underneath it.

Violet reacted first. "It's a good plan. Mary. All the newspapers will be there, and probably the Queen as well. Lots of politicians, of course. But what if Ayrshire doesn't win?"

"It won't matter," Mary replied. "I'll just go ahead anyway. It will make more of a point if it's him, that's all."

"Why Epsom?" asked Granny.

"Because I have this feeling that it's the right place. All those upper class people who mostly have no idea what goes on, and care even less. And also," she paused, "in a strange sort of way, it makes me feel that what happened to my mother was not entirely random and futile. I feel almost as if I am being led by her to make this gesture."

"Then you must do it." Heads nodded slowly in agreement with Valerie, who then added, in a tone that brooked no argument, "But I shall come with you."

Mary smiled at her friend. "I thought you might. You do realise that we might be arrested?"

"That would certainly draw attention to our cause," replied Valerie dryly.

"It would indeed," said Granny, "but it might be somewhat uncomfortable."

"I believe it will be worth the risk," said Valerie soberly.

"The day after tomorrow, then," said Mary. "And

we must leave early."

The rosy glow of the setting sun had disappeared and night was creeping into the garden as the group dispersed. Bidding her friends goodnight, Mary peeped in on her sleeping daughter before making her own way to bed. As she doused her candle, she knew that she was finally facing her own demons, and was going to overcome them.

"You look wonderful in that red hat," commented Valerie, "I think they would notice you even without the banner."

"It was my mother's favourite colour," replied her friend.

In fact, both women looked stunning. One of Annie Besant's friends had managed to get them tickets for the winners' enclosure so it was essential they looked the part. So far the day had gone smoothly, but they were aware of the tension stretching every bone in their bodies. The big race was about to begin. Mary took the folded banner from her reticule and held it close to her body in readiness.

As the horses thundered past Mary felt a resurgence of all her old fear and horror, but breathing hard she managed to subdue it and concentrate on what she had to do. The cheering reached a crescendo and the man in front of them turned in delight and said, "It's Ayrshire – my goodness, that will be a popular win!"

Everyone waited excitedly for the horse and jockey to enter the enclosure, and as they did, Mary stepped purposefully forward, flanked by Valerie. They had chosen the moment carefully. As the owner, wreathed in smiles, stepped forward to take the horse's halter,

Mary, smiling gaily, pushed through the cluster of people around him. They fell back, assuming, as she had anticipated, that she was a special friend. Before the Duke even had a chance to register her presence, she unfolded the banner and held it aloft.

Into the sudden hush she and Valerie both shouted, "Support the match girls, no more white slavery!"

The rumble of startled disapprobation began with a male voice saying, "Oh, I say, what is going on?" Valerie afterwards commented this was so inappropriate she nearly laughed. But then another voice called, "Remove these women! We don't want this nonsense at Epsom!" and the call went up for the police.

Within seconds two burly policeman had appeared and Mary and Valerie each found themselves taken by the arm and forced back through the enclosure. The banner dropped to the ground. But Mary observed to her satisfaction that the journalists were all scribbling like mad.

The women were escorted off the course, and warned by the police that they had committed a breach of the peace. They politely denied this, and Mary could see that the two policemen were finding it difficult to deal with such well-dressed and well-spoken ladies. There was some conversation with the Duke, who was looking their way. He finally nodded. It was the cue to release them.

"You've been lucky, ladies, His Grace will not press charges."

Mary didn't know whether to be glad or sorry but as they were escorted to the exit, heads held high, a voice behind them said, "Well done, ladies," and there was a smattering of applause. Not much, but enough to penetrate the curtain of hostility that surrounded them.

"*Some* support out there, then," whispered Valerie.

The next day the story was only eclipsed by the Duke's win, though even that was reversed in some of the papers. There were editorials in nearly all of them discussing the issue of the conditions in the East End, and the match workers plight in particular. Annie Besant sent a message congratulating them. The match girls had voted to come out on strike, and it was felt that Mary's action and the resulting publicity might help to tip the other unions into helping to support the strikers financially.

A few days later they learnt that this had happened, for the first time in the history of the unions. Mary was elated, especially when Elizabeth proclaimed, "I am *so* proud of you, Mummy".

The house and its occupants were thriving. Mary's network of like-minded and philanthropically inclined men and women was growing, and Violet's mother had agreed to take in what she referred to as 'some of your waifs and strays'. In fact, she was proving to be a tower of strength, talking to the traders in Covent Garden where she bought the flowers for her shop and sometimes hearing of possible positions for the girls before they became public. Unemployment was so high that they had learnt to move very quickly.

Violet and Harold now lived in the house next door to Violet's mother, and every evening their sitting room was turned into a classroom, as five or six women struggled to learn to read. The literacy classes were increasingly popular, as they increased job potential.

Evangeline had proved to be a star pupil, and had managed to find a job keeping track of the local chimney sweep's appointments. A clerking job like this would normally have been taken by a man so she was rightly pleased with herself.

One evening in early October, Mary found herself sitting in the garden enjoying a rare moment of solitude. Valerie and Anna were painting indoors, and Elizabeth was with them. All the other girls were out. It had been a good day. Cathy had brought a charming young man home and shyly announced that they were courting and she was to meet his parents that evening. Mary had been delighted to agree to be in *loco parentis* for Cathy when the visit was reciprocated the following week. Watching Cathy grow in confidence had been like watching the sun break through the clouds.

Mary was woken from her musing by the doorbell. With a start she realised that it had grown quite dark and the inevitable fog was already rising down the end of the small garden. She had grown quite cold. Pulling her shawl round her shoulders she went into the hall. Opening the front door, she was surprised to see a policeman standing there.

"Mrs Morrison?" he asked. She nodded assent. His accent was more educated than most of the police in this area. "I wonder if you could come with me? There's a young woman in some distress on the warehouse roof. She's got a small baby with her and she's threatening to jump. My colleague thought you might be able to help."

"Of course," replied Mary, reaching for her cloak and pulling the door closed behind her. "However did she get..?" but her question was lost as the man strode ahead of her. She found herself running to keep up. For what seemed like hours, but she thought was probably only about fifteen minutes, they ran through the thickening fog.

Finally they reached the warehouse. Mary looked upwards but could see no figure on the roof. "Where..?"she began to ask and then stopped. The silence was palpable. She was on her own.

"Constable," she called, "Constable, can you guide me to the girl, please, I can't see you or her through this fog?"

The officer appeared noiselessly at her side. "Well, it looks as if my colleague has resolved the matter. Perhaps we should go inside and make sure."

He took her arm and started to pull her into the building. Mary felt a abrupt chill of fear run through her. Suddenly his face was so close to hers that she could feel the warmth of his breath.

"You should know better than to go out alone at night, my dear. All those dreadful murders in Whitechapel. You really can't trust anyone any more. You are not at all careful, are you? I've been watching you for a long time, you know. A lady like you should know better than to consort with whores. I think the time has come to put a stop to you."

Mary could feel her panic rising as she frantically tried to pull away from him. "Constable, please let me go at once," she insisted, straining to sound authoritative.

He paused, his grip on Mary's arm tightening. "Don't let us be formal, Mrs Morrison. I've always thought of you as Mary. Especially when I've imagined this moment. Do call me Jack. Its how they always refer to me in the newspapers."

Mary never even managed to scream. The last thing she heard on this earth was his laughter. The last thing she saw was the flash of steel as the blade of the knife descended. God was merciful. She lost consciousness at that moment.

Part Two: Elizabeth

1903

Elizabeth let herself into the house and pulled off her boots with a sigh of relief. Padding along the hall she was surprised at the unusual silence but then she heard the sound of giggling from the kitchen.

"What are you laughing at?" she enquired, pushing open the door.

A grinning Rosalie held up a large drawing of Lord Salisbury, surrounded by some of the members of his aristocratic cabinet.

"You should be drawing for Punch," smiled Elizabeth, "None of their caricatures are as funny as yours."

"As all their staff are men, I don't imagine they feel as strongly as we do about the high levels of pomposity," said Rosalie's friend, Emily.

Elizabeth acknowledged the truth of this. It was not a bad Government, she thought, but nevertheless the status of women was still somewhere below that of convicts and lunatics, both of whom could retain the vote that was still denied to her sex.

"The meeting was good. Mrs Fawcett is a remarkable person. I think Mother would have approved of us joining her National Union."

Rosalie rose and came to put her arm round Elizabeth's shoulders. "Your mum would have approved of everything we've done, Lizzie. But most of all she would have approved of her daughter."

Elizabeth's eyes were moist. "It shouldn't still be hurting, should it? Nearly fifteen years, and I still expect her to be here when I come in. It's so stupid."

"No, it's not," replied Rosalie, "What happened was unbelievable and appalling and perhaps none of us will ever quite recover from it, but for you, it was the worse thing in the world. But you have struggled through and survived all that horror, and chosen to put on your mother's mantle and continue the fight. You are an example to us all."

"She's right, Elizabeth," said Emily. "Though everyone wishes that whoever did it had been caught and punished. That would have made it easier to put it all behind you. There's no doubt that the police really did work hard to try and find him. Your mother was so well respected even by those who didn't agree with her. I was sixteen when she died, and although I didn't know any of you then, I remember my mother and I both cried when we heard the news. We came to her funeral, you know, and we were staggered at the number of people who were there. Certainly half the East End, I should think."

It was true. Elizabeth, only ten at the time and holding Alice's hand tightly as they followed the glass-sided carriage, had never forgotten the silent crowds bowing their heads as they passed.

"We shall probably never know who or why," said Rosalie. "The whole area seemed to be full of maniacs at the time. And they never caught that other dreadful man. Thank heavens that all finally stopped."

They knew that she was speaking of what had

become known as 'the Ripper murders'. The police had declared that Mary's murder had probably been done by another hand, as it was believed that Jack the Ripper killed only prostitutes, not respectable ladies. Also, mercifully, Mary's body was found intact, whereas the Ripper routinely mutilated his victims.

Rosalie continued, "But you were right about the police. They were so helpful. There was one really well-spoken constable, John something or other, who was here so often I thought he was quite keen on Mum. Only then my real father turned up and we never saw him again."

Elizabeth smiled at her friend. The reappearance of Charles in Valerie's life had helped them all, practically and emotionally, to move forward with their lives. On returning from his exile in Australia, he had set about finding Valerie and his child. She had been right. He really did love her. The death of his father had enabled him to return to this country and find her. They had been married for twelve years now, and Rosalie had a ten-year-old brother, Percy, whom she adored. She divided her time between the family estate in Hampshire, which Charles had inherited, and what she thought of as her 'other' family in London.

There was a sound from outside and the door opened to reveal Granny. "I won't take my cloak off, I just wanted to pop in and find out how the meeting went," she said, sinking into a chair.

Elizabeth gave her a hug, before sitting in the chair opposite her. "Well," she began, "Mrs Fawcett gave us the names of two more women who have qualified to become doctors. It seems that once her sister had broken through that particular barrier, more and more of us are following suit. Thank heavens for Mrs Anderson, and the Royal Free."

"It's not enough, though," replied Granny. "Every hospital in Britain should be welcoming you with open arms. God knows there's a need for more doctors. We all know that there are still a lot of women who don't seek help when they need to because their husbands forbid them see a male doctor. There'll be no proper equality in anything until we have the vote. I sometimes think I shan't live to see real suffrage for women in this country."

"Don't you dare talk that way, Granny," said Elizabeth, blowing a kiss to her. "How should we manage without you? We'd all fall to pieces!"

"Nonsense. You always were prone to exaggerate," grumbled Granny, but they could see that she was pleased.

"Perhaps we should do something really drastic, like setting fire to the House of Commons, then they'd notice us," said Emily.

Rosalie looked at her. "You're only half joking, aren't you, Ems?"

The two women had discovered whilst at college that they shared a birthday and from this initial coincidence a firm friendship had grown. Both teachers, and committed advocates of universal suffrage, they were fervent followers of Mrs Fawcett, though Emily felt nothing was progressing fast enough. She was beginning to question the dictum that only peaceful protest would achieve the longed for end. Rosalie had inherited her mother's gift for drawing and her wickedly funny caricatures were circulated by Emily with much joy amongst the Suffragists, as they were now known.

Elizabeth had studied medicine, which she knew would have been unthinkable in her mother's day. Alice and Granny had taken her into their family and had guarded and cherished her after Mary's death. Along with Mary's friends and colleagues their determination that Elizabeth's education would be better than any of theirs had borne fruit. She had proved to be a natural academic, which was a particular joy to the scholarly Violet, and she had outclassed most of her fellow students regularly. As she was one of only two women in her year this might have made life difficult for her, but she possessed a modesty and charm that made her popular with both sexes.

Her namesake, Mrs Fawcett's sister, Elizabeth Garrett Anderson, had blazed a trail that had been her inspiration. But Elizabeth knew that she had not chosen an easy path. Though she had qualified and now worked at the Royal Free, many doors were still firmly closed to her. Violet's much older sister, Primrose, who had worked as a nurse and midwife at the hospital for many years, was often able to give her a helpful sense of perspective when Elizabeth was feeling particularly frustrated by the system. One evening, some weeks before, when the two of them had been travelling home together on the tram, Elizabeth confided how she would have loved to specialise as a surgeon, a seemingly impossible ambition.

Primrose sighed, and then chuckled. "Oh, Elizabeth. And *I* would have liked to have trained as a doctor. Which was absolutely out of the question in my day. It *will* all happen you know. Everything does move on eventually. Our mother would have loved to have been a teacher of horticulture. But it was unthinkable to my grandparents that she should do anything but stay at home and look after them until she married. However, Violet is a teacher, and her daughter, Kitty, our mother's granddaughter, will certainly go to college, assuming that is her wish. Violet and Harold are determined that she will have as many choices as her brother. Do you know, it is Kitty's ninth birthday next week, it doesn't seem two minutes since she was born. Once upon a time her future would have been mapped out for her, wife, mother, drudge. Well, probably a quite well-off drudge, but with a very limited, narrow life. Never a thinking, intelligent person in her own right. That situation is far less likely to happen nowadays. The world has started to acknowledge that we have the same brains as our 'masters'." Primrose leant over and grasped Elizabeth's hand. "Never doubt, my dear, that every step women like you and I take brings that day nearer."

Elizabeth knew that she was right. Primrose had devoted her life to nursing, often going out late at night to help at a confinement, with no expectation of any extra payment. The conditions in which many women gave birth were often horrific and one in four women died in childbirth. Infection and ignorance were rife. Only that day a woman had been brought into the hospital haemorrhaging badly. They had been unable to save either her or her baby. She left behind nineteen motherless children.

Elizabeth's fiancé, Stephen, was also a doctor, well respected and specialising in medical research. The two of them often talked until late into the night. Elizabeth told him, with some justification, that she could have both written and presented the papers that were so well received by his peer group with equal success, had she been allowed. To his credit, Stephen agreed with her, but Elizabeth wondered if he really understood her frustration at this unfairness. She was curiously reluctant to marry the tall, dark and handsome doctor, who had courted her so assiduously for nearly two years previous to asking her to be his wife. They had been engaged for over a year now. He was rich, intelligent, understood and respected her career, and he adored her. She did not understand her hesitation, and her friends, usually so quick to advise and support her, were unexpectedly reticent in this case. Stephen seemed content to let her dictate the pace of their relationship.

It was Emily who asked her now, "Well, Elizabeth, when are you going to put that gorgeous young doctor out of his misery and marry him?"

Rosalie threw her friend a quick glance, "Don't be a bully, Ems. Lizzie will tell us when she is ready. Anyway, we've got to go. On your feet." And she playfully pulled Emily up. "Mrs Pankhurst is coming to speak tonight about this new union of hers, and we are going along. It should be very interesting."

The two women having left, Granny, still determinedly cloaked, surveyed Elizabeth affectionately. "So, Elizabeth. I've known you, and loved you, all your life. I'm going to ask that question because your mother isn't here to do it. My dear, why aren't you setting a date for your wedding?"

Elizabeth sat silently. After a minute she said, "It's not because of what happened to Mummy when she married my father, although I know that's what everyone thinks. I've always known about that and what happened, but I see Violet with Harold, and Alice with Anthony, and anyway, lots of my friends are married and happy. And in any case, things are different now. This is 1903, and no-one could legally do what my father did to Mummy any more. But, the thing is, Granny, although it all seems so right and Stephen should be the perfect person for me, I don't feel sure. There is always this doubt in my mind."

There was a long silence as Granny sat there waiting for her to continue.

"We don't laugh, you see," Elizabeth said suddenly, "oh, Granny, I've only just realised. We don't laugh together."

Granny rose as majestically as her increasing arthritis would allow. "Then you should think hard about your next step, Elizabeth. Now come and give me a kiss, I must get back home, they'll wonder where I've got to. I think John wanted to pop in later and have a chat about the article he is doing for his newspaper on the hospital, will you be in?"

"Yes, of course," replied Elizabeth somewhat absently as she hugged Granny goodnight. "Yes, I haven't seen him all week. That would be nice."

As she let herself out of the house Granny found herself smiling indulgently. John would think that very nice indeed, she thought. Sometimes, she reflected, the onlooker sees most of the game. Either way, it felt like a very satisfactory afternoon.

1906

Rosalie's face was red with vexation. "Lizzie, you have got to help! Emily is coming back here and she has joined Mrs Pankhurst's Suffragettes. And I think she is right. I know that we have always tried to make sure that our demonstrations are peaceful, but where has it got us? I simply don't understand your hesitation, we have absolutely got to back her up, and join ourselves."

Elizabeth held up her hands in mock surrender. "Ros, calm down. The Suffragettes are becoming more and more militant, and God knows I understand why. But Mrs Fawcett still thinks that our Suffragist movement is really starting to work. And don't forget we have been with her almost since the beginning. We have managed to get the sympathy of a lot of MPs and influential people. I just want to make sure that we don't throw away everything we have achieved."

"Lizzie, look around you. Look at the poverty, look at the number of women on the streets, some of them working all day in the markets or the laundries and then going on the streets at night simply to feed their children. Dying during the sixth or seventh confinement because it's against the law for them to be given any information about contraception. The whole cycle then being repeated with their daughters. Sympathy is not enough, it is time for action. Don't forget, Lizzie, my mother and I really know what life on the streets is like. I want to see our sex *live*, Lizzie, not just survive until they drop dead from exhaustion or infection."

As Rosalie has intended, Elizabeth was shocked by Rosalie's mention of her past. It had been something she appeared to have buried deep in her mind for many years, and until this moment, Elizabeth had thought and indeed hoped that she might have no memory of her early, terrible experiences.

Taking Rosalie's hands between her own, she said, "I do understand. I heard that the Prime Minister made some patronising remark the other day about 'being patient but going on pestering'. As if we were a bunch of naughty children who might eventually get our reward. I felt, oh, belittled, I suppose. Oh, Ros, I think it's possible that John agrees with you, but before we commit ourselves utterly, I'd like to discuss it with him. Not be too hasty."

Satisfied that she had won the argument, Rosalie went upstairs to write to her friend. Emily was coming back to London to live next month, leaving her teaching post in Berkshire, and the friends were looking forward to seeing each other again.

Elizabeth stood looking out of the window. All her instincts told her that Rosalie was right. She was reasonably sure that John would think so too. Having married her childhood friend and companion six months earlier, she was blissfully happy, and it was as important to her now as it had been for most of her life to discuss almost everything with John. Perhaps a family conference, she mused. She loved the fact that Granny and Alice and Anthony now really were her family.

However, John's support for Rosalie was more hesitant than she had expected. "Of course, she's right, Lizzie. Every time we think we have made a giant step forward, it somehow gets swept aside within a week or so and we are back to where we started. The time has surely come for a stronger and more visible protest. But, and it is a big but, my darling, you must be prepared for a powerful legal response. My paper is one of the few that supports the Suffragists, but it did not support Mrs Pankhurst when she was sent to prison last year. Merely for interrupting a political meeting. I did think that Mr Churchill might have answered her when she asked him if he believed in votes for women. Even if he had only replied in the negative. It might have prevented the whole ghastly business that followed.

"The article I wrote calling her sentence an incredibly unjust over-reaction was cut to the bone if you remember. Had I not been a senior reporter I doubt if it would have seen the light of day at all. That was a warning bell. The movement has its first martyrs and there will be others. You must not underestimate how great the gulf is between Mrs Fawcett's Suffragists and the new and radical Suffragettes that the Pankhurst family has formed. I fervently believe that our cause is worth fighting for, but we must understand that this is a war, and we cannot predict the extent of the casualties."

Elizabeth was silent for a long time. Then, "Could you bear it if they send me to prison?"

Her husband held her gaze steadily. "If I knew that you were doing what you believed to be right, and had understood this might be the outcome, then, yes, my love. I know how brave you are. I also know that both of us grew up watching our parents finally coming to the conclusion that the only way forward was to gain the vote for everyone, man or woman. And that your mother realised it before most."

"She would join the Suffragettes, whatever the consequences, wouldn't she?"

It was more of a statement than a question, but John nodded silently.

"And," he said, "Granny already has, although mercifully she is not able to take much physical part any more. She and Mother have been distributing leaflets for a month or more."

Elizabeth was startled. "Alice, too? Why didn't I know?"

"You've been so busy, Lizzie. Nobody wanted to add to your load. I can't remember when we last all had a quiet evening round the fire. But, yes, of course they want to talk to you about the movement. Though they seem to have already made up their minds."

Elizabeth knew that she had been spending more hours at the hospital than at home. They were always understaffed and the Royal Free was the only place where many of their patients could get medical attention. Unfortunately they often sought it too late in the day.

"It seems that I have been a little tardy in asking for a family conference, then," she smiled. "But I think we'll have one anyway." She paused, then leaned forward and touched John's cheek. "I know that I do have to join. And that I will do whatever is required of me. I won't be able to live with myself, and mother's memory, if I don't."

He took her hand in his. "I've always understood that, my love."

The family conference took place the following evening. Elizabeth smilingly accepted that there was very little point in discussing the odds concerning the two suffrage parties. "We all seem to have made our decision, don't we?" Granny, Alice, Anthony, John and Rosalie all nodded firmly. "Well, what next, then? What's the way ahead?"

Unusually for her, Alice took the floor first. "We

had a letter from Edward today, sending you all his love. His regiment is still in the Sudan, but even out there he has heard about the Suffragettes and guessed we'd be involved. He says he worries that we will end up in prison."

"He knows we'll do what we think is right," said Anthony. That his younger son had chosen to follow in his footsteps was a source of great pride to him, and indeed, Edward already had his corporal's stripes.

"Well," said Granny, still feisty, if increasingly inhibited by her arthritis, "Next week, Keir Hardie is going to speak in the House of Commons. He may have the smallest party in the House, but he's a good man whose own experience has led him to believe in equal rights for everyone. Evangeline says he has put forward a motion advocating votes for women. He has always worked very closely with the Pankhursts. She thinks we should show solidarity and be there supporting him. Do we all agree to that?" There was a murmur of assent.

"Right, then," continued Granny briskly

"Let's get organised. No point in me coming, I'd just be an encumbrance. Elizabeth, can you get the time off?"

Elizabeth nodded.

"I'll come," said Alice.

"And me," added Rosalie, "Evangeline will probably want to come as well."

Evangeline had married her chimney sweep employer, Mr Timothy O'Leary, and now ran his business for him. Any idea that she might be inferior to him in any way was certainly not allowed to cross his mind. They suspected that Evangeline ran him with the same efficiency as she ran the business, but he appeared to thrive on it. Little Anna, still mute, but shining with happiness, lived with them and was adored by them both. She had begun to write delightful children's stories with wonderful illustrations, and Evangeline had found a publisher for her work, which sold well.

Anna would always be a child/woman, never totally recovered from the abuse which had stunted her body and left her silent, but she had found her niche. Granny privately thought that the eternal child had filled some of the void left by Chrissie in Evangeline's life. Not for the first time Granny reflected on the strange machinations of fate. It gave her faith in the future to see happiness emerge from such dual tragedies as these two had survived.

"I've a pupil near their house," said Rosalie. "I'll pop in on my way home tomorrow and ask Evangeline. Anna wanted to show me the story she's working on, anyway." Rosalie was making a decent salary teaching art to the children of the rich, which left her free to pursue the politics which were her real passion.

It was getting late by now, and they wound up with arrangements to arrive early for the debate in the House, so as to be sure of getting places in the Ladies Gallery. As they donned their outer garments, John said, "I'll be there, reporting for my paper. Good luck and here's hoping Mr Hardie can convince his fellow MPs."

"Indeed," replied Granny.

They were surprised at the number of women who had come to show support for the
Motion and delighted to see the Pankhursts were amongst them. The Ladies Gallery was soon crowded and they found themselves listening with excitement as

Mr Hardie began to speak. He was a passionate and lucid speaker, quickly making an excellent case for women's suffrage. The onlookers were angry when the barracking began from a few of his fellow MPs. The Speaker silenced the hecklers, but then the process of debating the proposed bill began. Some time later it was still going on without any obvious progress. The same questions, restructured, were hurled at the beleaguered MP. Amongst the more experienced watchers a voice was heard to say, "They are talking it out."

Elizabeth knew what this meant. A group who were opposed to the motion were stretching the debate until time ran out and it was too late to vote on it. Which, given the restrictions of parliamentary procedure, meant that it was effectively nullified. Elizabeth took a deep breath and shouted out loudly, "Shame on you! Give us the vote!" Beside her Evangeline and Alice unfurled a white flag with 'Justice for women' written on it in large green letters. They managed to push it through the grill and wave it frantically.

A voice just behind Rosalie called, "This is disgraceful, we won't be treated like this," just as the police appeared on the floor of the house. Pandemonium reigned, and the women drowned out the mockery of some of the MPs by joining in a rousing chant of "Votes for Women!" They continued to chant throughout their ejection from the gallery by the police.

Elizabeth was startled at the degree of force used by the police. As she was frog-marched outside, along with the others, the policeman who was gripping her upper arm pushed her violently as he released her, sending her sprawling onto the ground. For one unbelieving second, as he loomed over her, she thought he was going to kick her, but he drew back. From the venom in his expression, though, she was certain the thought had been in his mind. As she scrambled to her feet, facing him down, he spat at her, "Don't come back. Next time, it'll be charges. That's what you lot deserve. I'd have the lot of you put down." With that he departed back into the House.

Alice and Evangeline brushed her down, whilst Rosalie found her hat, which had flown off. Handing it back she said ruefully, "Well, girls, welcome to the seat of British democracy."

They waited on the embankment with a dozen or so other women for news of the proceedings. When it finally came they learnt that the debate had closed with no time for a vote. Silently they rose and began to make for home.

"No-one" said Evangeline, "expected it to be easy. Come on, everyone. Look lively. Mrs Pankhurst has a meeting planned for next week. No time to feel downhearted. What are a few bruises compared with what we are fighting for? Badges of honour, that's what they are."

Forcing smiles, they agreed. Elizabeth was relieved to find she had stopped shaking. Dear God, she thought, make me strong enough for this. That today's events were mild compared to what could happen, she had not a single doubt. Alice slipped her arm through her friend's, and the others followed suit. Linked together, the women strode towards the station, hats battered, but heads held high.

Less than two months later, they were making preparations for another parliamentary meeting, but with considerably more hope of a result. The suffrage societies had come together with various political and professional groups and were meeting the Prime Minister to press their claims for the vote. There were to be demonstrations all over the country, but especially in London. John's newspaper reported that over half a million women were now demanding this basic right.

Elizabeth and Rosalie had been nominated to be part of the deputation to Sir Henry Campbell-Bannerman, along with Violet and one of her teacher colleagues. All of them were thrilled to be in the company of such heroines of their movement as the colourful Annie Kenney, who arrived at their meeting place on the embankment wearing the traditional clogs and shawl of the Lancashire workers. Emily Davies came over and greeted Elizabeth. Mrs Davies had been a regular correspondent of Mary's, and Elizabeth had been brought up hearing the story of how she had once handed a petition to John Stuart Mill. She reminded Mrs Davies of this event.

"That was forty years ago, you know," said Mrs Davies, "and I'm not sure we are much further ahead. But thank you, my dear, for putting it into my mind. I might well mention it to Sir Henry today."

Rosalie's friend, Emily Davison, came running across the embankment toward them. Along with several hundred other women she was escorting the delegation as far as the Foreign Office, where they were to meet Sir Henry. "I do wish I was going in with you," she said.

"I think we have been chosen largely because of Mother's work," said Elizabeth.

Rosalie nodded agreement. "Don't worry, Ems, we

shall report back with enormous diligence," she grinned at her friend.

At that moment a policeman beckoned them in to meet the great man himself. The two girls found themselves at the back of the deputation and were having a job hearing or seeing what was going on. They knew that Sir Henry had a reputation for being a strong politician, but Elizabeth was surprised at how frail and elderly he seemed for one so newly appointed to the job. They were able to make out some of his words, and nudged each other joyfully as they heard, "You have made a conclusive and irrefutable case."

They did not catch what followed this, so were disconcerted when Annie Kenney, near enough to understand what was being said, jumped on to a chair and shouted vehemently, "We are not satisfied!"

As they turned and left the room they learnt from their companions that the Prime Minister had added, "It is more likely that you will succeed if you wait, than if you act now in a pugnacious spirit."

Exiting the Foreign Office crestfallen and indignant, the two young women were increasingly angry as they reflected on yet another patronising rebuttal. Rejoining Emily, the three of them found themselves swept along toward Trafalgar Square. An enormous crowd had already gathered there as word circulated that Emmeline Pankhurst was coming to speak. She soon arrived, and the crowd fell back to let her through. Standing on one of the great plinths, she reported on the meeting.

Her passionate refutation of the resulting advice rose to a crescendo with the words, "We have been patient too long. We will be patient no longer."

A great cheer went up and a sea of green, purple and white flags could be seen.

"This is the turning point," said Emily. "Look, hundreds, no, thousands, of people just here, in London. And heaven alone knows how many more across the country. We are not a minority struggling for recognition any more. We are half the population of this country. And today we have shown that we are not to be toyed with any more."

Elizabeth and Rosalie nodded agreement. Throwing decorum to the winds, they hauled each other up onto the back of one of Mr Landseer's lions and yelled with all their might, "Votes for Women!"

Battle was enjoined.

"I'll have her," said Granny. "I may be old and decrepit now but I can still look after a baby for a day".

Elizabeth sighed. "Granny, she may be only a year old, but she is into everything. John and I would never forgive ourselves if anything went wrong. You are certainly not decrepit, but let's be honest, you are not as agile as you once were."

"But I am. Well, nearly, anyway," said a voice behind them, and they turned as Alice came into the room. "I suppose this is about going to the Rally. I don't mind not going. I'll have Hyacinth. Granny and I can keep her occupied. To be honest, after the last time, I'm quite glad to have a good excuse."

John looked at his mother with amusement. "Mum, no one could possibly doubt your courage. Don't ever think that. But it would be quite a relief to have you at home for once. Sometimes I don't know who to worry about most."

Elizabeth nodded thoughtfully. "Alice, I accept your offer. Both your offers, in fact," and she bent to hug Granny. "Now, you all sit down and keep Madam Hyacinth amused while I say 'thank you' by getting the supper for us. No, you sit down, too, Alice. If I don't know my way about your kitchen after all these years I never will, and I have come prepared. We wanted to give you both a rest today."

Busy unpacking from her basket the fresh fish that they had picked up in the market on the way over, she reflected that Alice was looking very tired. She had been one of the fifty or so women who had stormed the Commons some months before, and had been thrown to the floor in the ensuing mêlée. Whether by accident or design they would never know, but before she could rise she had sustained several kicks. Some days later she was revealed to be in considerable pain. Elizabeth had insisted on taking her along to the hospital, where it was discovered that two of her ribs were broken. There was no doubt in Elizabeth's mind that the injury, and the manner of its delivery, had taken its toll on her mother-in-law, who was nearly sixty-years-old.

Elizabeth herself had been arrested for throwing stones at the windows of the Chancellor of the Exchequer's residence. Herbert Asquith was away at the time and her aim was not very good so, to her disgust, she had been let off with a caution. Soon after this she had realised that she was pregnant and had promised John and the family to abstain from taking part in any violent demonstrations until after the baby was born. However, now Hyacinth was finally weaned, she was eager to join in what promised to be the largest organised protest ever. Indeed, Mrs Pankhurst anticipated that upwards of two hundred thousand women would be present in Hyde Park on the day.

Finland had been the first country in Europe to enfranchise women, nearly two years previously, and the Suffragette movement had seen this as a beacon for their country and the rest of the world. But the prejudice against them was still immense. And the law showed no mercy. The women were left in no doubt that they were criminals, to be classed with thieves and murderers. A drunken brute could still beat his wife with little fear of retribution, but Suffragettes were to be regarded as the scourge of a civilised society.

However, the so-called civilised society reckoned without the strength and passion of its victims. Their overt physical frailty was deceptive, and their power of recovery often phenomenal. Evangeline had been a better stone thrower than Elizabeth and received a month's custodial sentence. She was the first person close to Elizabeth to be imprisoned. This was very much in Elizabeth's mind as she prepared their supper that night. Evangeline was due to be released the following day and her friends intended to turn out in force to welcome her through the gates of Holloway. When the meal was finished, they discussed the arrangements for the Hyde Park meeting, and then made their plans for the following day.

"We need to show her how special we think she is," said Alice.

"Indeed we do," affirmed Granny.

They arrived outside the prison early in the morning, holding their purple, white and green flags high. Evangeline eventually came through the gates.

She stood blinking in the thin sunlight for a moment. Dressed in his Sunday best, Tim, her (now retired) chimney-sweep husband, ran toward her with Anna at his heels. For a second Evangeline seemed as if she hardly recognised them. Then she fell into their embrace giving a cry that was somewhere between tears and laughter. Her friends held back until she came toward them, holding her husband's hand tightly, her other arm around Anna's shoulders.

They struggled to conceal their shock at her appearance. Her complexion was pallid to the point of yellowness, and her thinness was extreme.

"Just don't show me a mirror yet," were her first words as they gathered round her and smothered her in hugs.

Once home her husband banned them all until she was rested and bathed, and it was two days before they all came together again. John was determined to write her experiences for his paper. He was working for the *Daily Mirror* now, which had been launched a few years earlier specifically to cater for the 'tastes of Gentlewomen'. It had not taken into account that newspaper buying was almost solely done by men, however, and was forced to rapidly change its tactics in order to survive. But it was the first paper to have a section for and about women, as it had been the first to have a female editor, and was still considerably more sympathetic than most to the cause of the Suffragettes.

Evangeline certainly looked better today, Elizabeth thought. Some of her colour had returned, and her natural vigour was showing.

"Evangeline, are there too many of us? Would you prefer to take things more slowly?" she asked, looking round the tiny room in which were squeezed herself, Rosalie, Granny, Alice and John. Anna had taken Hyacinth off to play.

Evangeline, sitting close to Tim, shook her head. "No. I've been thinking about how to describe what it was like in there, and I'd sooner tell all of you at once. It's really hard to talk about, but…" Her words tailed off, then, looking straight at her friends, "It could be one of you next and it might help you to cope if you are a bit more prepared than I was."

She paused, obviously gathering strength.

"The main thing was the darkness. It always seemed to be dark. The sun never seems to get in through the tiny window; it's as if it can't push its way through the bars. The walls of the cell are dank and cold. They give you these clothes that are coarse and harsh to the skin and irritate you constantly. Everything is totally without colour, the clothes, the meals, just everything. The only break in the day is when the warders bring food round and it is so meagre and horrid that by the end of the first week you really don't care whether you eat it or not. The days and nights start to run together. You long for conversation. And you long for fresh air, but you feel so increasingly tired and languid it's almost too much effort to go to the exercise yard when your turn comes."

She paused again, and they waited silently as she searched for the right words. "When you arrive, you are buoyed up by your anger and your sense of rightness and all the unfairness. You think that will keep you going. But then you realise that you are surrounded by ill and feeble women. I suppose some of them are there because they have done dreadful things, but the sense of defeated and deadened spirits starts to pull you down after a while. It is hard to remember your purpose. You have to work hard at hanging on to the memory of all the injustices our sex suffer, and remind yourself constantly of what you are fighting for. You must not become a victim. That is what they intend. Staying strong and determined mentally is the only way to survive. And, as you se, I *have* survived."

She turned and smiled at her husband, then reached over and took Elizabeth's hand. "I'm afraid I may be getting too old for this, Elizabeth. But I hope your mother would feel that I've finally paid a bit of my debt to her."

Elizabeth's eyes filled with tears. "I think she would," she whispered.

In spite of Tim's request for her to stay at home, Evangeline insisted on joining the Hyde Park Rally. Anna was not fit enough for any real physical activity and promised to ply him with his favourite tea and pipe tobacco in return for his promise to sit for her. Evangeline had long wanted her to do his likeness, and he was finally persuaded that this was a good opportunity.

"Anna will distract him," she declared. "I must come with you, or the bullies will have won, won't they?" She was right, of course.

They could barely believe their eyes when they disembarked from the crowded tram at Marble Arch. On every side of the Mall were women, and quite a few men, streaming toward Hyde Park. On entering the park they found that it was a sea of white, green and purple, as were their own flags, which they unrolled with pride.

"Purple for freedom and dignity, white for purity

and green for hope," they chorused as they raised the banners high over their heads.

Platforms were being erected at intervals with willing volunteers helping to hold scaffolding in place. Everywhere there was music, bugles, trumpets, mouth organs and some groups of choristers singing their hearts out to the audiences that had clustered around them. The speakers on the platforms were using megaphones to make themselves heard and their passion and commitment were attracting large audiences. They were taking it in turns to celebrate the increasing public desire for universal suffrage, and to underline the wrongs at all levels of society that sprang from the lack of this basic right.

A small, pretty and extremely zealous Suffragette was attracting a large crowd with her rhetoric, "As a much greater lady than I once said, 'I know I have the body of a weak and feeble woman, but I have the heart and stomach of a King'. Join me, my sisters and brothers, in the fight to show the world that we will never, ever, accept the role of second class citizens!" As she lowered her megaphone and held out her hands to them they responded with a great cheer.

"Can't see much weak and feeble about her," commented John admiringly.

"It's like an enormous revivalist meeting," yelled Rosalie, over the noise.

And so it was, they laughingly agreed. Certainly, Elizabeth thought, there was a near religious fervour everywhere. Almost all of the huge crowd was sympathisers, though there were one or two ugly moments when trouble makers tried to stir up violence. For the most part this was easily dealt with, either the speakers or the crowd silencing the occasional heckler. However, one very drunk and belligerent man had obviously come with the intention of being disruptive and, as he was an extremely large man, everyone was very relieved when two burly policemen appeared and marched him off.

"But have you noticed," asked Evangeline, "the police seem to be protecting *us* today, for a change?"

Indeed, they had noticed. "However did Mrs Pankhurst manage that?" laughed Rosalie.

Elizabeth was convinced that Mrs Pankhurst could manage almost anything. She and John had been to several meetings where Mrs Pankhurst had spoken, and they had come to realise that she was the most extraordinary orator. Not only could she deal with hecklers in a quite remarkable fashion, turning their interruptions to her own advantage, but she was able to convey her ardour and dedication with an almost majestic dignity. "Thank goodness she's on our side," John had once remarked, only half joking. Elizabeth knew exactly what he meant.

The four of them, Elizabeth and John, and Rosalie and Evangeline, found a place under a tree where they had a good view of the chief speaker's platform.

"We should be able to hear all the good speakers," said John, "because the crowd goes quiet when they take the platform. Not everyone is able to captivate their audience, however earnest and heartfelt their convictions."

He had been busy trying to record everything in his note-book from the moment they arrived, but he knew that trying to catch the mood of optimism would be the most important thing.

"But that is so often reflected in tiny details, rather than big events," he confided to Rosalie.

"I noticed that you have been watching the people in the crowd rather than the speaker," she replied. "I did wonder about that."

"Well, it's the reaction to what is said that is important, isn't it?" he asked with a grin. "You can be the most erudite person here, but if no-one listens, you are wasting your time. See," he pointed to a dais some way from them, "look over there. Someone is gathering a crowd before she has said a word!"

Rosalie grabbed Elizabeth's arm. "Lizzie, look who it is. It's Emily. I didn't think we'd be able to find her in this crowd but I suppose I should have guessed that she'd make sure she was seen and heard!"

They pushed their way nearer to her, but were unable to get close enough to hear what she was saying, although, as if to bear out John's words, her audience listened in rapt silence, broken only by the occasional 'hear, hear'. As she climbed down from the dais, there was a huge round of applause and some enthusiastic cheers, so they knew her speech had been well received.

Rosalie and Elizabeth frantically waved their banners high in the air, jumping up to catch Emily's eye, which they eventually did. She waved acknowledgement and gestured for them to meet at a point below some trees, slightly apart from the mass. When they finally made it through the crowds, they came together with much embracing and laughter and flopped down on the grass.

"Come on, Emily," said John, theatrically poising his pencil over his notebook, "what did you say to arouse such fervour in your audience?"

"You always exaggerate, John, and I know when you are teasing me," laughed Emily, "but they did like it, didn't they? I only said what we all know, that it is dreadful that a wealthy woman can employ male servants, who are totally reliant on her for their livelihood and for directing their duties, and yet they are entitled to vote and she cannot."

"But what caused that commotion, Ems, there were cheers and some boos when you held up the Union flag?" asked Rosalie.

"Ah, yes," said Emily with a slight smile, "that was when I said that Queen Victoria should have been ashamed of herself for saying that women should not be involved in politics when she was the most powerful person in the world."

"My goodness," said Evangeline, "Emily, you are a brave girl! Good for you!"

The others nodded soberly. The Queen had been very popular, and although her son, Edward, might not enjoy quite the same reverence as his mother, the monarchy was usually considered by most people to be above criticism. It took nerve to say such things, however true they were.

A sudden hush fell over the spectators, and the group on the grass scrambled to their feet, standing on tip-toe to see what was happening.

"It's Mrs Pankhurst," reported John, "they are helping her up on to the main platform. I musn't miss this, excuse me, ladies," and so saying he grasped an overhanging tree branch and swung himself aloft.

The vast crowd seemed to sense that something special was about to happen. Gradually all the noise ceased, until the whole of that huge park with its thousands of occupants was silent. The small figure of Emmeline Pankhurst waited quietly and confidently for the noise to cease. Someone well out of sight blew a bugle and was quickly hushed. Her speech was not long. The Government, she said, must surely be convinced by the sheer numbers of people, both men and women, here today, that public opinion was on the side of universal suffrage. She spoke simply and effectively and concluded with a resolution calling on the Government to bring in a bill to enfranchise all women without delay.

The response was overwhelming and exuberant. The park reverberated with cries of 'hear, hear'. Many of the men threw their hats into the air. The bugles rang out and the banners were waved. Regarding the sea of white, purple and green from his tree top perch, John found himself thinking that perhaps the struggle that had dominated his and Elizabeth's lives since infancy was finally over.

Dropping from the tree, he hugged his wife. "They can't ignore this, my love," he said. "Look at all these people – we've done it! At last, we've won!"

Elizabeth held him tightly. Naturally more cautious, she smiled up at him and replied, "Wouldn't that be wonderful?"

Linking arms with Rosalie, Emily and Evangeline, they joined the exodus from the park, marching to the tune of *The British Grenadiers* and singing lustily:

> *Some talk of votes for women,*
> *And so it soon will be,*
> *Of wrongs that will be righted -*

Just wait and you will see!

1909

Evangeline's description, accurate though it had been, could not begin to describe the horror of being imprisoned, thought Elizabeth. The thin light filtering through the high window only served to illuminate the dirt and dampness of her cell. She wondered how Emily and the others were faring.

Their 'crime' had been handing out leaflets to the crowd at one of Lloyd George's meetings at Limehouse. They had been incensed by a legal ruling earlier in the year that had denied a woman the right to divorce her husband, even though he might be a self-confessed adulterer who refused to support either his wife or his children. Conversely, a man had little problem divorcing his wife, on an often trumped-up charge of adultery, but the law did not regard this as unbalanced. As a result, many women were left destitute, often with several children to feed and clothe, and no possible way of bettering their lot. The Suffragettes had been hoping for matters to improve, but this new judgement was a massive retrograde step. As if to emphasise the legality of it, their attempts to publicise such injustice had resulted in their arrest. Their increasing demand to be treated as political prisoners, which in truth they were, was denied.

Elizabeth had been arrested, along with several others, and at Thames Police Court the following day had received a custodial sentence of two weeks. She was horrified to hear that Emily had been given two months. Emily had smashed several panes of glass on her arrival at the prison and had been rushed away from the other women. Rumour had it that her cell was the worst one in the prison, with water running down the walls. Elizabeth wondered how she could bear it. Already the three days she had served felt like a lifetime.

She was missing John and Hyacinth and all the family badly. She reflected that sometimes she barely saw them anyway, when the hospital was under-staffed, as it often was, but that was not like this separation. Then, she knew that she was being useful, and doing the job that she loved. To some extent, it was her choice. This was like being in another world, where time seemed to have stopped. She was beginning to understand how quickly you could lose touch with reality. Or even discern what reality was. Putting her head in her hands she found that she was shivering uncontrollably. This kept happening to her and she knew it was not just the cold. But it's better than crying, she thought grimly. She was determined not to give her captors that pleasure.

During her walk round the exercise yard a fellow demonstrator, who she knew only slightly, murmured to her that Emily was going to refuse to eat. Elizabeth was shocked.

"What, anything?" she whispered back.

"Yes," came back the reply, "she says that they can't let us starve to death, so they'll have to release us. Some of us are joining her."

Elizabeth contemplated the unspoken invitation and then nodded. "Yes, alright." With a grimace, she added, "The food is so vile anyway. I keep having these dreadful attacks of nausea."

Her companion glanced at her sharply, but at that minute the warder called out, "No talking over there. Walk apart please. Two minutes left, then back inside with you all."

Once more around the high walled yard, nearly as dark as it was inside the building, and Elizabeth found herself back in her cell. When her supper of some unidentified gruel with a hunk of grey bread appeared, Elizabeth left it untouched. She announced to the grim-faced warder, "I shall not eat until my unjust imprisonment is ended." The warder took it off without comment. Elizabeth repeated the procedure the following morning. She was becoming conscious of pains in her stomach. The food was again cleared without comment.

Later that day, to her amazement, Elizabeth found herself outside the prison along with half a dozen fellow Suffragettes, blinking in the sunlight. Emily materialised beside her, suffused with joy.

"It worked, Lizzie! Now we know how to deal with them!"

John wrote a hard-hitting article describing what was happening to the Suffragettes in prison, based on Elizabeth's experiences, but his editor pruned it mercilessly. He was told he must be more careful not to give offence. John bit back the angry words that he would have liked to have said. Common sense told him that his articles would not see the light of day at all in any other paper. At least the *Daily Mirror* was giving the cause some exposure.

He wrote regularly for the Suffragette newspaper, which was entitled *Votes for Women*, but his words were both anonymous and unpaid, and to some extent he was preaching to the converted, of course. But it made him feel better about the other journalistic compromises he was forced to make.

Violet was another regular correspondent. She felt that it enabled her to make a contribution to the cause. Although still only in her fifties, her health was increasingly fragile and she was often plagued by attacks of dizziness and breathlessness which left her weak for days. She had been quite old to have a first child when Kitty was born, and Elizabeth privately thought that she had never fully recovered from the infection that had nearly taken her life after Harry's birth the following year. Kitty, now fifteen, was longing for her parent's permission to take her mother's place in the rallies, but Elizabeth understood their reluctance to give it all too well.

"I know how I would feel if it was Hyacinth," she told John.

"Indeed. I don't think I can bear to contemplate the thought of you both risking your life and liberty together," he replied soberly, "Thank God, Hyacinth is still much too young for that worry."

Elizabeth was conscious that the Suffragettes attacks on property were becoming more and more violent. She often thought back ruefully to the Hyde Park Rally. How easily the Government had ignored them. Reportedly two hundred thousand people had been there, cheering for universal suffrage, but as far as Parliament was concerned, it seemed that it might never have happened.

Rosalie was back from spending her summer in Berkshire with Valerie, and mortified that she had so far escaped arrest. Elizabeth was struck by the incongruity of her chagrin that she had not yet been imprisoned.

"Ros, darling, trust me, you don't feel like a hero dressed in a hospital chemise, shivering with cold, and being pushed about by warders."

But Rosalie was convinced that she had missed a fascinating experience. More worryingly, she was determined to put this right.

Even Emily, more militant than any of them, remonstrated with her, "Ros, going to prison is the bit we'd rather not have to do. It's not an end in itself. It's just the result of trying to get people, politicians in particular, to notice our cause."

"But," said Rosalie "they notice you more when you've been in prison."

This was true. Some of the women had begun to wear a badge cast in the image of prison bars, to show that they had been incarcerated.

"Done time," said Granny, with her usual gritty humour.

"Well, then," said Rosalie, as if that settled everything.

"You might have your chance very soon, Ros," said Emily. "We've decided to intensify the harassment. We are going to organise several simultaneous attacks on various political targets, which should keep us on the front pages of the papers and possibly force this pig-headed Government to take us seriously at last. Apparently I shall be throwing stones at windows in Whitehall. How do you feel about coming with me?"

Elizabeth and Rosalie recognised bravado when they heard it. A quick glance passed between them. The two young women had known each other so well for so long, that sometimes they were almost able to read each other's thoughts. Elizabeth spoke first. "Emily, dear, you know how we feel. Wither thou goest... well, almost!"

The three women laughed quietly together. Then, "Thank you," said Emily quietly.

Elizabeth reached over and took Emily's hands in hers, "I was a bit of a failure last time I tried this stone throwing business, but we will come with you and try again. Who knows? This time, I might even manage to break a window or two."

Emily rose to her feet. "I must go, but thank you again. We will discuss the details when I know more." She hugged them both.

Rosalie saw her to the door. When she returned, Elizabeth was sitting looking at one of Anna's drawings of Hyacinth. "Alice and Granny see more of her than I do," she remarked ruefully, replacing the likeness on the mantelshelf.

Rosalie knelt in front of her. "Lizzie, you don't have to come. You've been looking a bit peaky lately, and anyway, the hospital needs you."

Elizabeth regarded her steadily. "Thank you, Ros. But my mother taught me that if you find excuses, even valid ones, for not doing what you know, deep down, is your duty, then you have failed. Not anyone else. Just yourself. And then you become less than yourself. So I shall be there. Throwing stones. Inaccurately, probably, but throwing them, nonetheless."

There was silence between the two women. Then Elizabeth sighed. "Oh, Ros! No-one understands, do they, how hard it is for women like us to break windows, to defy the law, to participate in any act that society regards as hooliganism?"

"Our families do," replied Rosalie stalwartly, "and, in the end, their judgement of us is the only one that matters. And the rightness of our cause."

"Yes," said Elizabeth, "and so we shall screw up our courage once more then, I think."

A commotion in the hall heralded the arrival home of John and Hyacinth. They had been spending the afternoon with Granny, who was finding it harder now to get out and about. Elizabeth put a finger to her lips. "Not a word. I'll tell John later." Rosalie nodded.

Four days later Elizabeth stood shoulder to shoulder with Rosalie and Emily, part of a team that had been sent to Whitehall. Other women were marching on the House. Bracing herself for the task ahead, Elizabeth found that they had arrived at a point near enough to throw their cache of stones at the windows of the building. Their brief was to create damage. This time her aim was true, in spite of her nervousness. She heard the window shatter and saw the glass splinter. Crowds began to gather to watch them, whether to support or jeer she was never to know, as suddenly they were surrounded by mounted police.

The horses and their riders seemed huge. They milled among the women, who stood their ground, their stones almost all gone, holding hands in a line as they waited to be arrested. The noise from the horses and the crowd was beginning to block out all thought. Elizabeth could feel the sweat dripping down her back. Rosalie had been thrown to the ground in the melee and her dress had been ripped as she rose. Emily saw a dropped stone and dived almost under the hooves of a horse to retrieve it. She aimed it at the nearest window, but a passing kick from a policeman, high above her on his horse, caught her on the shoulder and caused her to lose her balance. As she hit the ground the stone fell from her grasp.

Incensed at this brutality, Elizabeth grabbed the stone and threw it with all her might. This time it met its target. She felt a grim satisfaction. She turned to pull Emily to her feet and saw that Rosalie was holding her ground as an enormous black horse reared and waved its hooves inches from her face. The policeman on its back was laughing with sadistic joy.

"They have been given permission to terrify and hurt us," she thought as she grasped the hands of her friends again. "This is the Government's way of dealing with us. Treat us like animals. Or even less than animals." This last thought was prompted by seeing the same officer patting his horse affectionately as he moved away from them.

It was almost a relief when they were finally arrested. They were taken together with over a hundred demonstrators to various police stations. The following day John was in Bow Street to see Elizabeth and her comrades sentenced to a week's solitary confinement. He blew her a kiss as she left the court. He was aware that they had all made the decision to refuse food during their imprisonment.

Alice was waiting with Hyacinth when he returned home. He clasped them both tightly. His mother and his daughter. Not a religious man, he prayed to a God that he only half believed in, to keep his beloved wife safe.

Alice read her son's mind with her usual perception. "They're doing it for us all, love," she said. "And they are right. You know they are. Everything else has failed. We all want a better world for Hyacinth. And every other little girl in the land."

John nodded. Alice's practicality and compassion had informed his life, as had Granny's. He just wished that he was the one in prison.

"I want you to come home with me this evening," said Alice. "No," she stopped him as he began to demur, "not for your sake, for mine. Your dad is with Granny. She had a fall yesterday. We didn't let you know because we thought you had enough to worry about. But we think..." she hesitated, and he could see that she was struggling not to cry, "We think this could be it, John."

When they arrived back at his childhood home, John and his mother were met by Anthony. "She is still with us, but only just, the doctor says. She wants to speak to John."

Slipping into the darkened room John sat quietly by his grandmother's bed. He picked up the gnarled and spotted hand on the quilt and put it to his lips.

Granny did not open her eyes so he was startled when she said, in a weak, but still clear voice, "I was beginning to think you wouldn't make it, lad. No, don't interrupt, I haven't got much voice or much time." She paused, visibly gathering strength to continue. "I know where Elizabeth is, of course. I want you to tell her from me that I am so proud of her. A long time ago, I learned what it was to suffer public disapproval when *my* mother helped Mrs Beaton to set up her soup kitchens."

She gave a faint chuckle, "People always have to find something wrong with you if you put yourself out to help others. Mary found out all about that when she started to help the street children. And Alice, my dear daughter-in-law, your mother, risked a great deal when she broke the law by helping Mary to get away from that awful man."

She opened her eyes and looked at him, "Tell Elizabeth that, in the end, it will all be worth it. And you remember that too. Now, give me kiss, and get your mum and dad up here." Her mouth curved in a smile as he kissed her forehead. Her voice was now so faint he had to lean close to catch her words. "You're a good man, John. You have been a great joy to me, dear boy."

Elizabeth left prison seven days later, her fast unbroken. Her resilience was such that two days later she attended Granny's funeral. Edward was unable to come as he was still abroad with his regiment, but the family were amazed and touched by the number of people who attended. Even Cathy, whom Elizabeth had not seen for several years, was there. Married now, and with three children of her own, she put her arms round Alice. "Without you and Granny and Mary, I don't know what would have become of me. I owe you all my life."

Valerie and Charles came down from Berkshire with Percy. Rosalie and her mother wept unashamedly together. But running through the service was a feeling of love and respect and thanksgiving for a life well lived.

Afterwards Elizabeth said to John: "I think she would have liked it, don't you? It was the kind of 'Goodbye' that seemed right, somehow." He could only agree.

Two days after the funeral, her strength seemingly built up again, Elizabeth told John that the Suffragettes were planning another demonstration that weekend. She did not tell him about the increasing nausea she was suffering as she put it down to the hunger strike of the previous week.

John held his wife tightly. "I sometimes wish that I didn't have such a brave wife," he whispered into her hair.

Five days later Elizabeth was back in prison, and refusing to eat again. None of them had contemplated the horror of what was to happen next. Elizabeth was asleep when they came into her cell. The wardress, a burly woman who Elizabeth had not seen before, shook her awake. "So you haven't eaten your food again?" She gestured to the table under the window which held a tin plate with bread on it and a mug of water. Elizabeth made no answer and started to turn away from her on the narrow shelf that served as a bed. Before she could move, another wardress appeared with a wooden chair, which she placed in the centre of the tiny cell. The two women ordered Elizabeth to sit on it. Sleepy and worn out from lack of food and fresh air, Elizabeth did as she was bid.

As soon as she was seated two more wardresses entered the room, with two men behind them. Elizabeth recognised one of the men as the prison doctor. As she began to formulate a question, she found herself pinned down by the four women, one of whom used her hair to jerk her head backwards. The pain was excruciating, and the stomach pains that were becoming familiar to her shot through her body. She opened her mouth to protest but before she could, a hand was clamped over her mouth and the doctor began to force a tube, which appeared to be about two feet in length, up one of her nostrils.

Elizabeth realised that they intended to force feed her. She struggled to evade them but the dreadful sensation as the tubes progressed up her nose and down her throat left her helpless. Her ear drums felt as if they were going to burst. When almost all of the tube had been pushed into her body by way of her nostrils, she was forced back onto the bed. The wardresses held her down with an iron grip, while the doctor stood on the chair, holding the funnel end of the tube over her head.

He began to pour amixture of egg and milk down the funnel. The pain was unbelievable. Deciding the process was not fast enough, he pinched the nostril with the tube in it, and then squeezed her throat to accelerate the process. Finally satisfied that she had received enough nourishment, they removed the tube. The doctor then used his stethoscope to check Elizabeth's heart. That she was nearly unconscious worried him not at all. As they gathered up their appliances and prepared to withdraw from the cell, the doctor remarked to his companions, "That'll teach her. Right, where's the next one?"

Elizabeth staggered from her bed, almost crippled with the agonising pain in her throat and ears, and a dreadful burning sensation in her chest. Reaching for the chamber pot under her bed, she began to vomit.

Three days later John arrived at the prison gates to fetch his wife. His horror knew no bounds when he saw her. She was gaunt and deathly white, except for the purple bruises that appeared in profusion on her face, and he suspected on other parts of her body. He ordered the cab driver to take them straight to the hospital.

Throughout the night he paced the hospital corridors. At dawn, one of Elizabeth's colleagues told him that his wife had miscarried the child that neither of them had realised she was carrying. He sat by his wife's bed and they wept together for the life that never was, and now never would be. And for the children they had just been told they would never have.

When Elizabeth was fit to be left for a few hours he went home. The dawn was just peering through the windows of their home. He began to write. He described the assault on his wife in detail. When he had finished writing he took the copy round to his editor, who read it then and there.

He finally raised his head and looked at his exhausted reporter. "Yes," he said. "Yes. In this case, John, I think we should put the cat down firmly amongst the pigeons. Go home now. The storm will break tomorrow."

Dropping off at his parent's house to collect Hyacinth, he was allowed to go no further.

"Bed," ordered Alice, after one glance at her son. "I'll pop Hyacinth round to Evangeline, and I'll go and sit with Elizabeth at the hospital. You can tell me more later."

So when Elizabeth woke, it was her surrogate mother who held her hand, and soothed her bruises with pads soaked in witch hazel. And wiped away the tears that slid down her cheeks as she lay there silently, her poor sore throat and chest not allowing her to sob.

John's article came out the next morning. The other papers picked up the story and the press was in uproar. Words and phrases such as 'outrageous' and 'an affront to the dignity of females' were bandied around. Questions about the treatment of Suffragettes were asked in the House. The MP's were vastly amused by these questions. Incredibly to many, there was considerable laughter in the House. Mr Gladstone, the Home Secretary, said that his Office had authorised the treatment to stop these women killing themselves. It wasn't his fault if the press couldn't see that.

Eventually allowed home, Elizabeth hugged her daughter. She met John's eyes over Hyacinth's brown curls. "I must go on, darling, you do know that?"

He was always aware that her early childhood, spent in hiding with her mother from her brutish father, had taken its toll on Elizabeth. He also knew that growing up in a home that had become a refuge for a succession of beaten and desperate girls was never far from her mind. Their mutual history meant that he understood better than anyone the events and emotions that had shaped this woman who was dearer to him than life itself. He reflected wryly that he had grown up surrounded by courageous women. How could he wish Elizabeth to be anything else? He knew that things could never be quite the same between them again if he tried to persuade her to be less than she was.

"Of course you must, my love," he replied.

Then he went into the garden and discovered that the nails on his clenched hands had penetrated the skin. His palms were bleeding. As was his heart.

1913

Violet and Harold looked at Elizabeth in horror. "Elizabeth, you can't mean that. You have to help us.

Kitty is only nineteen. When we ordered her not to go, she just got up and walked out of the house, and we haven't seen her since. But I know she would listen to you." Violet's voice broke and she reached for a lace-trimmed hanky. "I'm sure you know where she is. Oh, I *hate* all this violence. We never expected it to be like this. I know she was with Emily and Rosalie last week on one of Mrs Pankhurst's so called 'guerrilla raids'. I just can't believe that setting fire to Kew Gardens is going to achieve anything."

"Rather the opposite, I should think," interjected Harold.

Elizabeth looked at them steadily. "Aunt Violet, I can't help you. Even if I knew where Kitty was, which I don't. And you shouldn't ask me to. Of course I know how you feel, I have a daughter too, don't forget, and I confess that I pray daily that we will have attained our ends before she is old enough for me to have to face what you are facing. But, if we have not, then face it I will, because I believe our cause is as just as you and mother thought it was all those years ago."

"But we didn't expect it to come to this," repeated Violet. "We thought that when there were enough of us they would listen."

"No," said Elizabeth. "That's what we *hoped* would happen. And it hasn't. Asquith's Government is throwing every foul weapon at the Suffragettes that it can think of. This 'Cat and Mouse Act' is just their latest ploy. Letting the women who are on hunger strike out of prison, then re-arresting them as soon as they have eaten. But can't you both see that it is the result of public revulsion at the force-feeding? Looked at one way, it is a victory."

She could see that they were unconvinced, but she continued vigorously, "Our support grows all the time. Women came from all over the world to join our last big march, sixty thousand of us, from aristocrats to factory workers." Elizabeth paused. She had been one of the seven hundred women who proudly carried banners displaying a silver arrow and proclaiming, 'From prison to citizenship'. Every one of the seven hundred had suffered imprisonment fighting for the right to vote, some many times.

She crossed to her mother's old friend and put her arms round her. She felt so frail nowadays. "Dear Aunt Violet. You've fought for the cause all my life. You've been a splendid example to us all. Don't make Kitty feel guilty about wanting to carry on your work."

Harold gave a sigh. "Vi, I hate to admit it but she's right. Everyone has to carry on with the fight in their own way. We can't deny Kitty that freedom. Look at Valerie's girl. Rosalie is skin and bones, in and out of prison, and still she keeps at it. Along with that friend of hers, Miss Davison."

"Emily has taken more punishment than any of us," said Elizabeth. "Do you remember when she barricaded her cell door with her bed to stop them feeding her, and they put a hose pipe through her cell window and flooded the room? The water was over her shoulders before they stopped."

"She's certainly plucky," mused Harold. "I seem to remember she took them to court for that, didn't she?"

"She certainly did, and she won. The court awarded her damages," asserted Elizabeth proudly.

"Yes, laughable damages. And look at her now," said Violet wearily, "Still barely recovered from throwing herself down those stairs in the prison. That exploit has to have been all of 18 months ago. And what good did it do?"

"I think," replied Elizabeth, "that you are much too clever not to know that we can't always see, when we are in the middle of a fight, which of the battles will ultimately have the most importance. Emily's courage is undeniable."

"I think she is quite mad," said Violet, rising to her feet and preparing to leave.

"No, you don't, Aunt Violet," said Elizabeth firmly. "Anymore than you think Rosalie is, or that I am. You just want to protect Kitty. I expect your mother felt the same when you went out at night in the London fog to help the street children. Especially after my mother's murder. She must have been through hell worrying about you. But I don't remember that her worries stopped you. In fact, as I recall, you were instrumental in exposing Bramwell's atrocious practices to the police, and without you he probably wouldn't have been brought to justice. That meant a great shadow was lifted off the East End. You can't have a monopoly of heroism, I'm afraid. You have to let Kitty have a look in."

Violet halted, halfway to the door. She turned to Elizabeth. "Oh, my dear, you are your mother's daughter," she whispered.

"And so is Kitty," replied Elizabeth.

A reluctant smile curved Violet's lips. "If you see her, tell her that we love her. And she can come home any time. We won't try to stop her again."

Harold took his wife's hand. "Well said, Vi."

When they had gone, Elizabeth gathered herself

together and prepared to go to the hospital. They were desperately short staffed again. Sometimes she was so tired that she slept at the hospital rather than return home between shifts. She thought it ironic that Mary's determination to make conditions better for her daughter had meant that she, Elizabeth, had often seen little of her, and now history was being repeated with her own daughter. But she comforted herself with the thought that at least Hyacinth had a loving father.

She hoped that she had been right to defend Kitty to Violet. The girl was so young, but then, so were many of the Suffragettes. Without a doubt, the women *were* fighting a war, and there were increasingly casualties. A few months before Elizabeth had taken part in a raid on the West End. The Suffragettes were thoroughly sickened by Government taunts that they were not expressing themselves forcibly enough – this from the Ministers who had been more than ready to make concessions to the miners when they took militant action to make their point just weeks before!

Armed with hammers, the demonstrating Suffragettes had descended on Oxford Street and had left a trail of broken windows from Piccadilly through to the Strand. As always, they neither attempted to resist arrest nor tried to escape. However, during the ensuing arrest of well over a hundred protesters there were many examples of the police brutality that they had learnt to expect. Not only were the women and girls manhandled roughly, many sustaining injuries that required medical treatment, but they were frequently subjected to sexual assaults. Their clothes were ripped unnecessarily, and many officers took sadistic pleasure in pulling them along by their breasts.

Elizabeth herself had been victimised in this way and knew that, worse than the pain, was the attempt to humiliate and demean. She noticed that the more obviously middle class women were almost always picked out for this treatment. She had been startled to see Rosalie spit in the face of a policeman who was treating her this way.

Afterwards, she determined to bring herself to do the same if the situation arose again. As she said to John, "We are so conditioned. I was almost more shocked at Rosalie's behaviour than the policeman's. Isn't that absurd?"

Elizabeth wondered where Kitty was. She was fond of the clever, feisty girl and knew that Hyacinth adored her. She wondered if Kitty had told her parents yet of her ambition to follow in her Aunt Primrose's footsteps and become a nurse when she finished at college. She hoped, wherever the girl was, that she would be careful.

In fact, at that very moment Kitty was sitting in Emily's rooms discussing with her and Rosalie how they would bring about an event that was destined to rock all their worlds.

"What," asked Emily, "is the thing that you are most frightened of every time we have a protest rally or a demonstration?"

"The police, of course," replied Rosalie, adding mischievously, "Well, and those ladies who use their hat pins to scratch on pillar boxes. I'm always afraid one of them is going to take my eye out."

"Ros, will you please be serious," said Emily, laughing in spite of herself, "Don't make young Kitty giggle or we will never get anything sorted out."

It always gave Rosalie pleasure to see her friend

smile. Since one of Emily's friends had died of heart failure after a violent confrontation with the law, her determination to bring about justice for her sex had left even less room for laughter in her life.

"Sorry," she apologised. "Right. Though it was a serious answer. The police are such brutes."

"I think that the very worst thing is the horses," said Kitty. "I am so scared when they rear up over me. They are so big. Sometimes I just want to run away and hide. And I hate the smell of them, and the noise they make. But I know it's not the animals, it's the way they are used. To intimidate us. And then the police pretend when they hit us with their crops it's not on purpose."

She pulled back her sleeve to show a livid scar. "Look. That was when that sergeant used his whip on me. A real custodian of the law, I don't think. He was aiming for my face, but I got my arm up in time." Her chin wobbled and her eyes filled with tears at the memory.

Rosalie put her arm round her shoulders. "Oh, Kitty, you don't have to come on the demonstrations."

"Yes I do," replied Kitty stoically.

Emily looked at the two of them abstractedly. "You're right, Kitty. It's the horses. Do you know, you have given me an idea. They use the horses to frighten us, so why don't we give them a dose of their own medicine, and use a horse to get us the sort of publicity that even the King couldn't ignore?"

"What do you mean, Ems?" asked Rosalie.

"I'm not sure," replied her friend. "But it's the Derby soon, and the King's horse is running, of course. I wonder if we could..." she lapsed into silence, but Rosalie jumped into the breach.

"Oh yes, Ems! Like Aunt Mary and Mother did at the Derby. They cornered the Duke of Devonshire in the winner's enclosure and waved their banner and it got an amazing amount of publicity. It's a splendid idea! I'll help any way I can."

"And so will I," chimed in Kitty.

Emily got to her feet. "Then I'll try to think of something that will make even more of an impact than that did."

Rosalie looked up at her. Something in Emily's demeanour was suddenly worrying her. "Ems, nothing too drastic, please."

Emily laughed down at her friend. "Come on, Ros. Perhaps it's time our movement had a martyr."

Rosalie reached for her hand. "Emily, what are you talking about? You are worth far more to us alive than dead."

Emily looked at her gravely. "Sorry, Ros. Didn't mean to frighten you. No, I just meant ...well, I don't know what I meant, really. But I will do my best to come up with something that will make a huge stir, I promise you. That is what we really need to do now. Kitty, are you staying here tonight?"

"If I may," replied Kitty. "My parents are treating me like a child at the moment."

Rosalie walked slowly back home. Letting herself in, she was pleased to see John in the drawing room, pushing Hyacinth on the rocking horse that was her favourite toy. She wondered whether to talk about the conversation she had just had, but decided to wait until Emily's plans were properly formed. She knew how he worried about them all. 'No point in adding to his worries unnecessarily,' she thought, as she went to join them.

Rosalie was working on a portrait when Kitty came round the next day. Elizabeth had just arrived home from an extended shift at the hospital and was delighted and slightly relieved when she opened the door to her.

"Your parents are very worried about you, Kitty," she told the girl, having given her a hug and taken her through to where Rosalie was painting. "You should, at very least, assure them that you are safe and well. I believe they have come to understand that you are doing what you feel you have to do."

"Oh, Elizabeth," said Kitty, "You've been talking to them. Thank you, thank you, thank you! I have missed them so much, and I hate them being cross with me. I'll go and see them when I've told you both about Emily's plans for the Derby."

Elizabeth looked at her questioningly. "The Derby? What's this about then?"

"Well," said Rosalie, "Emily's been inspired by what our mothers did, Lizzie. She is suggesting that we should try to use the Derby again to get some publicity for the cause. After all, we don't seem to be making much progress at the moment, and all the press will be out in force for that." Turning to Kitty, she asked, "So what has Emily come up with, Kitty?"

Kitty was bubbling with excitement. "She thinks that as the horses come round Tattenham Corner, we should all suddenly wave our Suffragette flags like mad. It will probably be enough to startle the riders, and with luck they'll have to abandon the race. Think what an impact that would have, people from all over the Country follow the Derby, and would hear about what had happened. Perhaps if their precious race was sabotaged then they would finally begin to understand how serious we are."

Elizabeth and Rosalie were silent for a moment, then Rosalie said, "But, Kitty, might that not be dangerous for the spectators?"

She and Elizabeth were both remembering Mary's story of Elizabeth's grandmother, Dora's, accident all those years ago at Epsom. Mary had never doubted that it had been responsible for both her parents' early deaths.

"Will we have a chance to talk to Emily?" asked Elizabeth. "Derby day is only a few days away now, and I think that we should discuss it with her further. We don't want to risk anyone being injured."

Rosalie nodded agreement. "I'll go round there now. You go and get some sleep, Lizzie. You've been up all night at the hospital and you look tired out."

Returning just as Elizabeth was up and about and getting tea for Hyacinth, Rosalie admitted that she had been unable to find Emily.

"Typical of the woman. Comes out with a plan, then disappears so that we can't talk her out of it. I'm not happy, Lizzie. I certainly don't want Kitty waving a flag at that rail. I'll make sure that she and I are a good bit away. We'll concentrate on being in sight of the Royal Box, I think, then we can wave our flags from there. If Emily's plan fails then at least we will have made some sort of protest. I'll get as many of the others as I can to come with us. How about you?"

"I think I'm on shift, but I'll be there if I can. John will be there for his paper, anyway. I know that Alice is having Hyacinth that day, because she is taking her to a fair in the park, Hyacinth has been talking about it all week."

Rosalie laughed. "She's turning into a proper little chatterbox, isn't she?"

Elizabeth looked at her quizzically. "Do you ever regret not marrying, Ros?"

Rosalie was silent for a moment, then, "Sometimes. If I had met someone that I felt
I could really trust. Someone like John, I suppose. But after everything that happened..," her voice tailed off.

Elizabeth nodded. "Good job you've got a share in Hyacinth, then," she joked, deliberately lightening the mood, "So, do be careful, my dear friend. Take care of Kitty *and* yourself at the races."

"I will," promised Rosalie with a smile.

Rosalie, Kitty and John joined the crowds at Epsom early on Wednesday. It was a beautiful day and it was impossible not to be caught up in the gaiety of the event. John had a pass to the winner's enclosure, and the two women stationed themselves within sight of the Royal Box, as planned. The purple, green and white flag was rolled into Kitty's parasol, to be liberated at the right moment. They searched the crowd for a sight of Emily, and were finally rewarded. She was on the opposite side of the course, but waved merrily across to them. Her whole manner was so bright and cheerful that Rosalie felt a surge of relief, which made her realise how worried she had been about Emily's intentions.

A sudden hush in the crowd was followed by the start of the cheering as all the spectators egged on their favourite. Rosalie found herself laughing at the sheer joyfulness of the event. She glanced across the course at Emily, who was also smiling and holding what looked like a card up to her lips, and then she was frozen with horror as she saw her friend slip under the rails just as the King's horse rounded the corner.

She heard herself scream, "NO, Emily, NO!" but her voice was lost in the surrounding din. Time seemed to slow down. As if in a dream, Rosalie saw her friend run into the middle of the racecourse directly in the path of the horse. As the horse reared, throwing the jockey, Emily was seen to be lying motionless on the ground.

Rosalie was never to know whether Emily was trying to grasp the reins of the King's horse, or whether she meant to throw herself under its hooves. Later, when the course was finally emptied, she and Kitty went to look for whatever it was that Emily had been holding. Rosalie thought it might have been a letter, and wondered if it had been meant for her. So many scraps of paper were lying around it was a hopeless task. Whatever it was, it had gone forever. The only thing anyone was sure of was that, six days later, the Suffragettes had their first martyr. Emily had died without regaining consciousness.

The news of Emily's death sped around the world. In spite, thought Elizabeth, of the concerted effort on the part of the parliament and the press to negate and even ridicule it. Thousands of men and women sent wreaths from all over the globe. On the day of her funeral, a vast procession moved slowly across London, watched silently by tens of thousands more. Ten bands played funeral music, and a bodyguard of Suffragettes all dressed in white with black armbands flanked her coffin, which was draped in purple. A dozen clergy walked at the head of the procession. All over the country young women dressed in white and older women in black took to the streets to pay tribute to their gallant heroine.

Elizabeth and her friends walked sombrely in time to the music. Later, with a few of Emily's other close friends, Elizabeth, Kitty and Rosalie went on the train with the coffin to where Emily was to be buried, in the family grave in Northumberland. At the funeral, Kitty, who along with them all had been strong throughout the day, finally burst into tears.

Rosalie put her hand on the girl's arm as they left the church for the burial. "No, Kitty. Don't cry. Be proud of her. Hold up your head and let the world see your pride. Emily will be a beacon for our cause. She will be remembered with gratitude by a great many women forever. She was smiling when she ran out onto the course, I saw her. She rightly knew that millions of people would understand the seriousness of our position through her actions. She gave her life to put an end to the intolerable suffering of so many women in this country, and everywhere. The story of her courage will live in history forever, whatever nonsense may be promoted by our politicians. I believe her entire life was leading to the moment of her sacrifice."

Only later, in the privacy of her room, did Rosalie allow herself to weep for her friend.

A few weeks later Alice, Elizabeth, Rosalie and six-year-old Hyacinth joined fifty thousand other women taking part in the Suffragette Pilgrimage in Hyde Park. Violet and Kitty walked beside them, holding hands tightly. Many husbands, fathers and sons cheered them from the sidelines.

Elizabeth had been asked to address the meeting. The crowd fell back to make way for her. Standing on the dais, and looking out at that vast throng, a sea of women dressed in white, purple and green, she felt near to tears. A hush fell as she began to speak.

"My fellow fighters, it lifts all our spirits to see so many of our sex here today. As each and everyone of us are aware, the battle still goes on. Sometimes it is hard to continue. Occasionally, we even wonder if the pain and indignities we have been forced to suffer are too much to bear. But we are the lucky ones. We are the women who already have some freedom or we would not be here today. So I ask you never to forget that we are fighting to change the laws of the land. That is what the right to vote really means.

"We fight for the hundreds of thousands of women in our society who are forced to work long hours and are paid a pittance for doing so – and often that pittance has to be handed to their husbands who drink it away while the women watch their children starving. We fight for the women who are deprived of any proper education so that they are unable to claw their way out of the brutal and poverty-stricken lives they lead. We fight for the women forced into prostitution, often by their own fathers, whose lives are governed by fear and humiliation. We fight for the women who are not able to join us today because their lords and masters would not dream of letting them. We fight for the majority of our sex whose role in life is to be the slave, the chattel, of a man. All the while this country is ruled by men who believe that women are inferior beings in every way, then fight we must. Whatever the cost."

Elizabeth took a deep breath. "I would like to finish by quoting our gallant friend and fellow fighter, Emily Wilding Davison. Emily said, 'Rebellion against tyrants is obedience to God.'"

Elizabeth held high the flag she was holding beside her, and with a cry of, "Votes for women," she stepped off the platform to deafening applause. As she found her way back to her group, who hugged her and patted her on the back, Hyacinth took her mother's hand and looked up at her. Elizabeth had to bend to catch her daughter's words.

"Does that mean it's finished, Mummy?" asked the child, "Does it mean you'll never have to go away to the prison place again?"

Elizabeth held her daughter closely. Whatever the cost, she thought. For us all.

Part Three: Kitty

1914

"Oh, Mummy, don't worry. Everybody says it will all be over by Christmas, and Harry will back home with us, covered in medals!"

Harry glanced affectionately at his sister and said, "One thing you can always be sure of, Ma, that's Kitty's tendency to exaggerate. But I'm sure she's right about the war. After all, we have to teach these Germans a lesson, can't let them ride roughshod over a neutral country like Belgium, can we?"

Violet contemplated her two children. She and Harold were modestly amazed that they had managed to produce two such lovely specimens. Kitty was small, dark and vivacious, and Harry the complete antithesis, tall, fair and, although quieter than his sister, possessed of a sense of humour that made him an asset to any gathering.

"In the end," she said, "you'll do what you think is right, and I applaud that. But allow me some sorrow that you are both going to be leaving us so soon. I hardly have to tell you how much I shall miss you."

"At least," said Harold's voice from the doorway, "Harry will be in Edward's regiment."

Harry turned to greet his father with delight. "You've been to the War Office, Dad. However did you manage to pull that off? How absolutely spiffing!"

"Chap was an old pupil of mine," said Harold, winking at his family while somewhat self-consciously smoothing his moustache.

Violet knew how difficult he would have found doing anything that smacked of nepotism, but she had begged him to put in a word on Harry's behalf. Edward had been one of Harry's heroes for as long as anyone could remember. One of his great treats when very young had been to visit Alice when Edward was home on leave. He would sit, mesmerised, listening to Edward and his father, Anthony, comparing soldiering stories. Harry had always known precisely what he wanted to do when he grew up.

To Alice and Anthony's great joy Edward had risen to the rank of Captain. So to Second Lieutenant Harry Granger, just down from Sandhurst and off to defend his country against the Hun, joining his hero's regiment felt like the final affirmation that life was going his way.

"So when are you off, Sis?" he asked Kitty.

Kitty had just finished her probation period at the Royal Free, and was joining the nursing staff at the Royal Victoria, the Military Hospital on the south coast.

"Next month," Kitty replied. "It's such a good hospital, I'm lucky to have been accepted there. And even if there are not many casualties from this war, at least I'll feel as if I'm doing my bit. You will be careful, won't you, Harry?"

"Always!" replied her brother with a grin. "We'll have to make the most of our last few days of freedom, though. Are we both invited to Phyllis's party tonight?"

Kitty giggled. "We certainly are. She may be my best friend but I sometimes think it is you she's really interested in!"

Just after seven o'clock that evening Kitty and Harry, decked in what Kitty so aptly described as their 'glad rags', finally departed for their party with considerable noise and gaiety. Violet and Harold waved them off before settling down in front of the French windows that looked out onto their small but pretty garden.

"That was good of you, darling," said Violet.

Harold did not pretend that he misunderstood. "Comfort to me, too, to know that Edward's keeping an eye on him." He sighed. "All this hysteria, Violet. As if going to war was some kind of game. Let's hope Kitchener is wrong. He thinks we're in for a long haul. I'm afraid he might be right." He paused. "So what's happening with our other war, then? What does Elizabeth think we should do, follow Mrs Pankhurst or listen to Mrs Fawcett?"

Violet had spent most of the previous day discussing just this with her friends.

"Elizabeth and Rosalie both think we should help the war effort. I must say I tend to agree. Mrs Fawcett's pacifism is admirable, but I think we must do what we can to ensure victory, after all, that must benefit all of us, men and women."

"Kitty has obviously made that decision already," said her husband, "But, thankfully, she is too young to be sent abroad, even if she is qualified."

Violet stared into space. "If only Harry was."

"I know, my love, I know," replied her husband.

Kitty and her friend Phyllis went with Harry to the station. Violet and Harold had been more than willing to say their farewells to their son at home and leave it to the younger ones to fight through the troops massing at the station on the first leg of their journey to Europe. The atmosphere was both rousing and uplifting. A band was playing the popular tunes of the day and many of the young volunteer recruits were joining in, singing *It's a long way to Tipperary* with great gusto.

Looking round, Kitty could see many older faces smiling bravely. Mothers were kissing their sons goodbye with glistening eyes, but the overall mood was of pride and patriotism, which mirrored her own feelings precisely. Standing on tiptoe to give her tall brother a last hug and kiss, her eye was caught by another figure standing watching them.

"Oh, Harry, there's Lawrence. I shall leave you to Phyllis's tender mercies, which I'm sure you'll both enjoy, and go and have a word." Smiling gaily at her brother, she whispered, "Take care".

He hugged her tight. "Of course," he whispered back.

Kitty waved to Lawrence, and they both pushed through the crowd in an effort to get near enough to speak. Glancing back, she saw that Harry had Phyllis in a close embrace. Kitty's exit had been tactfully timed. She knew that since Phyllis's party the previous week, their relationship had galloped apace, to their mutual delight. The war had certainly speeded life up, she thought.

Lawrence finally reached her and grasping her hands he pulled her through the throng toward him. "Kitty, what a piece of luck! I was looking for Harry, and I confess I was half hoping I might see you before we left."

Kitty laughed up at him. "I bet you say that to all the girls."

"No," he replied, "Only very pretty nurses called Kitty."

Kitty could feel her face colouring. She was an accomplished flirt and had known Lawrence, a fellow officer cadet of Harry's at Sandhurst, for some time. But just recently they had been thrown together socially on several occasions, and she suspected that she was beginning to feel something deeper than friendship for him, but with no clue as to whether he reciprocated her feelings. This was about to be resolved, however.

"I say," he stammered, his sophistication of the last moments rapidly evaporating, "I have been wondering, well, it would sort of, well, make a chap very happy if..." he tailed off, leaving Kitty looking at him quizzically, but with the beginnings of a twinkle in her eye.

"Yes?" she encouraged him.

"Well," he took a deep breath, "Kitty, can I write to you? And perhaps, if we both get leave together..?"

Kitty took his hands in hers. "I would love you to write to me. And I promise that I shall write back. And let's hope we meet again soon. I should really like that, and I am sure Harry would be delighted too."

Lawrence's face cleared. "Dear Kitty, I have been wanting to ask you that for weeks. Do you think that I..? He stammered to a halt again, then, "Might I kiss you goodbye?"

"Oh, yes!" replied Kitty, throwing her arms round his neck and caution to the winds, for at that moment the call of 'All aboard, please,' rang through the station.

Within minutes the train was pulling out, leaving

billows of dirty smoke in its wake. But standing side by side, waving long after it was possible that they could be seen, Kitty and Phyllis both realised that, mingled with their sadness at the parting, was the beginning of a joyful hope.

This farewell scene was repeated the following week when Kitty boarded the train for Southampton. Wishing her 'Godspeed' and waving her off, as well as her parents were her Aunt Primrose and Elizabeth. Just as the train was leaving, Rosalie came tearing through the barrier, and, running alongside the train, she pushed something into Kitty's hands. "A farewell present, with love," she shouted.

When she finally settled back on her seat, Kitty became aware of the curious glances of the two other girls in her carriage. She could see by their uniforms that they were also bound for the Royal Victoria Hospital. She carefully unrolled the tube that Rosalie had given her, and gave a gasp of surprise. There, staring up at her, was Emily's face. Not for the first time, Kitty marvelled at Rosalie's talent. Under the picture Rosalie had inscribed: 'To inspire you if the going gets hard'.

Kitty eyes filled with tears. She held it up to show to her companions.

"Isn't that..?" one of them began.

Kitty nodded. "Yes, that's Emily Wilding Davison." She added proudly. "She was my friend. And one of the bravest women who ever lived."

And she will indeed be my inspiration, she thought. For the rest of my life.

1915

Royal Victoria Hospital,
Nutley,
Hants.
Dear Elizabeth,
I hope you don't mind me writing to you, I know how busy you must be at the Royal Free. It's just that sometimes I think I shall go mad with pretending, and you are the only person that I can really tell the truth to. It seems to me at the minute that everyone in the world is lying to someone else in an effort to make them feel better.
Lizzie, it is appalling here, the wounded and dying are arriving constantly throughout the day and night. We have to keep the men on stretchers in the corridors while we wait for someone else to die. We never have to wait for very long. The air is filled constantly with screams and moans and, almost worse, the careful speech of the conscious: 'Nurse, Nurse – can you help me – I can't see anything'. And we can't help them, Lizzie. We can't give them back their eyes any more than we can give them back their arms or their legs or whatever else this fearful war has taken from them.
Yesterday we had a man who had lost his whole face. Can you imagine, Lizzie, his whole face? I stood by his stretcher and tried to sound bright and cheerful and I held his hand while I told him that everything would be alright. Alright. With no face, no eyes, no nose, no ears. Alright. I heard myself prattling on and then he gave this cry and, Lizzie, he was dead. Thank God, I thought, he's dead. No

more pain, no more half life, I didn't know whether he was able to hear or think or – anything. I just rejoiced that he was dead. Sister asked me to write to his wife, as I was the last person to talk to him. His wife. Apparently he was nineteen years old and he married his girlfriend before volunteering. So I sat last night and wrote this letter saying how brave he was and how he died fighting for his country and how proud we all should be of him.
And it was all lies.
He died in agony. Confused and faceless. How could I leave her with that, Lizzie? So I lied. I lie to Mother and Father when I write. I lie to Harry and I know that he is lying to me. But if we dared to write the truth then I would be censored and he would be shot. Because this is war is an obscenity. Are they going to go on fighting until there are no more young men left to kill? I think that is just what they are going to do.
And in the meantime we talk of patriotism and victory and it all being over soon.
While the smell of death and urine and suppurating wounds fills the hospital, and we wait to find out which of the next blind and faceless victims is one of our own loved ones. And that is the other demeaning factor. That every time I realise that the poor dying soldier writhing on the stretcher is not Harry, or Lawrence, or Edward, I feel this overwhelming relief. At least he's not one of mine. How can we survive such callousness, Lizzie? How can I live with myself knowing that I am grateful that this is someone else's brother or lover or husband?

I always wanted to nurse. I watched you and Primrose helping to make the world a better place. But this is a picture of hell.
A week ago a lad came in with both legs and half an arm shot away. He was blind, and had lost his lower jaw. He begged me to put him out of his misery.
I did, Lizzie. I won't tell you what I did, and I know you will never ask. I shall live with it for the rest of my life. God forgive me, but even as I weep over this letter, I know that I would do it again.
Pray for me, Lizzie,
Your friend,
Kitty.

1916

It was the cold, thought Kitty. She had been ready for the dirt, and the lack of equipment, and even, in some small measure, for the fear, but nothing had prepared her for the biting, excruciating pain of the cold. It was her turn to do the night guard duty, and although her coat was theoretically rainproof, the snow had seeped through the seams and frozen her skirt and jumper. She was aware of moving with a curiously stiff walk as she tried to keep the garments from touching her body. At least the three layers of woollen underwear she had on were still reasonably dry. Her feet weren't too bad, she reflected, thanks to Violet's insistence on spending a fortune on her boots. But, oh God, the pain in her hands. When they warmed up they were on fire with chilblains, but that was nothing to the sheer agony of when they were just this side of frozen.

Her fingers had warmed slightly in the cook-house where she had been boiling the water used to thaw out the petrol filters from the cars. To her relief all the four cars that were her responsibility had started immediately she cranked them up. The vehicles were fitted out as ambulances, enabling them to accommodate stretchers, and were always on standby. If they were not turned over every hour throughout the night then, in this freezing climate, the radiators would burst, or even the cylinders.

She was glad that Grace was sharing the shift with her. Although not a lot older than Kitty, she had been out here longer and was more adept at managing the cars. Kitty had heard her swearing quietly into the night just now at an old Vulcan which was refusing to start, but the subsequent sound of the engine coming to life had borne witness once more to Grace's expertise.

When Kitty had volunteered for the FANY's she had exaggerated her competence with regard to her mechanical skills. A quick lesson in running repairs from her brother Harry, home on leave, and her careful though somewhat meagre driving experience had been enough to get her through the BRCS driving test. Her father had declared this a fluke but Kitty knew that both Harold and Violet would have been relieved if she had failed. Having Harry at the front was difficult enough for them, without their daughter being in the firing line as well. But they had, she knew, been proud of her when she had been accepted by the corps, and even more so when she had sailed through her probation period.

The light was coming up over the camp and the noise of the guns was starting up spasmodically. She hardly noticed it anymore. She heard a shout from the main hospital, and several of the girls came running out. Grace called over to her, "Barges coming in!" and, without hesitation, Kitty slipped behind the wheel of the nearest car, thankful that her ministrations had enabled it to start smoothly. The girls coming out of the hospital were pulling on layers of outer garments as they ran – no-one ever took much off at night – and the other three vehicles started off only slightly behind her.

Kitty knew that the arrival of the barges heralded the most seriously wounded soldiers. The canals were used more and more to transport the men, enabling them to have a smoother passage than on the hospital train with its unavoidable jerks and spasms. Once the FANY's were alerted by the field telephone, it was their job to meet the barges, collect the injured and often dying, and convey them back to the hospital.

Kitty dreaded the calls, knowing that every dip or bend in the road could cause a scream of anguish from her passengers. But she had learnt not to show her own distress as she administered rudimentary first aid before loading the stretchers into the car. Although she had acquired most of her knowledge about automobiles since she had been in France, when it came to helping the wounded she was one of the relatively few trained nurses in the corps and knew her composure and experience were valued by the others.

She was about halfway back to the hospital with her cargo of eerily quiet, grimly heroic soldiers when one of them started to call, "Help me, Nurse, help me".

Unable to lift her attention from the unlit and unmade road, Kitty tried asking him about his life back home and thought he was listening to her as he fell silent again.

"Are you married?" she asked, desperately trying to distract him, when another voice cut across her.

"'e was, love. But she's a widow now. Thanks for trying with 'im, though. I know I'd rather go 'earing your voice than not. What about a song?"

Though she had to make a tremendous effort to suppress a sob that seemed to be forcing its way up through her chest, Kitty tremulously started to sing *Pack up your troubles in your old kit bag*' and was rewarded by hearing the other two of her patients sing the odd word with her, until they drifted off to sleep. She continued singing until they arrived back at the camp, where other hands were waiting to help unload.

"All of them gone, Kitty, sorry," said one of the helpers.

Kitty left her 'ambulance' and went in to the cookhouse. She poured herself some of the stewed liquid that passed for coffee and went and sat near the stove. She was twenty – three-years-old and often felt more like a hundred. She sometimes thought that she had no tears left to shed. She was wrong. It seemed that however familiar one became with death, the capacity to mourn was infinite. Perhaps she should be grateful for that. As she murmured out loud over and over again, "I am so sorry, I am so sorry," the tears ran unchecked down her face.

A blast of freezing air shot through the hut as Grace came in. "Kitty, Sister Havers wants you down on the ward."

Kitty gulped down her coffee and passed her mittened hands over her cheeks to dry them.

"Come here," said Grace, as she produced an

incongruous lace hanky to wipe the younger girl's face. Putting her hands on Kitty's shoulders she looked at her affectionately. "We do our best. It's all we can do. Even though it's mostly not enough. We all cry, Kitty. It sometimes feels as if the whole world is crying. And that's why we are going to do another concert next week. Cheer ourselves up, as well as the lads. Smile, please."

Kitty obediently pasted a smile on her tear stained face.

"That's better," said Grace. "Can't have you walking about the wards looking like Mona the Misery. Off you go. Oh, hang on, a letter came for you." She handed the envelope to Kitty.

A quick glance revealed it to be from Lawrence. Kitty put it safely into the inner pocket of her greatcoat before fighting her way through the bitter winds back to the hospital.

Sister Havers greeted her crisply with, "Kitty, one of the men just brought in is asking for you. I wouldn't have called you from your transport duties but he is very ill. He says his name is Captain Edward Meredith. Do you know him?"

"Oh yes, Sister," gasped Kitty. "My brother Harry is in his regiment."

Sister Havers looked at her sharply. "You may go and speak to him straight away. Then come back and see me here."

Kitty made her way down the ward until she found Edward. His eyes were closed and one splinted arm was lying on top of the gray blanket. The just-replaced bandage round his head was already pink as blood seeped through it and Kitty quickly retraced her steps to the cupboard where dressings were kept. Standing over Edward, she unwound his bandages and began to staunch the flow of blood again. It was a large wound but Kitty could see that it was clean. It was his tortured breathing that worried her more than the head wound and, examining him more closely, she saw that under his collar another dressing was concealing a throat wound.

He opened his eyes and stared at her blankly. For one dreadful moment she thought he was not going to recognise her, then, "Kitty – wanted to see you," he mumbled, reaching for her hand. She bent toward him. "Harry's a Captain, now. Wanted to tell you myself. Only good thing about having bought it. Seeing you. Telling you myself. He's a good boy..." and he fell back, half asleep, half unconscious.

Kitty, her mind in turmoil, finished re-bandaging his wound. So Harry was alive and presumably well, at least, he had been when Edward last saw him. She tucked the blanket round Edward, still fully clothed as that was the best way to keep warm, and touched his forehead in a caress. His eyelids fluttered but he did not wake.

"Oi, Nurse," said a voice from the adjoining bed, "Can I have some of that?"

Kitty turned with a smile and realised that she had been so focussed on Edward that she had been oblivious to the rest of the ward. The quiet moans of some of the patients were so much a part of her life now that she barely noticed them. "Cheeky!" she admonished the man, moving to tuck his blanket in and being rewarded with a grin. She recognised him as the man whose lower leg had been amputated the day before.

"How are you feeling?" she asked.

"O.K." he replied "They'll have to send me back to Blighty now, so I reckon it's worth half a leg to get me out of this hell hole."

Kitty wondered if Harry would feel the same way. She hadn't seen him for nearly a year. On that last leave there had been a stillness about him, an aura of sadness underneath his delight in being home with his family, that Kitty had understood all too well. The one brief afternoon they had spent together had been their only chance for honest discussion. It had been so painful that after their first exchanges they had retreated to their own thoughts, each knowing that to say too much was to risk exposing how fragile their courage was, not only to each other but to themselves. How could they admit what they both recognised, that they were involved in nothing more or less than a war of attrition, with men being fed endlessly into the war machine? For a soldier to voice such a thought almost certainly meant death as a traitor by firing squad.

Kitty made her way back to Sister Havers. "He wanted to tell me that my brother has been promoted."

Relief flickered across the Sister's face. It undermined morale when the girls heard bad news of their nearest and dearest out here. "Right, Nurse. Back you go. The ambulances are still needed, we haven't managed to get all the wounded off the barges yet. But you may come back to see the Captain when you come off duty."

This was a concession, Kitty realised, and she acknowledged it gratefully. Pulling her scarf over her nose and mouth she fought once more through the blizzard, which showed no sign of abating, and climbed back into her 'ambulance'. Grace was just drawing out again, so she tried to keep her in view. The winds were buffeting the side of the vehicle, making it difficult keep on the rutted and potholed road. Her mind was full of Edward. He had been nearly nine when she was born, which had made him seem very old to her when she was a child. But the gap in their ages had inevitably narrowed as she grew older and, with Harry, she had looked forward to this handsome soldier's visits when he came home on leave.

How close all their parents had been, she reflected, as she peered through the snow obscuring most of the windscreen. Elizabeth, Violet, Alice and Valerie had been like a large family, their children playing and growing up together. The thought that Edward might die of his wounds was like a knife in her stomach.

"Don't let him die," she whispered, "Please, don't let him die".

It was late afternoon before Kitty was told by one of the duty officers to go and get some sleep. Her shift had by now been thirty-six hours long and Kitty was dropping with exhaustion. A quick look in on Edward reassured her that he was no worse.

Finally back in the dormitory she shared with eleven other girls she took out of her pocket the letter she had carried with her all day:

'My dear girl
Yesterday was the anniversary of that wonderful
day when we last met. Such a hurried three days –
but, thank God, you managed to get leave, too. Now
that I know that you care as much for me as I for

*you, I believe that I shall have the strength to get through all this and come home to be with you. Harry and I are both well. He sends his love to you, of course. I am looking forward so much to introducing you to my mother and my sister. I know that they will love you as I do. My sister, Frances, has become a VAD and is working with the Red Cross somewhere out here. She met Phyllis recently and the two have them have become good friends. How brave you all are. But you, my love, are the bravest and cleverest girl in the whole world.
Love from your own
Lawrence. xxxxxx'*

Holding the letter close to her heart, Kitty at last lay on her bed and slept. It seemed she had barely nodded off when she was being shaken awake by Grace.

"Come on, Kitty. We're on early duty because of the concert tonight."

Kitty rolled over and squinted at the little clock by her bed. It was five o'clock in the morning. She had been asleep for twelve hours. Still half-drugged with sleep, she made her way to the wash house, and performed some rapid and rudimentary ablutions. The biting cold made taking too many clothes off a suicidal venture.

She had forgotten about the concert. Ten of the girls were going down the line later to perform '*The Fantastic FANY'S'* for the several hundred Guardsmen who were resting there. The concerts had become a regular and highly valued part of life at the front. The girls had made themselves a range of costumes, mostly glamorous, but sometimes comic. They wrote and performed a variety of sketches and were often amazed at the talent in their midst, both as writers and performers. Kitty's corps boasted two professional dancers as well as a classical singer, so they were in constant demand. As well as being able to hold a tune, Kitty played their rather ramshackle piano so she was an integral part of the group.

However, several hours on the wards stood between her and the evening performance. She hoped no more barges would arrive today. The incessant roar of the cannons seemed nearer. It didn't do to think about that. Soon after her arrival she had helped to evacuate a hospital in the face of the German counter-offensive. The screams of the wounded, being moved in every possible conveyance, and the proximity of the gun fire as the Germans approached had caused the horses to stampede. Kitty had narrowly avoided having her car overturned by them. She would never forget her terror.

The wind seemed to have abated slightly, and she arrived at the hospital less breathless than the previous day. Shedding her coat, she straightened her uniform cap and decided that she had time to visit Edward before reporting for duty.

She could hear his breathing before she reached the bed. He was lying in virtually the same position that she had left him the previous night. The blood had stopped seeping from his head, but the hand poking out from his bandaged arm felt cold and was not a good colour. She found a piece of blanket and wrapped his hand in it. Gently pulling his shirt away from his throat wound, she was filled with foreboding. The wound was even more extensive than she had thought.

"We are going to operate," said a voice behind her.

She turned to see Dr Janssens. The Doctor was a short middle-aged Belgium with a ginger beard that was curiously at odds with his grey hair. He was known to be a skilful surgeon as well as a compassionate man. Kitty respected, as well as liked him, so she felt immediate relief that Edward was under his care.

"Will he..?" she stopped abruptly, knowing that the question forming on her lips was unanswerable and unfair.

The doctor bent over Edward. "We will do what we can, Kitty. We are all in God's hands."

Reporting to Sister Havers, Kitty found that she was assigned to the burns ward. This was the hardest ward to cope with, rows of white bandaged faces with hollows for the eyes of those who might be able to see. The occupants of these ghostly cocoons tried hard not to cry out in agony when their dressings were changed. Kitty and an unqualified but experienced FANY worked their way down the ward.

Although Kitty could not ignore the dreadful disfigurement revealed when the bandages were lifted, she had the good nurse's knack of being able to see past them to the real person, and chatted as if she was changing a plaster on a grazed knee. Her matter-of-fact attitude combined with her gentle and sympathetic touch made her a great favourite with her patients, though she was unaware of this. Her relief arrived to release her earlier than usual with the message that Sister wished them all luck with the concert. She poked her head round Edward's ward but was told he had gone to the operating theatre.

Grace and the other girls were waiting for her back at the dormitory. With the help of three recuperating

Tommys they loaded the ancient piano on the back of a lorry, gathered up their gear and were on their way. They had only about ten miles to drive but they were very aware that the condition of the roads as well as the current weather conditions, it was now blowing a bitter gale, could mean that this could easily take them an hour and a half.

They rehearsed their songs and sketches as they sat on the floor of the bouncing lorry. They had to yell above the noise of the asthmatic old vehicle so that Daphne, their driver, and Beryl, the navigator, could hear their cues. By the time they reached their destination, merriment reigned and spirits were high.

"Well," said Daphne as they disembarked, "we certainly think we're hilarious, so let's hope they do!"

And they did. Six hundred men laughed and cheered and stamped their feet and applauded so enthusiastically that the girls gave encore after encore. Kitty had not experienced such joy and gaiety for a very long time. The FANYs ran through their repertoire twice, and finished with an exhilarating rendition of their special version of *The Road to Mandalay*. Then Kitty asked if any of the men would like to sing a solo.

A certain amount of jocular scuffling ensued, then a very bashful looking young subaltern was frog-marched onto the makeshift stage. Laughing, Kitty asked him what he was going to sing. As he bent toward her in the rather dim light, they recognised each other simultaneously.

"Kitty!" he exclaimed, "I thought it might be you, but I was right at the back and I wasn't sure."

Kitty was wreathed in smiles. "Percy! I didn't even know you were here yet."

Elizabeth had told her that Valerie's son was forsaking Oxford to join up, as were so many of his fellow students, but she had forgotten.

"Only got here last week," he confided.

The barracking from the audience was growing louder, and grinning at Percy, Kitty launched into *Roses of Picardy* which she and Percy had sung together at a 'family' party Valerie and Charles had held one Christmas. The other girls grouped round the handsome officer and his tenor voice soared through the tent, bringing a lump to many a throat in the audience.

When the ballad was over there was a moment of silence before waves of tumultuous applause filled the tent again. After an encore of the song, which the audience joined in, an officer leapt on to the stage and asked the girls to finish on a rousing chorus of *Pack up your troubles* which they duly did. There were many willing hands to help load up the lorry, giving Kitty and Percy the chance for a few words.

He told her that his parents had not wanted him to volunteer and she nodded. But they both knew, he added, that he had no real choice. Rosalie had wanted to volunteer as a war artist and had been furious at her rejection, not on grounds of her sex, but that she was too old. So she was working on the trams in the day and had started drawing classes for some of the convalescing shell-shocked soldiers in the evening. She had a theory that it would help them, Percy explained, and to everyone's surprise she seemed to be right, so she was getting some official backing now. Charles had turned most of their Berkshire estate into a convalescent home and Valerie was following her daughter's lead with some of the shattered souls and finding similar success.

Kitty recognised how proud he was of his mother and sister and was pleased for them all. She told him that Edward had been wounded, but apart from saying that Harry and Lawrence were both well, she added little. He is still so new, she thought as they hugged farewell. So new, and fresh, and innocent. He still believes in this war.

Feeling the jollity of the evening retreating, she jumped on to the lorry and they waved goodbye. The girls fell silent until Beryl's voice was heard from the front of the creaking vehicle singing: *Keep the home fires burning.* One by one they joined in as the lorry ploughed through the night.

Sister Havers was waiting for Kitty when they arrived back. Edward had died on the operating table. The Padre had made arrangements to bury him in the cemetery they had made behind the hospital. He was one of eleven patients who would be interred the following day. Sister gave Kitty permission to attend.

Kitty nodded dumbly. She found her way back to the dormitory like a sleep-walker. Grace glanced at her and a few minutes later was pushing a mug of hot tea into her hand. The rest of the girls continued the business of bedding down, but were now silent, respecting her grief for her friend. Kitty knew that several of them had lost brothers, and that one of the girls had lost her husband.

'But why aren't I crying?' she thought. 'Why aren't I sobbing for this man I have known all my life and loved and respected? Why just this numbness?'

She thought of Alice and Anthony, so proud of their soldier son. John, always gently teasing his younger brother. Harry with his hero worship for Edward, the gallant soldier.

I must write, she thought. The Padre would, of course, but she must as well. She walked to the small cupboard which held all their writing things and became aware that she was still holding the mug of tea. Standing with it incongruously half-way to her lips she felt a great shudder go through her, and a cry that was barely human issued from her lips. In an instant her friends and colleagues were round her, leading her back to her bed, holding her while she sobbed, sobbing themselves.

Sobbing for all the loss, for all the pain, for all the horror that surrounded them. Sobbing now, so that they could somehow draw strength from each other and rise yet again tomorrow to face the day in front of them.

1917

Amiens.
Dear Elizabeth,
Because of some political machinations that I don't quite understand, it seems that we are working for the French now. Apparently our services were volunteered to their Bureau of Motor Sections and we were sent here to Amiens. But, quelle surprise, the British were furious that the French – or was it the Belgians? – hadn't asked the right people for permission to use us, and we were ordered out of the British Zone. It all seems to me to be pretty typical of this war. However, it's an ill wind... The French are paying us the princely sum of 10 francs a day and have issued us with fur coats, very

welcome! They also give us a 'washing allowance' and feed us, so it is all preferable, if one is honest. In fact, none of us give a hoot whether we are working for the British, the French or the Belgians. Our job remains the same. We collect the wounded, who arrive in a never- ending stream, from the hospital trains, administer what help we can and drive them to the hospitals. On the way there, we to try not to get either them or ourselves killed by shells, cannons or snipers. It definitely concentrates the mind.

The other day I got stuck in the mud. None of my cargo was conscious enough to realise that we were in trouble, so that was a comfort. I was trying to reverse out with no discernible luck when Daphne came up behind me. She stopped her taxi- cum-ambulance far enough away so as not to get hoisted with the same petard, strode over to me, reached up her skirt and produced, of all things, a petticoat. This she removed, laid under my wheels, and hey presto, I was off again. What a woman – I must ask her if she was wearing it for just such a purpose – I haven't even seen one for years!

I haven't had news of Harry or Lawrence for some time. I know everything gets held up, but if you have any news of them I should be grateful for it. I don't like to mention this to my parents in case...well, you know why. I am due some leave soon, and shall see you all.

My love to John and Hyacinth,
Kitty.

Amiens
Dear Elizabeth,
Thank you for telling me. I would rather know than not. I imagine my parents are loath to send me so much bad news while I am so far from home.
If there ever was a God, he must have died too, I think.
Kitty.

1918

Kitty heard the church bells ringing before she was properly awake. Disorientated, for a brief moment she thought she was back at the front, then she remembered that she was at home and in her own bed. She had been leaving Waterloo station, just returned to England on two weeks leave (whether or not you want it, Sister had said when she had demurred) when she had heard the news vendor's call.

"Armistice! Armistice! Germany signs the armistice. Get your paper here, read all about it. The War is over. Armistice! Armistice!"

Collapsing on one of the station benches, she had read the news three times before it sunk in. I suppose that means we have won, she thought. Two young /old men in khaki uniforms came and sat on the bench beside her.

"Do you mind, Miss?" one of them said, "There's a great queue for the paper now, and me and my mate are just on our way back. Is it true?"

She handed him the paper. The two men read it in silence. Finally, "Well, then. There it is. Over at last." And they politely handed her back the paper and boarded the train.

She understood perfectly. It was as if all emotion had been drained out of them. We are the generation that has seen too much, too soon. She wondered if she had said it out loud, as a middle-aged lady scurried past her waving the paper, pausing to give her a perplexed look. Too much, too soon. And, she added to herself, I suppose *we* are the lucky ones. The survivors. Hefting her bag, she had begun the walk to the tram.

Her last leave had been marked initially by Violet and Harold's determined efforts to be cheerful. They had arranged visits to the theatre, supper parties and social events ad nauseum. Anything to avoid talking about Harry. They had not known that Kitty and Lawrence had an 'understanding', so although saddened by his death it had not resonated with them as it otherwise might have done. The charade was finally ended during a visit to *Chu Chin Chow*, when in the middle of an uproariously laughing audience Kitty glanced at Violet's motionless form and saw the tears cascading down her mother's cheeks. Kitty and Harold rose in unison and led the unresisting Violet out of the theatre.

At least they had been able to share their anguish and desolation after that, though Kitty hoped her parents would never fully understand the death of hope and the depth of the disillusionment that she and Harry had known.

Almost worse was her visit to Alice and Anthony. Elizabeth and John, deeply grieving themselves, had accompanied her. She had told them how Edward's last words had been to express his pleasure in Harry's promotion, and how loved and respected he was by his men. She was unable to think of anything else to say that might alleviate their pain or her own.

Afterwards, on their way home, Elizabeth had squeezed her hand and said, "Well done, Kitty. It will help them to know that you were with him near the end."

She could only nod mutely, thinking of Lawrence and Harry, dying in the mud. She lay awake at night, praying that it had been quick for them both.

The church bells were the first indication that the country was about to honour Victory Day, as the Government had named today, in style. Glancing at the clock she saw that it was nearly eleven o'clock. Her parents had let her sleep late. She guessed her chronic exhaustion must be more obvious than she realised. Suddenly, as she was dragging herself out of bed, the most enormous noise filled the air. Instinctively she ducked, covering her head with her arms, before remembering that this was part of the celebrations. She had forgotten that they were due to start at eleven o'clock with the nation-wide firing of maroons. As the echoes of the maroons faded, they were replaced by the sound of many bugles playing a ceremonial 'all clear'.

Dressing hurriedly, she heard a knock at the front door. A minute later Violet called up to her, "Hyacinth is here for you, Kitty".

She had promised to go with Hyacinth and John to Hyde Park. Elizabeth was on duty at the hospital. Kitty wondered if that was coincidence, or part of a strategy to make her join in the festivities. Perhaps her family and friends were aware she certainly would not have had anything to do with them if she had been left to her own devices. Smiling slightly, she realised that she had probably been subtly coerced. Well, possibly they had a point, she conceded. There was nothing to be gained by staying at home being miserable.

An hour or so later, as she and John held Hyacinth's hands tightly between them in the milling crowd, she was glad that she had come. The elation of the public was contagious. A group of women munitions workers burst on to the streets whooping with joy, led by two girls waving tambourines. They invaded the open car of a rather staid Staff Officer, causing considerable mirth among the onlookers. Any uniformed soldier spotted in the throng was ambushed and garlanded, and the buses, overloaded with more returned warriors, were decked with flags and streamers. Two lads ran alongside one of these with a flag declaring: 'Welcome home, our heroes!'

Allied flags flew from hundreds of hastily improvised flagpoles on the roofs of the buildings. The high spot of the occasion was a sighting of the King and Queen as they made an informal drive down Whitehall to the Park. John hoisted Hyacinth high on his shoulders as they drove past, and his eleven-year-old daughter was convinced that the King had given her a special wave. And who could say that he had not, thought Kitty, as she looked at the girl's flushed and excited face.

Kitty was struck by the number of women pouring out of the shops and factories and offices. She hadn't fully realised how many women were doing jobs during the war that once would have been only available to men. She recognised a certain irony in this situation. All around them the singing and revelry continued unabated. Some of the young boys were waving blackout curtains that they had torn down. Along with every one else, Kitty had been shocked to hear of the aerial bombing of civilians. She knew that the first German raid on London's East End the previous year had killed one hundred people and injured four hundred more. Anthony's batman, finally retired, had been mortally injured in the raid. One of the bombs had fallen on a school and killed ten children, one of them the daughter of Phyllis's milliner. To bomb innocent children seemed the final obscenity to her.

Hyacinth sometimes had an almost uncanny ability to tune into her thoughts. "It's all over, Auntie Kitty," she whispered into Kitty's ear. "Be happy." As she hugged Hyacinth in response, Kitty met John's eyes over the child's head. She knew that he was also remembering their absent loved ones.

"I'm not sure," she thought, "that I shall ever again know how to be happy."

Just over a month later, Kitty went with Elizabeth, Alice and Violet to the polling station. She was still only twenty-five-years old and therefore not eligible herself to vote. But as she watched the others enter the building her head was full of Emily, and her sacrifice. She found herself communing silently with her dead friend, as she waited for the return of the older women.

'At last, we have the vote. Not on equal terms yet, but that will come. You helped to achieve this. But a whole generation of beautiful young men are lost forever. How many millions dead, Ems? I wonder if we will ever know. What kind of world is there for those of us who are left over? If we had been able to help shape the world could we have prevented this war? Something else that we will never know. Wherever you are, Ems, help us. If you can. Help us to use this vote, that you gave your life to achieve, to see that nothing like this ever happens again. And to make sure that this really is the war to end all wars.'

1923

Percy regarded his wife affectionately, "It seems that the destiny of our families is always to be explaining to the children why Mummy is in prison."

"Percy, darling, that is just not true," replied Kitty, hoisting twelve-month-old Julian into his high chair. "Here, pass me Charlotte, they behave better if we put them opposite each other."

Percy deposited a kiss on his daughter's forehead before handing her over. "It's just that looking after the twins might be considered enough for most people, you know. Certainly would for me."

Passing him a spoon Kitty began to supervise the administration of what could only be described as mush to the two children, expertly feeding Julian with one hand and wiping his chin with the other. She noticed with some amusement that Percy still managed to drip almost as much down himself as he deposited in Charlotte's mouth, but forbore to point this out. Time for a little tact, she thought, aware how few husbands and fathers would contemplate, let alone enjoy, this operation.

"I have no intention of going to prison. But Marie wants me to help in the clinics, and I feel I must. Anyway I don't think for a minute that they'll prosecute us. It's all hot air. If they were going to do it, they would have done it by now. But, after all, why do you think I a married a lawyer?"

"Because you took pity on me after my tenth proposal?" grinned Percy.

They smiled at each other. Certainly Percy had been persistent, but also gentle and patient. They had both had a lot of healing to do as they edged their way back into civilian life and had found that each gave the other the proverbial shoulder to cry on. Their shared experiences had been the basis for a friendship that had eventually flowered into love to the delight of both their families.

Kitty said,"Suzanne looks after the twins just as well as I could, better, probably. We are lucky to have her. And to be able to afford her."

They had indeed been lucky to acquire the Norland-trained Nanny. She had come to them through one of Elizabeth's colleagues, whose own children were now all at boarding school. She was charming and efficient and Kitty daily counted her as one of life's blessings. She had not contemplated continuing nursing after the twins were born, but the invitation from Mrs Stopes to help in her revolutionary birth control clinic had provided an irresistible challenge. As one of the first State Registered Nurses, and possessing her own car, a homecoming present from her parents after the war, Kitty had accepted a position as District Nurse and Midwife in London's East End in 1919.

The job had been a revelation to her. Everywhere she found poverty, overcrowding and ignorance. Along with many others, she had expected the new free clinics set up after the war to improve the acknowledged poor health of many women and their children. That was before she had seen some of the clinics. For the most part they were dark, damp and depressing. Even worse was the effect of the obligatory registration which many people regarded as an intrusion of their privacy. It was not uncommon for Kitty to be told that, "My ol' man says we're not 'aving that lot know our business.'

She had learnt to remove her uniform on arriving at a confinement, screwing it up so the bugs would not invade it, and placing it in a hat box she carried for the purpose. The nurses were constantly cautioned that they must never let their clothes touch the walls for fear of infestation. In these conditions, often with six or seven small children sitting in the one room the family lived in, Kitty would try to make the mothers as comfortable as she could. She carried piles of newspaper in her small car as this was often more hygienic than allowing the mother to give birth on the bare and dirty mattress shared by the whole family. It was not unusual for the bedclothes to be pawned on a Monday, and retrieved on payday. Sometimes she found herself frantically trying to keep the bed bugs from crawling up the birth canal as they fell from the ceiling on to the writhing form on the bed.

There were no anaesthetics for these women. She had been warned when she began that the rich had anaesthetics and the poor had a knotted towel to pull on. Kitty had thought she was dead to feeling but found she was not. As more and more women begged her for help and advice on how to avoid yet another pregnancy, Kitty found that she was still capable of immense pity, accompanied by a mounting fury at the conditions these people were forced to live in.

Paradoxically, her anger had helped to bring her back to life again. After a particularly difficult birth, which had resulted in the death of a malformed baby, Kitty found herself unburdening her frustrations to her aunt. Primrose had finally (and rather unwillingly) retired, but loved to be 'kept in touch' by Kitty.

"It's as if getting the vote has made no difference. So many of these people live in squalor, the husband gets and keeps most of the money while the wife has baby after baby, some of whom live and some don't. I see these women trying to keep body and soul and family together on less per week than I'd spend on a hat. What did we fight for, if it's made no difference?"

Primrose looked steadily at her niece. "It *has* made a difference, Kitty. It's made a tremendous difference to people like us, who can choose our careers and are not beholden to any man. But we are the educated ones, and, if I dare point it out, the better off ones. We are starting from a higher base in every respect. So now we have to try to make it count for those who have no concept that any other way of life is possible for them."

Kitty sighed. "It's like that man in the story who kept pushing the stone up the hill, and every morning found it had gone back to the bottom."

"I know," replied her aunt. "It is both absurd and callous that it is still illegal for us to try to teach them about any kind of pregnancy prevention except abstinence when most of these women don't have much choice about that."

That conversation had been very much in Kitty's mind when a few weeks ago she accepted Mrs Stopes' invitation to join the team in her Holloway clinic. She had discussed it at some length with Elizabeth, who she knew had mixed feelings about Mrs Stopes.

Elizabeth, as always, went straight to the point. "I

think you should support the clinics in every way, Kitty, but be wary of Marie. I think she is doing the right thing for the wrong reasons. I've known her for years, and she thinks the so-called lower classes should be prevented from breeding too much in case they overwhelm the upper classes. In other words her own 'class'. She advocates birth control as a form of 'racial progress. I don't think I need say more!"

Indeed she did not. As Percy put it, "Watch your back and keep your head down." Kitty thought that might be anatomically difficult but took the point.

Her first day was disappointingly slow. However, just as she was beginning to think that no-one would come and she might as well pack up and go home, two women, shrouded in headscarves, slipped furtively through the door together. Kitty stepped forward to greet them. Before she could say anything, one of them looked at the heavily-curtained windows of the clinic.

"You can't see through them, can you?" she asked. "Only Jim'd kill me if he knew I was here."

"No, indeed," Kitty reassured her. "You're quite safe here. All we want to do is advise you."

She started by making the two women a pot of tea. She had been told by one of the other helpers that the suggestion that this was a social occasion often aided relaxation. They were all aware how desperate, and how frightened, most of their visitors were. Kitty was one of the few qualified nurses staffing the clinics, as the medical profession was officially hostile to their aims.

As they sipped their hot tea the two women began to talk to her. They were sisters. Elsie had four children under five and had been told that a fifth would kill her.

Her husband had sent the local priest round to see her when she repeated this to him. The priest had told her severely that to die in childbirth was a glorious end for any woman. When she asked him who, in that case, would care for her other children, he had simply said, "The Lord will provide", prayed at her and left. Elsie found she was unconvinced.

Janet, the younger sister, also had four children, her last one being born with a withered leg. She had found the sixpence needed to take him to the doctor, even though that had meant pawning her wedding ring, and buying the family less food for the week, but, although sympathetic, he could do nothing. He told her he thought that it was due to her lack of nourishment when she was carrying the baby. Her only crumb of comfort lay in his assurance that the child could eventually be fitted with a calliper which might eventually help him to walk.

Janet had recently found she was pregnant again. She had tried to abort the foetus by inserting knitting needles into her vagina. The resulting haemorrhage was so violent that she had been rushed to hospital and was lucky to be alive.

The two women told their stories and then sat back, looking trustingly at Kitty. With a sudden sense that perhaps, in some small way, she really could help to change the world, she reached into her bag for a Dutch cap and began to draw a diagram.

Part Four: Hyacinth

1925

Hyacinth was in love. She had never been in love before but she absolutely knew that this was the real thing. After all, she had read lots of books and they all talked about how your 'pulse quickened' and your 'heart beat faster' when you saw your loved one, and those were precisely her symptoms.

Hyacinth had left school the previous year with no clear idea of what she wanted to do with her life. All she knew for sure was that she did not want to be a doctor like her mother. "Honestly," she confided in her friend Daisy, "I just never see my mother. She's always at the hospital. I do see a bit more of Father, but he is forever writing something, and smiles at me vaguely and pretends he is listening to me. I see more of my Auntie Kitty than I do of them, especially now she's got four children and doesn't work at the clinics anymore."

The two girls caught each other's eyes and giggled. It was an ongoing joke between them that Hyacinth's Auntie Kitty had helped at the notorious 'birth control' clinics whilst seeming to be always in an 'interesting condition' herself. Neither girl was quite sure what her work had involved, any more than they were familiar with the mechanics of becoming 'in an interesting condition', but Hyacinth had overheard Percy gently teasing his wife on the subject, and Kitty's eventual laughing agreement that it might be less than tactful for her to continue.

"I suppose I feel the urge to repopulate the world," Hyacinth had once heard her mother say to Percy.

Hyacinth had not understood what she meant and as an accidental listener had not liked to ask. She and Daisy had mulled the remark over but come to no satisfactory conclusions. Daisy was three years older than Hyacinth, but had grown up in a less 'modern' household and regarded Hyacinth as very worldly. Hyacinth was happy to go along with this, whilst aware that it was something of a delusion.

The myth had been perpetuated to some extent when Hyacinth had eventually found herself a job on the staff of the BBC, as assistant to the director of women's programmes. John had been able to get her the initial introductions through his contacts on the paper, but Hyacinth had made the most of her opportunity. Her department was responsible for nearly two hours of entertainment on the radio for six days a week, and although Hyacinth knew she was just a glorified tea maker at the moment, she was learning fast. She had no doubt that one day she would run the department. Her friend, spending her days helping her mother with occasional voluntary work, and waiting to meet 'Mr Right', envied her.

It had been at Daisy's twenty-first birthday party that Hyacinth had met Toby. It was a very posh party, held at one of London's top hotels. Hyacinth had been allowed to buy a new dress for it, and she had chosen a very daring purple beaded dress with shoulder straps and the hemline just above the knee. When she showed it to her mother, Elizabeth had loved it.

"Oh, darling," she said, "I would have given my eye tooth to have worn that at your age. Everything was corsets and boots in my day. You look so pretty."

The thing that neither Hyacinth nor her mother had realised was that the dress was heavy. *Really* heavy. Beads could be a bit of a liability, Hyacinth was beginning to understand. Dancing a frantic Charleston with Bobby Raikes, Daisy's rather pompous cousin, she became conscious that the dress was not made for such energetic pursuits. She didn't know whether to be glad or sorry when it became obvious that she was shedding some of the beads. Fortunately, Bobby was too intent on showing his own prowess to notice.

When Hyacinth eventually collapsed onto one of the cane chairs surrounding the dance floor, she was startled to hear a voice behind her say, "I believe these belong to you."

Turning, she found quite the best looking young man she had ever seen, proffering her a handful of all too familiar beads. Hyacinth was her mother's daughter. Covered in embarrassment she might be, but she was not going to show it.

"Thank you so much," she smiled, taking the proffered beads and slipping them into her bag.

"As a reward, I wonder if I might have the next dance?"

"Indeed, it will be a pleasure," responded Hyacinth, successfully subduing her rapidly increasing heartbeats. Or at least, this was how she described the scene to Daisy later.

And that was how it began.

1927

"I simply can't believe that you and Daddy can be

so unreasonable." Hyacinth struggled to stop her voice wobbling. She was twenty-years-old and was absolutely not going to sound like a child.

Elizabeth gave a deep sigh. "Oh, darling, we just want you to be sure. We are happy for you and Toby to be engaged, if that is what you want, but we must insist that you wait another year before marrying. Toby can't begin to support you, Hyacinth. Your job is all very well, and I can't tell you how pleased we are that you have done so well at the BBC, but you couldn't possibly keep the two of you on your salary. And suppose you start a family, how would you manage then?"

"Toby is just waiting for the right opportunity. He is beginning to think that perhaps the flickers might be worth a try. We met Mr Novello at a party last week and he was very encouraging. He thought that with Toby's looks and training he would be sure of landing some good parts. Even though it's not real acting, it would tide him over for a while."

Elizabeth felt her heart sink even further. She liked Toby well enough, but wondered several times a day why her daughter could not have fallen for a man with a proper job. Toby was an actor. Against the wishes of his family, he had auditioned for, and been accepted by, RADA. The famous Royal Academy of Dramatic Art had been set up some twenty years before by Beerbohm Tree, an actor Hyacinth knew had been a great favourite of her mother's, so she mentioned this often. To no real avail, John and Elizabeth were quite set against the marriage until Toby had proved himself in his chosen career.

Unfortunately, although Toby was working steadily

in the theatre, all his parts so far had been negligible and certainly not very lucrative. "I come through the French windows, waving a tennis racquet, calling 'Anyone for tennis?'" he complained, "Then some ingénue jumps up, says, 'Oh, super,' and we both trot out again until the last act, when we stand around holding hands and looking goofy, while the older actors get all the good lines and we say, 'Ooh', at intervals to prove we are listening."

Hyacinth thought he was wonderful whatever he did, and proudly took her parents along to one such show and, although they would not have told her so for the world, they had been less than impressed by Toby's thespian skills. He had managed to fumble one of his ten lines and then left a pause so long before another that they feared he had forgotten it altogether.

"I can't help feeling that it's only his looks that have got him this far," remarked John, in the privacy of their bedroom that night. Elizabeth agreed. "So let's hope someone writes a play needing an affable young man who happens to look like a Greek God," she laughed.

Several hours later John sat bolt upright in bed and reached for his reporter's notebook, always kept beside the bed. It can't be that difficult to write a play, he thought, as he began to scribble. Two days later the sound of the typewriter clacking away non-stop had made both Hyacinth and Elizabeth curious.

"What *is* Daddy doing?" asked a bemused Hyacinth. But her mother was equally mystified. A week or so later, John emerged from his study, announced that he had to go into the office, and left. As soon as he had gone the two women rushed into his study and searched for clues. There were none.

"Whatever he's up to, he doesn't mean us to know. At least, not yet," said Elizabeth thoughtfully.

When John came home that evening he was irritatingly unforthcoming in response to probing from his wife and daughter.

"Sort of smug, even," mused Elizabeth to Kitty.

"Not really like John," replied her friend.

"I know," said Elizabeth. "It's all really out of character."

Elizabeth was working less hours at the hospital now, and found that she enjoyed being with Kitty's young brood.

"I suppose that I never really had time to enjoy Hyacinth," she said, piling the two youngest boys between the twins on the back seat of Kitty's car.

"Well," replied Kitty with a grin "Whatever the reason, believe me, I'm grateful. Suzanne is wonderful, but I have to let her have a day off sometimes! Right, then, kids, off to the park."

Sitting by the Serpentine later, watching the children play, Elizabeth and Kitty were surprised to see John walking by the lake in animated conversation with a middle- aged man who looked vaguely familiar. As they came nearer, Elizabeth rose to her feet and waved, catching John's eye. He hurried over to her, bringing his companion.

"Elizabeth and Kitty, I should like to introduce you to a former colleague. This is Mr Tyrone Guthrie."

The introductions made, Elizabeth was startled to hear Mr Guthrie say, "Well, John, that is settled then. No royalties, but I'll audition the young man next week. I'll be in touch." And he was gone, striding off through the park, leaving them regarding John with puzzled expressions.

"Alright, I'll come clean," said John, watching the rapidly departing figure of Mr Guthrie. "I've written a play. After all, I've been a writer all my life, and we both love the theatre. How hard can it be, I thought? Well, to be honest, it wasn't. Tyrone Guthrie used to be an announcer and I often wrote his reports when he was working for the BBC. We got to know each other tolerably well. But now he's gone back to his first love, the theatre. He likes my play, it's a romance about an aristocratic and extremely handsome young man who is engaged to a princess but who then falls in love with a servant. It's all very silly, but, though I say it myself, rather well written. And Rufus, the hero, is exactly the kind of part for Toby. So, he will be invited to audition and we keep our fingers crossed. If he gets the part, he'll have to go to Scotland with Tyrone's troupe for several months. And if he's good enough they might ask him to join the troupe. Either way, Hyacinth will have to do without him for a bit, which won't be such a bad thing, and hopefully domestic harmony will be restored."

Elizabeth gave her husband a hug. "I've always known you were a genius."

"Well, let's cross our fingers it works," he replied.

Hyacinth was ecstatic when she heard that Toby had landed the part. She was mildly amused that her father was the author of the play and thought that both he and Toby were lucky to have found each other.

"Isn't it wonderful that Toby inspired Daddy to write a play?" she rhapsodised to Daisy.

Daisy thought so, too. "But won't you miss him if

he's in Scotland?"

"Yes, of course I will. But I've got a promotion, and I am going to be very busy. I've been asked to help set up a series of afternoon programmes about the Suffragettes. It's going to be great fun to do. Mummy's promised to let me interview her, and so has Kitty, and she is going to ask Aunt Rosalie if she'll talk to me when she comes to stay with her and Percy. Kitty says Aunt Rosalie knows more about Emily Davison than any of them, and I want to do a whole section about her. I think I may have got this job because of what Mummy and the others did, but I'm going to show them how good I am. So you see, I shan't have time to be miserable. And now Toby and I are properly engaged, we can both save like mad for when we are married."

"Goodness," said Daisy enviously, "You really have got it all planned out, haven't you?"

Hyacinth laughed, "Sorry. I am a bit full of myself, aren't I? But it's so super that it's all turning out well. I know how lucky I am. In a couple of years, Toby will be famous, I'll be established at the BBC, and we can be married and everything will be just heavenly!"

"Gosh," commented Daisy, "Nothing ever seems to go wrong for you, Hyacinth."

1930

"Oh, no!" said Hyacinth, reading the memo on her desk for the umpteenth time, "Look at this, Susan." She handed the note to her colleague. "I simply don't understand. Everyone knows that I should have had the last promotion and now I've been passed over again. And I am doing more and more stuff that is just secretarial. My Suffragette piece was an enormous success, why, even *The Times* described it as 'a new and thought provoking departure for women's programmes'. So why am I being treated as some sort of pariah? Miss Williams passed me in the corridor this morning and could barely say 'hello'. I was counting on getting that job. We really need the money. Toby hasn't had a decent part for months, only one really good offer since our wedding and then the company went broke. We can't go on letting our parents support us."

Susan read the memo carefully before handing it back. "I suppose that with so much unemployment there is just more competition for the posts. Perhaps we should just be grateful to be here."

Hyacinth stared at her. "I *am* pleased to have such a good job. But I also know that I work jolly hard, and that I am very good at it. Who has been given this post, anyway?"

Susan buried herself deeper in the paperwork on her desk. "I'm told that it's Miss Gray."

Hyacinth was stunned. "What? That woman who keeps trapping me in the corridor and picking my brains? That's ridiculous. She knows nothing about running this department. I saw she'd applied but I didn't think she stood a chance. I'm going to ask Miss Williams what's going on."

Susan looked up sharply. "Hyacinth. Don't. You can't afford to lose your job anymore than I can. Who knows what goes on in their minds? Forget it. Let's just get on with this project. It is very important that we get it right, for the parents of those poor children."

Reluctantly, Hyacinth nodded in agreement, temporarily distracted. They had been given the task of setting up interviews with some of the people connected to the dreadful accident that had happened in a Glasgow cinema on New Year's Eve. Seventy-one children had died, most of them crushed to death when the nine hundred children crammed into the cinema had panicked and tried to run from the building when smoke filled the auditorium. In fact, the fire had been extinguished very quickly, but jammed doors and the lack of adult supervision had contributed to the tragedy.

Hyacinth and Susan had been asked to report on the safety aspects of the disaster, and then discuss their relevance to the increasing popularity of cinema matinées for children. It was unusual for their department to be given anything as potentially controversial and they were very conscious it must be handled with considerable tact.

"This certainly does give you a sense of perspective," commented Hyacinth, as she began to go over her notes again. "One couple lost all three of their children. Makes my troubles seem a bit petty, doesn't it?"

On her way home that evening Hyacinth mulled over Susan's words. She knew it was good advice. She would be mad to throw up a job she loved and needed, and their joint research today had underlined that. But she still felt resentful and undervalued at being passed over for promotion, as she told Toby when they were eating their supper together that evening.

"Never mind, old girl," he said. "I've got some perfectly spiffing news. My agent told me today that the walk-on part I did in that film of Ivor's caught someone's attention. They want me to audition for a film in America!"

Hyacinth choked on her food, causing Toby to rush round the table and thump her on the back. When – in spite of his ministrations – she had recovered, she threw her arms round his neck.

"We've been home for ages, why didn't you tell me straight away, you pig? I've been maundering on and you had this wonderful news!"

"Well," said Toby, a bit sheepishly. "The thing is, I've already accepted. Then I thought we ought to talk about it first and you might be a bit... well, a bit put out."

"You mean I can't come too?" asked Hyacinth. "How long is it for?"

"If the audition is rot, I'll be back almost before I've gone. But if it goes O.K., they are talking about six months. It's what they call a biblical epic, and they want me to play a Roman Centurion who is converted to Christianity. It's the third lead and they are paying an awful lot." He named a figure that left Hyacinth gasping.

"So if you get it, we could easily afford for me to come and join you. But then I'd have to give up my job at the BBC."

Toby nodded. "That's the fly in the ointment. I know how you love the job, for all the ups and downs you've had."

And, thought Hyacinth, we can't be certain that we won't need my salary in six months' time. "We'll think about it, sweetheart. When do you have to go?"

"Well, actually," replied her husband, "the day after tomorrow."

Hyacinth hid her shock at the immediacy of their separation. "Well, then," she said calmly, "We'd better let the parents know and then start doing some serious packing."

In the office the following day even the austere Miss Williams was impressed with Hyacinth's news. "He's certainly a very handsome young man," she commented as she swept through.

Susan and Hyacinth looked at each other and giggled. "I didn't know she'd noticed," said Hyacinth.

"Well, at least that's something cheerful," said Susan. "But I'm afraid she came in with the bad news before you got here. It appears that they've taken the cinema story away from us. It's gone to one of the other departments. "

"Oh, no," said Hyacinth "Why? Who's doing it?"

"Guess. Upstairs, of course. They've decided it's too important to be left in the hands of women, who after all, should be at home washing-up."

Hyacinth had never heard Susan sound so bitter. "I can't believe it. After all the work we've put in. And we were doing a good job with it. I'm going to make a stand."

"Please don't, Hyacinth. It won't get us anywhere, and you might get us into trouble. We have to hand over all our notes to Miss Williams. Mine are in the top of my bag, get them and put them with yours. I've got this stimulating article to research on the right length for a fashionable woman to wear her skirts."

Half-heartedly Hyacinth gathered up her own notes and located Susan's capacious bag which she had thrown onto a chair. As she began to delve into its contents, Susan suddenly came shooting across the room toward her, saying, "Don't worry, I'll get them…" and, startled, Hyacinth dropped the bag and its contents on to the floor.

A tiny leather purse fell at Hyacinth's feet. Stooping, she picked it up. As she rose she was astonished to see her friend back away from her.

"Oh, please don't tell," came the other girl's anguished whisper.

Hyacinth's bafflement must have shown on her face. As Susan, recovering some composure, reached for her property, it dropped to the floor again. The two young women watched as if mesmerised as a gold ring fell out and rolled across the room. Silently, Hyacinth retrieved it and handed it to its owner.

"Why?" she asked. "Why the secrecy? Why didn't you tell me you were married too?"

Susan's face was scarlet with embarrassment. "I would never have got the job if they'd realised. So I just said I was Miss. No-one questioned it. Gerry lost his job at the bank last year. He can't find anything else, and we're behind with the rent. You mustn't tell anyone, Hyacinth. I need this job badly."

"But the BBC has a policy of equality for all, including married women."

"*Did* have, you mean. Before the depression and all the unemployment. Now they think that married women should be at home, supported by their husbands. They say we are taking jobs that the men need and we don't. Oh, Hyacinth, can't you see, that's why you haven't been promoted. You never will be. It's difficult enough for single women. But you don't stand any chance at all if you're married. That's why I have to keep it secret."

Numb with shock, Hyacinth handed Susan the ring. All sorts of incidents were going through her mind. "I think I have been very stupid," she concluded. "Don't worry, of course I won't land you in it. Your secret is as safe as houses with me."

Picking up her own bag she walked out of her office and then the building, without a backward glance. Arriving home, where Toby was making his usual shambolic attempts at packing, she sat on the bed and watched him with a smile playing round her lips.

"Leave it, darling." she finally said. "I'll do it tonight. For both of us. I'm coming with you."

Toby let out a loud whoop of joy. "Really?"

She nodded and replied with a laugh, "Look out Hollywood! Here we come!"

Two days later the young couple were aboard *Britannica*, embarked for New York and what they confidently expected to be the biggest adventure of their lives. Elizabeth had been slightly concerned as, although the *Titanic* disaster had been eighteen years earlier, like so many people she had lost a colleague who had been aboard.

"I wish they weren't going on a White Star ship," she had confided to John.

But Hyacinth and Toby were thrilled that the film company had booked them passages on the most popular liner of the day, with its acres of light wood and splendidly modern interior. The voyage was everything they could have hoped for and when they finally arrived in New York they had a full address book and numerous invitations to visit the friends they had made. They were to stay in the famous Algonquin Hotel, as Toby's audition was to take place in New York. As they fell into bed that night Toby remarked drowsily: "I say, old thing, this is the life, what?" What indeed, thought Hyacinth as she drifted into sleep.

The following morning a car arrived to take them across the city to a small studio. They arrived a few minutes early, and the director explained to Toby the effect he hoped to achieve. An actress had been booked to play opposite Toby. Hyacinth had taken him over his lines so often that she knew them as well as he did. The scene was the first meeting between the centurion and the girl who would eventually convert him to Christianity. Though not long it was obviously a crucial piece.

Toby was taken off to have his make-up applied and a costume adjusted to fit him. But his opposite number had still not arrived when he returned. Hyacinth thought her husband looked amazingly handsome in his centurion's costume. They went and sat in an unobtrusive corner whilst waiting for the actress to arrive. After another half an hour, during which their presence seemed to have been totally forgotten, Hyacinth was increasingly aware that Toby was becoming more and more nervous. She wondered if these people had any idea how much might depend on this audition for them.

Leaving Toby reading over the scene yet again, she went to find the director. Putting on her most winning smile and politest manner, she asked him if there was any news of the girl. The director, a short and slightly plump man with a perpetually harassed manner, looked at her for a moment as if trying to remember who she was.

Then, in a loud voice he hailed a boy who came scurrying across the room. "Hey, Jimmy, go and check out that broad, she should have been here hours ago." Jimmy went running off, presumably to find a telephone, thought Hyacinth.

Another hour passed and the actress still had not appeared. Even more worryingly, Jimmy seemed to have vanished as well. The director approached Toby, who was pacing up and down, holding his by now shredded script.

"I guess we're going to have to call it off, kids," he said. They looked at him with horrified expressions.

"Until when?" asked Hyacinth.

The director shrugged. "Who knows?" he replied.

"But we are over here specially to do this," said Hyacinth, her eyes filling with tears as all their expectations seemed about to crumble into dust.

"Say," asked the director, whose name was Saul, "are you over from England, then?"

They nodded.

"I thought I recognised those cute accents," said Saul. "My mother's second cousin, she lives in Boston and she's married to an Englishman who sounds just like you. Name of Harris. Monty Harris. Do you know him?"

Somewhat taken aback, they had to admit that they did not.

"Just thought you might," said Saul. "Hey, I've had an idea."

He turned to Hyacinth. "Why don't you fill in? Do the scene with, er..?"

"Toby," said Hyacinth, staring at him for a long moment as she thought about this outrageous idea. "All right," she said finally, "Why not? I know the part, after all. Let's give it a go."

An hour later, made up and costumed (a glance in the mirror told Hyacinth that she looked very fetching), she was being told where to stand, and the camera man was 'lighting' them. Poor Toby was sweating profusely by this time, a combination of nerves and the heat from the lights. The make-up girl magically appeared and powdered him down. Finally, the audition began. Hyacinth was glad that Toby had done the small part in the Ivor Novello film the previous year, which had given them both some experience of what seemed a rather laborious process. They did the short scene seventeen times before Saul finally declared a 'wrap'.

"You were terrific," he said to Hyacinth. "You Brits are very popular at the minute and you both sound so classy. Voices are all the thing now, only Mr Chaplin is still holding out against the talkies. I guess he don't sound too good."

Hyacinth wondered whether to point out that Charlie Chaplin was also a 'Brit', but decided against it. Saul promised them that the audition would be on its way to his bosses that evening, and they that would be contacted in a couple of days. Returning to the Algonquin in the studio car they held hands tightly.

"Was I, you know, O.K?" stammered Toby.

"I thought that you were wonderful, darling," Hyacinth reassured him.

He hugged her. "They'd have called it off if you hadn't stepped into the breach, though. You were so brave to do it."

"Or desperate," she replied with a giggle. "I had this awful vision of going back home with our tails between our legs and trying to explain that nothing had happened."

"I was absolutely petrified. Were *you* very nervous?" asked her husband.

"Dreadfully," replied Hyacinth, but she knew it was a lie. She had been nervous of letting Toby down but to her surprise she had found the whole process most enjoyable.

"Well," said Toby, as the chauffeur leapt out of the car to open the doors and the Algonquin's commissionaire appeared to usher them into the hotel, "Let's hope you never have to do it again."

1932

"I simply cannot believe that they are expecting me to play second fiddle to a four- year-old child. I absolutely, definitely, totally, will not do it."

Mike regarded his star through a haze of cigar smoke. "Sweetie, I think you should think very carefully about this one. There are contractual difficulties if you refuse. Also, this Shirley Temple not only sounds like a nice kid, she is becoming very popular. The papers are calling her 'America's Princess'. Turn this down and you might get trampled in the rush of people trying to take your place."

"I don't care. I want a film that will make them take me seriously. I'm fed up with all this light-weight stuff. And I will not be a stooge to some curly-haired toddler."

"I think you should talk to Toby before we go any further. Where is he?"

"I have no idea. Out impressing some out-of-work starlet, I imagine. It's him you should be talking to, anyway. He's supposed to be my manager." Hyacinth moved away from her dressing table after carefully checking her make-up. "Deal with it, Mike. That's what you get your ten per cent for. Get me something meaty. Something to prove I'm a real actress."

Mike left the rambling, Hacienda type Bel Air bungalow, waving to Maureen the housekeeper as he passed. But are you a real actress, Hyacinth, darling? he wondered. That Hyacinth radiated an almost eerie luminosity in front of the camera was undeniable. One influential newspaper had published an article only last week comparing her to Garbo and Louise Brooks and posing the question: 'Why does the camera love these Europeans so much?'

But Mike thought that the other two women were probably actresses of much greater ability than his client. Deep down, he suspected that Hyacinth's stardom was a fluke. She had captivated the studio boss, Jacob Goldberg, when he saw her in Toby's audition, and he had cast them both immediately. The film was a minor success, and Hyacinth a major one. The studio had paired them opposite each other again, but the second film was a flop. Toby had not had another part yet, but Hyacinth had gone on to have an unexpected hit playing the mousey cousin of the heroine in a screwball comedy. The studio was dangling a very lucrative contract under her nose. Unfortunately Hyacinth seemed to have no concept of how tenuous fame could be in Hollywood, reflected Mike, and was holding out for a clause that would enable her to choose her own parts. Mike thought hell would freeze over before the studio would allow that.

He went to look for Toby. For all the woodenness that Toby had shown on screen, Mike had a gut feeling that he was the real actor out of the two Brits. He knew that Toby had never quite overcome his discomfort with the banality of the script. Either way he was becoming fond of the young man who displayed the warmth and amiability that seemed to have deserted his wife. He found Toby beside the swimming pool, watching the antics of the two black children who Mike recognised as the housekeeper, Maureen's, son and daughter. Toby looked up at Mike and grinned.

"I know, I know. Theoretically they should be sweeping the leaves in the yard. But they're kids, for heaven's sake, Mike. What is it with this country? Unemployment everywhere, but black kids are expected to do this stuff for nothing, just because their Mum works for us. Let them play, I say, we can easily employ someone to tidy the garden – oh, sorry, the yard!"

Mike nodded. "Agreed. But your neighbours and, perhaps more importantly, your employers, might take issue with you. You could be a bit too radical for comfort."

"Think I'll risk it," replied Toby. "There's a chap came round yesterday asking for work and I've already given him the job."

"Is he black?"

Toby looked puzzled. "No. White fellow. Says he's an actor. Then, they all are in this town, aren't they?"

Mike laughed agreement. Everywhere you went, an aspiring actor popped up, waiting to be spotted by a talent scout and given the break that would change their lives. Unfortunately the movie industry was struggling as hard as the rest of America to survive, and with audiences dropping drastically, there was a lot of belt tightening going on. To be unknown increasingly meant staying that way.

"How's Hyacinth?" asked Toby, slightly sheepishly. "She was in a right old mood this morning over this Shirley Temple thing, so I sort of bunked off."

"So I see. Well, not that much improved, I'm afraid. I'd stay here a bit longer if I were you."

"Sometimes," said Toby, "I feel as if I hardly know her any more. Oh, I am terribly proud of her, she is brilliant. But she's like a different person. Perhaps I am a bit jealous. She's doing so well, and all I seem to do is lay about, chatting to some of the friends we made on the trip over. Anything on the horizon for me, Mike?"

"Not at the moment. But I've got my spies out on your behalf, don't worry." Mike turned to go. Then, "Toby."

"Yes? What, old bean?"

"Toby, just don't let it get around that you've got a white chap sweeping the yard and two black kids in the pool, eh? Be careful. You and Hyacinth, well, you might be more vulnerable than you think. This isn't London."

Toby stared after his retreating form. Of course it's not London, he thought. Swimming pool, enormous garden (even though they call it a yard here), what is the dear chap on about? A yell from the pool distracted him.

"I'm coming," he shouted in reply, as he dived into the pool to chase his giggling companions.

1933

"Please let me in, Hyacinth. Tell me what's wrong. Come along, old girl. Whatever it is, we can sort it out between us." Toby pulled ineffectively at the bedroom door. Then he squared his shoulders in the way he had when playing the centurion, about to die for the sake of his love. "Hyacinth, I am not going away until you open this door."

Silence. Then to his relief he heard the key turning in the lock. Throwing open the door, he stepped back in alarm. "My sweet, what has happened to you?"

Hyacinth's face was a swollen mass of bruises, from the purple beneath her eyes to her puffed-up lips. She shrank away from him and backed on to the bed. Toby approached her cautiously. He sat beside her on the bed and took her hand.

"Sweetheart, have you been in an accident?" Hyacinth mutely shook her head.

"What then? Why can't you tell me?"

He could feel that Hyacinth's whole body was trembling. He knew that she had gone to see Jacob Goldberg that afternoon, and he had been reading by the pool when the car returned. He'd thought that she had just gone to get changed, until Maureen had come to get him.

"Mr Toby, I think you should go to Miss Hyacinth. She's not feeling too well."

One look at Maureen's expression had caused him to drop his book and dash into the bungalow, only to find the door locked and to hear his wife's sobs. Hyacinth looked up at him now, her pitiable face wet with tears.

"He raped me, Toby. Mr Goldberg raped me."

Toby went rigid with shock.

Hyacinth continued between sobs, "He told me he wanted to see me about that part I wanted so much, you know, in the Somerset Maugham movie. I thought he was going to tell me that they had decided to cast me, but when I got there his butler showed me into this room and then, before I realised what was happening he..." Hyacinth put her hands over her face and shuddered uncontrollably before continuing, "he locked the door behind me."

Gently her husband put his arms round her. She rested her head against his shoulder, her body racked with deep, gulping breaths, childlike and beyond tears.

"Darling," he murmured, "You're safe now. But you must tell me everything"

"I feel so dirty. I thought you'd never want to touch me again. Oh Toby, I can't bear it. How can you ever love me now?"

"Sweetheart. There is nothing and no-one in the whole world that could make me stop loving you. But I must know everything. Take a deep breath and tell me exactly what happened."

Hyacinth began to talk in a whisper, her head still resting on Toby, her eyes cast down so he could not see her face.

"The room was dark. First of all I couldn't see anything, but when I heard the door lock I began to panic. Not badly, I still thought someone was playing a silly joke. Then I saw that it was a bedroom, and Mr Goldberg was sitting on the bed in his dressing gown.

"He said..." Hyacinth stopped and took a deep gulp of air. "He said 'Dear Hyacinth, I think it's time that you and your nigger-loving husband found out who calls the shots out here.' And then he just lunged at me. I started to scream, but he laughed and said, 'Yell away, who do you think is going to come to your rescue? Carry on, Miss Brit, I like it that way.' And then..."

Hyacinth paused for a long time "he…he…"

Toby held her, hardly breathing himself, waiting.

"And then … he ripped at my dress and … he…and I hit him. Toby, I hit him in the face as hard as I could. But he kept hitting me back …and laughing… while he was…doing it. When he'd…" Another long pause. " When he'd … finished … he threw my clothes onto the bed. He just said, 'Get dressed. The car is at the front.' And he walked out of the room.

"My dress was all torn and I was trying to hold it together. I ran through the house and the car was there. It was the butler driving it. And…and just as we were pulling off Mr Goldberg came and stuck his head through the window and said that if we called the police they would laugh at us, and he would make sure that the whole of America knew that I was a whore, and you were a pimp."

Toby wiped his wife's battered face carefully with his handkerchief. "Darling, I'm going to call Maureen to come and be with you for a minute. I have something to do."

Toby went into the sitting room and examined the list of addresses and telephone numbers that he had pasted into their address book when the couple had disembarked from the Britannica on their arrival in America. To his relief he found himself speaking to the person he needed straight away. Coming from the bedroom, Maureen heard him say, "And he is in California now? Thank you. I am so grateful to you, dear chap."

Maureen knocked at the open door. "Mr Toby. I know what happened today. No," she held up her hand. "Please hear me out. Louis, Mr Goldberg's butler, he is my friend. My special friend. Louis works for Mr Goldberg because it is the only job he can get. My husband, he ran off a long time ago because there was no work here anymore. Not enough to keep two kids. As you know, I worked for the lady who lived here and then when you came, you took me on along with the house, and I think it's been good for us all, hasn't it? You trust me?"

Toby nodded. Maureen continued. "Louis rang me. Before Miss Hyacinth left the house. It's happened before, you see. Please don't go over there, Mr Toby. Mr Goldberg is like a god in this town. He'll have you killed, and he'll never, ever have to answer for it."

"Maureen, I know. I understand more than you think. Go and pack our bags, please. Just some clothes and stuff. Hyacinth and I are leaving tonight. And so are you. Don't ask any questions, please. *You* must trust *me*. We've made a ridiculous amount of money out here, and I want you and the children to have some of it and go. Before the morning. Tell Louis you'll contact him later. Now, I have some more phone calls to make." And he turned back to the telephone.

A week later at Southampton docks, Hyacinth was in Elizabeth's arms. "Oh my goodness, darling," said her mother, "Whatever happened to your face?"

"Oh," said Toby, before Hyacinth had a chance to reply, "she should have seen you a week ago, shouldn't she, darling? Fading fast now. Fell off a horse."

"I didn't even know you could ride," said Elizabeth.

"Oh, Mummy," replied her daughter, "There's a lot you don't know about me."

"I suppose there must be, but anyway, I do know

that I am so glad that you are home safely," said her mother. "Your father wanted to come to meet you, but he's been covering the Goldberg murder for his paper all week. My goodness, that was near where you were, wasn't it? They think someone called 'Baby Face Jo' had something to do with it. How horrid. That poor man. Shot in his own swimming pool."

Alone in their bedroom in her parents' home, Hyacinth asked the question that had been burning in her brain for several days, "Toby, you made it happen, didn't you? I don't know how, but I know you did."

Toby came and put his arm round his wife. "Don't ask too many questions, my love. We made some useful contacts on the voyage over, and I stayed in touch. Like in war, sometimes vermin have to be exterminated."

Hyacinth looked up at him. "Do we have the right to make that judgement, Toby? I mean, I know that what he did to me was unforgivable. I would have killed him myself if I'd had the courage and the means when it was happening, but I couldn't have done it later. I keep wondering what he was like with his family? He might have been the kindest man on earth to them. And to all intents and purposes, we murdered him, didn't we? "

Toby looked at her for what felt like a long time. "You didn't, Hyacinth. I may have done. And if I had, I certainly wouldn't be making any apologies for it. End of story."

Hyacinth felt a chill run through her. I don't know this man, she thought. He's my husband and yet he's a stranger. "What are we going to do now, Toby?" We've got the rest of our lives ahead of us, and we're quite rich. Where do we go from here?"

"Could you bear to go back when the fuss has died down? We're not linked to anything, no-one has any inkling what that devil did to you. Louis has disappeared – well, he's in New York with Maureen actually, but only we know that. We wouldn't have a problem. It's just that I've been sent a script for a film that tries to show how difficult life is for a Negro in the USA, and it's all seen through the eyes of a visiting Englishman. Mike is behind it, of course. It's a wonderful script and a terrific part. And there's a great role for a woman, if you're up to it."

Hyacinth felt her stomach turn over at the thought of returning. For a dreadful moment she thought she might be sick. Then she remembered her mother in prison, being force fed. Hearing the stories of Kitty at the front line in the war. Both triumphing over adversity. Ultimately, turning it into something positive in their lives.

'I *will* not let that man turn me into a victim,' she thought. Looking at her husband, she felt she was seeing him for the first time. The moment of truth, she thought. Either I believe he's a monster, or that he's a good, brave man.

But what were her alternatives? Divorce was out of the question. Even if she had grounds, or felt she really wanted to leave him, which she didn't think she did, she knew that in England a divorced woman was a social outcast. And what he had done, however dreadful, he had done for her. Or that was how he would view it.

Suddenly she remembered overhearing Alice talking to Anthony about Mary. "A prisoner in her marriage to that wretched man." The words had stayed in Hyacinth's head, because although Elizabeth had often told her stories of her grandmother, her grandfather, Daniel, was rarely mentioned.

'A prisoner in her marriage.' The words hit her like a tidal wave. Then, 'What nonsense,' she thought, looking at her handsome, loving husband. Bracing herself, she smiled at him, "As long as I can be with you, my love."

1934

The applause was deafening. Hyacinth looked up at Toby on the stage and grinned. She rose to her feet with the rest of the audience and clapped her hands high in the air. He winked slyly down at her and almost imperceptibly raised one shoulder. She nearly giggled. He knew she was more worried about her gown slipping down than the award she might or might not win. But he held his own statuette firmly in his hand and quelled the audience easily as he stood and looked out across the rows of seats.

He is so much *more*, Hyacinth thought. More than she had ever suspected. Perhaps she was, too. Without doubt, the horrific events of the previous year, which could so easily have destroyed them, had moulded and shaped them into two different people. But what kind of people? Had two wrongs made a right, she sometimes pondered? Would she ever really know Toby? Perhaps actors, like chameleons, played the part that was expected of them at any given time. Either way, she had made her choice and any reservations she might have would stay her secret for the rest of her life.

Into the silence Toby began to speak, "Thank you. I thank the many of you who have made my wife and I so welcome here. It is with enormous humility that I accept this award tonight on behalf of the thousands of Negroes who live in America."

Toby stepped off the stage. Was it her imagination or was the applause slightly more muted now, wondered Hyacinth. Ten minutes later the auditorium went wild again as Hyacinth mounted the podium. It was the first time a husband and wife had received these awards. Hyacinth smiled down at her husband.

"My appreciation is immense, but I have to tell you that this will be my last movie as an actress." A gasp went round the audience. "As you know, some time ago, I was under contract to Mr Jacob Goldberg. I am sure Mr Goldberg would be delighted to know that, due to the success of *America the Free*, Toby and I have bought the company he left behind. Goldberg Studios will be renamed Hytobe Enterprises, and will be dedicated to making movies that pursue the freedom of persecuted minorities everywhere and anywhere. Many of you are aware that in England I cut my teeth with the British Broadcasting Corporation. I am returning to my first love and I shall be Hytobe's first producer. I ask you to wish us well in our enterprise."

Holding the statuette high, she left the stage. The audience was on its feet again. As she regained her seat next to Toby, he rose and kissed her.

"Funny old world, dear heart," he whispered in her ear.

Part Five: Charlotte

1937

The worst part of being a twin was that everyone treated you as if you were only half of a person. Charlotte loved Julian passionately but right now she didn't care if they never did anything together again. How could he be so selfish? Her mother had a letter from Aunt Hyacinth this morning asking if the twins would like to go out and stay with her for the summer. Charlotte was beside herself with excitement. Not only were Aunt Hyacinth and Uncle Toby the only people that they knew who were rich and famous, but they lived in Hollywood.

Charlotte wanted to be a movie star. As her friend Clara said, 'Well, who doesn't?' But Charlotte had known since she was tiny that it was her destiny and with her fifteenth birthday approaching she was certain that this was fate finally taking a hand. So she could hardly believe that now everything seemed to be going horribly wrong. Julian, ensconced in his wretched public school, had already made arrangements to spend the summer touring with the school's rotten cricket team and declared he couldn't let them down.

"Why can't I go without him?" she demanded of her parents.

Kitty and Percy looked at her in amazement.

"Go without your brother?" said Percy. "But Charlotte, darling, you are twins. You've always done everything together. You'd miss him. Besides, he'd look after you. It's a long journey."

"I don't need looking after; I am quite capable of looking after myself. Anyway, we go to different schools," argued Charlotte. "I don't see him for weeks on end. Why can't he stay here and play his silly old cricket and I'll go and stay with Aunt Hyacinth?"

Kitty looked thoughtful. "I do see what you mean, Charlotte. I would worry about you doing that journey on your own though, darling. Unfortunately, neither your father nor I can drop everything and go with you at the moment. What with work and the rest of the family, we are both up to our eyes in stuff. But it does seem unfair to stop you going because Julian doesn't want to."

"Oh Mummy, please let me go. I'll be absolutely fine on my own."

Kitty looked at her daughter. Charlotte certainly appeared capable of crossing the Atlantic without qualms. Fifteen going on twenty was how John had laughingly described her the other day. Not only was she intelligent, she was tall for her age and strikingly pretty. But, although her frequently expressed stellar ambitions might have suggested otherwise, she had a fund of common-sense which helped to keep her feet on the ground.

"We'll think about it," Kitty said.

Charlotte gave a whoop of delight.

"But," cautioned her mother, "No decisions yet, so don't bank on it. Get ready for school now."

"Will you talk about it today?"

Percy looked up. "Perhaps. Now do as your mother says."

Charlotte dropped a kiss on her father's head as he

bent back over the morning paper, and danced out of the room.

As soon as the door closed behind her he turned to Kitty. "I'm not very happy about it, you know."

Kitty nodded agreement. "I share your misgivings, darling. But she is right. If Julian wanted to go as well, we would almost certainly have said 'yes' straight away. And yet, to be truthful, she is much more grown up than him."

"I think that may be what bothers me," replied Percy, only half joking.

"We'll talk tonight," said Kitty. "I must go." Giving her husband a quick hug she gathered up her Gladstone bag and departed.

Kitty had been working for several years for the local branch of the Women's Health Committee and her sphere of duties covered everything from birth control to basic hygiene. Her main occupation was finding other women who could sympathetically give practical advice where it was needed. So much illness and disease in her sex was still caused by extreme poverty, but Kitty understood the need to tread softly. Pride was not confined to the well-heeled, and nothing was achieved by those who ignored this basic dictum.

As she jumped into her car, Kitty tried to forget her domestic problems and concentrate on the work in hand. Thank God she still had the faithful Suzanne. Kitty adored all her children but she occasionally admitted to herself a suspicion that full-time motherhood might have been a nightmare for her. Ironic when she spent so much time trying to help others to cope with that very scenario.

She was often reminded of how much she missed

her own parents. Harold had never been the same after Harry's death. Kitty knew how much Violet had worried about him, even while she was trying to deal with her own grief. Harold's long and debilitating illness had seemed to Kitty almost an extension of his sorrow. As if his whole body had slowly broken down. Violet had outlived him by a mere two years.

Kitty had not realised that along with her sense of loss would come the strange and intimidating realisation that she was the oldest one in her family now. No-one left whose greater experience and wisdom she could call on, who would listen to her troubles and soothe her. That was her job now.

She was aware that the role came more easily to her in a professional capacity than with her own family. Probably, she thought, because at work she could be more objective, less emotionally involved. Ah well, to each his own, she mused philosophically, as she drew up outside the clinic. 'You can only do your best,' was Percy's constantly repeated dictum when she agonised over a perceived shortcoming and, cliché or not, she knew he was right.

Charlotte, meanwhile, was in the school cloakroom discussing the injustice of life in general with her friend Clara. "If Julian wanted to go, and I didn't, they'd say 'yes' straight away. And Mother is supposed to believe in equality between the sexes! Huh!"

Clara nodded in sympathy. "You're right about that. Leonard is going to stay with my Aunt Moira in New York next month and no-one questioned him going on his own. Well, actually, my gran will be going too, but she'll only be interested in flirting with all the rich old widowers on board. Well, that's what Daddy said anyway."

"Your relations are such fun," sighed Charlotte, enviously. "Mine are really boring. Don't you mind not going?"

"Aunt Moira only asked him, not me. I'm supposed to be going out there next year, I think. Obviously she can only stand us one at a time!"

Charlotte grinned at her friend. "She's the one with that rather dishy American husband, isn't she?"

"She sure is," replied Clara, and hearing the lesson bell, the two friends exited the cloakroom, giggling and exchanging what they believed to be 'Americanisms' in more and more bizarre accents.

"Oh, Charlotte, I really am sorry. It's only because we care about you. We've talked and talked about it, but your father and I agree that we still think it's too far for you to go alone." Kitty tried to put her arms round her daughter, but Charlotte shrugged her away angrily.

"I think you are mean. Mean, mean, mean and I hate you – I hate you both!" With this, Charlotte ran from the room and could be heard sobbing as she mounted the stairs.

"I'm not sure we handled that too well," remarked Percy.

Kitty sighed deeply. "I'll have to let Hyacinth and Toby know. It is a pity. But I think it is the right decision, don't you?"

"We can't let Charlotte having a tantrum change our minds. We are doing what we think is best. So that's that."

However, as it turned out, it was not. Kitty came in

the next evening to discover Percy in earnest conversation with Mrs Battersley, Clara's grandmother. The two women had the slightest of acquaintances, having only ever met at various school functions, so Kitty was surprised at the visit.

Percy rose to explain. "Kitty, darling, Mrs Battersley has called to make us a splendid offer. It seems that she and Clara's brother are off to America for the summer to stay with relations. Charlotte has been emoting all over their house, and Mrs Battersley has offered to keep an eye on her on the way over, if we were to change our minds."

"Well," said Kitty slowly, "That is really good of you. In fact..." she glanced at Percy, who nodded in anticipation, "I can see absolutely no reason for refusing your generosity. I think we shall accept immediately, and thank you from the bottom of our hearts for saving us from what promised to be a very difficult summer."

"I'm delighted to be of use," smiled their benefactor. "I'll leave you to pass on the good news to Charlotte, and we'll get together to finalise arrangements in a couple of weeks."

So it was that a few weeks later an ecstatic Charlotte found herself bound for America. Coincidentally, she was aboard the same ship that Hyacinth and Toby had crossed the Atlantic in seven years before, and was as mesmerised by the sheer luxury of it as they had been. Clara's brother Leonard seemed less so. Charlotte was beginning to realise that Clara's family was much better off than her own. Leonard seemed very sophisticated, though whether as a result of his being two years older than her, or his slightly more affluent life style, she was not sure. Mrs Battersley settled immediately into several friendships and Charlotte was amused to realise that they were, as predicted by her granddaughter, all with elderly, unattached gentlemen.

On their second day out, Leonard saw Charlotte watching his grandmother as she promenaded along the lower deck. Mrs Battersley carried a large parasol and was escorted by four eager admirers, all vying for her attention. Smiling, Leonard joined Charlotte at the rail. The two adolescents barely knew each other as Leonard, like Charlotte's brothers, was away at school for most of the time. Although they had exchanged pleasantries, each was still shy in the other's company.

"Grandmother was the most eminent debutante of her day," he remarked, "Mother says she was a famous beauty. I think if people have been very good looking, they have a kind of gloss, a sort of special confidence, that they never quite lose, even when they are old, you know."

Charlotte turned to him, surprised at his perception. "Yes. Yes, I think you're right." She was picturing her Aunt Rosalie, her father's sister, who was a lot older than her father, but still had striking features and carried herself in such a way that people always turned to look back at her.

Leonard, hands in pockets and looking down at the deck, broke the short silence. "Do you fancy a game of quoits?"

"That would be lovely," replied Charlotte, feeling her cheeks go red. Her tendency to blush for almost no reason was the bane of her life, but Leonard, looking up and meeting her eyes, thought she looked charming.

"Spiffing," he said, "See you on court in twenty minutes?"

At dinner that evening they sat together like old friends, laughing and joking. Leonard's grandmother, glancing at them over the bowed head of one of her conquests, noticed their new found ease with pleasure. One thing less to worry about, she thought. Not that worry was a major factor in her life.

A week later they docked at New York. The evening before, laying entwined with Leonard in one of the lifeboats, Charlotte was shocked at the strength of her passion. At least, she thought that must be what it was. Her body felt quiveringly alive to every touch of Leonard's fingertips and she daringly allowed him to touch her breasts and was startled at the feelings this engendered in her.

Pulling herself upright, she put her hands on his chest and pushed him semi-playfully away. "No, we mustn't. Please, Leonard."

Leonard moved away from her. "You're so beautiful, Charlotte. But you mustn't tease a fellow, you know. Girls get a bad name for doing that."

"I don't know what you mean," replied Charlotte, with absolute truth, "How am I teasing you? It was you who kissed me first and it was you who suggested we come up here where it was private."

"Yes, but you wanted to, didn't you?"

"Of course I did. You know that I love being with you. This whole week has been magical, like a dream, hasn't it?"

He nodded, gently stroking the hair back off her face. Charlotte sighed with pleasure, and continued, "It's wonderful up here, just you and me sort of hanging between the sea and the stars as if there is no-one else in the world."

She lay back and let Leonard kiss her again, giggling as he nuzzled her neck. Then, he took her hands and moved them down his body, whispering, "See what you do to a fellow."

Charlotte's head felt as if it was going to spin off into the sea. Leonard was now touching her in a way that made her protests very half-hearted but she knew this was not what ought to be happening between them. She was further bemused by not having any idea what might happen next.

"Oh, Charlotte," whispered Leonard, moving his hands up her skirt, "I know what to do. The chaps at school talk about it all the time. I'll be very careful. It will be alright, I promise you."

Almost before she had a chance to think, Leonard was on top of her, and Charlotte felt her knickers being yanked down. Her efforts to protest were smothered by his mouth on hers and a vague feeling that it would be impolite to resist. The next moment she felt a pain that seared through her body like a knife. She screamed, but his face on hers muffled the sound. Seconds later he pulled himself off her.

Charlotte lay dazed, a strange wet feeling between her legs.

"I say, are you alright? I hope I didn't hurt you?" Leonard was pulling his trousers on and looking at her with concern. "Charlotte, you were wonderful. Was it good for you, too?"

He helped her gently up into sitting position, and she nodded mutely. Carefully he helped her tidy her clothes, and handed her down from the lifeboat. Outside her cabin, he kissed her with a kind of reverence.

"Are you sure you're OK? It *was* great, wasn't it? Better even than they say. Sleep tight. See you in the morning."

Charlotte locked the cabin door. Going through to the lavatory she discovered the blood between her legs. She mopped it carefully with a towel. Then she went and laid on her bunk. She stared at the light in the ceiling until her silent tears obscured it completely.

It was nearly five months later, back at school in England, that a biology lesson made sense of something that had been puzzling her. Charlotte realised that she was pregnant.

1938

Charlotte was horribly aware that it was Julian she was going to miss most of all. Not that she saw much of him nowadays, but they had never had secrets from each other before. As far as she knew.

Leonard's avowal that 'the chaps at school talk about it all the time' was burnt into her brain and she doubted that she would have been able to confide in her twin, anyway. He might indeed have such conversations. He would hardly tell her if he did. Even her younger brothers might, for all she knew. Her perceptions had been irrevocably changed. She felt isolated.

She wondered if it would have been different if she had a sister. Until recently Clara had filled that place in her life, but she was about the last person Charlotte could turn to now. She was full of her family's plans to move to a rather grand house in Yorkshire, recently inherited by her father. Charlotte hadn't seen Leonard since the day they disembarked at Liverpool. Their return journey had been an uncomfortable affair, with Charlotte staying in her cabin for much of the time to avoid him. At meal times they hardly spoke, not daring to meet each other's eyes.

Just before Christmas, when the revelation of her condition caused Charlotte to cast frantically about for a confidante, she thought about going to see Aunt Elizabeth, but rejected the idea when she realised that Elizabeth would have felt bound to tell her parents. Charlotte was desperate to keep the truth from them. The thought of their disappointment in her was more than she could bear. In the past she had giggled with her school friends at stories of girls who were 'no better than they ought to be' without any real idea of what was meant by the phrase. In any case, she had always assumed it was something that applied specifically to domestic servants, never to her own class.

She occasionally thought that she might have been able to tell her Aunt Rosalie, but as luck would have it Rosalie was taking some students on a prolonged tour of Florence, and would be away for the whole winter. As Charlotte's panic and despair grew, so did her determination not to burden her family with her shame. Christmas had been a nightmare. At least she had stopped being sick every morning, having to lock herself into the bathroom and praying that no-one would hear her. The jokes about her increasing tubbiness were hard to shrug off.

"Leave her alone, it's only puppy fat," Kitty had remonstrated with her brothers, and Charlotte had been hard pressed not to cry out, 'No, it's not, Mummy –

can't you see what's happening to me?'

But now her plans were made. Julian was going back to school today. She had hugged him so hard that she knew he was quite embarrassed. "I say, Sis, no need to go overboard. See you in the Easter vac."

But he wouldn't, of course. Charlotte knew that he might never see her again. She had agonised over the note to leave for her parents. Eventually she had decided that anything she might say other than a brief farewell would inevitably bring them face-to-face with the truth and defeat the purpose of her disappearance. That this disappearance might cause them much greater pain and hurt than knowing the real reason for her flight never crossed her mind. She was quite sure that her intended action was not only the best, but the only course of action open to her, so her final effort read:

'Darling Mummy and Daddy,
Please don't try to find me. I love you and the boys more than I can say.
Forgive me.
Your loving daughter,
Charlotte.'

Two weeks after her sixteenth birthday, and now more than six months pregnant, Charlotte left her parent's house stealthily in the small hours of the morning. With her she took with her life's savings of nearly £26 and a small case containing some of the clothes that still fitted her. She walked to the station and asked for a ticket to wherever the first train of the day was going. The man in the ticket box barely looked up as he asked, 'Single or return?'

"Single, please," replied Charlotte, trying not to shiver, though whether with the cold or with the effort required not to turn and run back home she was unsure.

Some time later she was in Hastings, a town on the South Coast. Walking south from the station as the dawn started to appear she saw the sea in the distance, and what she recognised as a pier. Arriving under this just as it was light she sat down on the pebbles and gazed out at the sea. Charlotte's intention had been to look for lodgings until her baby was born. She could not think beyond that. For the first time it occurred to her that she could put an end to her troubles by simply walking out into the water.

It was a revelation to her. It seemed so obvious she could not think why it had not occurred to her before. She rose slowly to her feet, and taking off her coat, left it with her case on the beach. Falteringly at first, but with increasing purpose, she began the walk to the water's edge, where she shed her shoes.

It was so cold. Beyond her imaginings. The first roll of the water over her stockinged feet made her gasp for breath. However, the very chill made her more determined. The churning pebbles in the shallows hurt her feet. But surely this final penance shouldn't be too easy, she thought, as she pushed her way into the sea. It was quite calm, and although she could see some white-tipped waves further out, they were dispersed long before they reached her. Clenching her body and mind against the numbing cold she pushed out toward them.

She was up to her waist when she felt it. The kick in her stomach was so hard that she nearly lost her balance. For several weeks she had been feeling a sensation like the fluttering of wings in her tummy, but she had thought it was indigestion. In that moment she realised that her baby was moving. That it was protesting. That it must have hands and feet to protest so physically. For the first time it acquired a reality. A baby. Her baby. She said it aloud, standing with the water swirling round her. "My baby." She repeated it. Her hands went to her protruding stomach protectively. It kicked her hard again. For the first time in months, Charlotte laughed out loud. How could her unborn child be so insistent? How could she possibly deny it?

She turned, and now walking with the tide, regained the beach quite easily. She collapsed onto the pebbles, frozen and shivering. She had not been aware that she had moved so far to the east. The pier seemed quite a long way off, and she realised that her shoes were probably underwater by now. Suddenly she was overcome by tiredness.

"Sorry, baby," she murmured, laying just beyond the water's edge and drawing her legs up under her. "Must just rest for a minute…" Fatigue descended on her like a cloak, combining with the cold to drift her into a protective unconsciousness.

It was the sound of singing that caused her to open her eyes. She found herself in a very small room, with one small window through which rays of thin sunlight were shining. She was not cold any longer. In fact, she was very warm indeed. The singing was glorious. She wondered if she had died, after all. If so, it really wasn't so bad, she thought, and snuggling down into the warmth she slept again.

The voice was kind, but insistent. "Come along, child, sit up please. Time for some nourishment."

Charlotte was gently but firmly grasped by the shoulders and shaken awake. Bending over her was a figure in flowing robes and a strange headdress.

Charlotte pulled herself up in bed and gazed at the apparition. "Are you an angel?" she asked sleepily.

The apparition chuckled in a very human fashion, "No, child, I'm Sister Mary Angelica of the Order of St Agnes and I am trying to get this soup down you. Now, will you please concentrate on drinking it?" She placed a large ladle-like spoon in Charlotte's hand and held a bowl of delicious smelling soup under her chin. "You've been quite poorly and you've not eaten for several days. You and that bairn you're carrying are in desperate need of some sustenance, so come along."

Charlotte did as she was bid, feeling herself grow more wide awake with every mouthful. Soon the whole bowl was gone.

"There, now," said Sister Mary, "That'll bring the roses back to your cheeks. What's your name, child?" Without waiting for an answer she carried on, "When the fishermen turned up here at the convent with you, all soaking wet and half drowned, we thought we were going to lose you and the bairn. You've had a fever for over a week now, but your temperature went down last night."

Charlotte's hands went to her stomach. "My baby! Is my baby going to be alright?"

"As far as we can tell," replied her benefactor. "It's a lively little thing. Now, we are not going to ask a lot of questions, my dear, we've a fair idea what took you to that beach."

Charlotte felt her cheeks flame, but Sister Mary put up her hand in a conciliatory fashion. "This is not a place for judgements, so just tell me if there is anyone I can contact. Anyone who should know where you are?"

Charlotte shook her head vigorously. The nun looked hard at her, then sighed. "But you do have a name?"

"Chloe," replied Charlotte.

"Right," replied Sister Mary, "Well then, Chloe, snuggle down now and get some more sleep. If you are up to it you can join us in the refectory for lunch later. Sister Bernice has looked out some clothes that should do for you. Just come down the stairs and follow the clatter of the dishes."

Charlotte lay down. So she wasn't dead. She did feel very tired, though. How strange to find herself in a convent. Now she was on her own she thought of all the questions she wanted to ask. She wished she hadn't had to lie about her name. As sleep overcame her once more, she wondered drowsily if fibbing to a nun meant that you went to hell.

The clothes were strange but comfortable. As Charlotte pulled on the long brown loosely elasticized skirt, and smoothed the smock-like top over her increasing bulk, it occurred to her that these clothes had been worn by others in her condition.

"Well, baby," she whispered, "it looks as if we might have come to the right place."

As directed, she was led to the refectory by the noise of clashing saucepans and cutlery and the hum of muted voices. Sister Mary rose to greet her. There were six nuns sitting round the rectangular table, and another two moving around serving them. A girl, dressed in similar garb to Charlotte, and obviously very pregnant, was also seated at the table. Sister Mary found

Charlotte a seat and another smiling nun appeared from the kitchen with a dish of some kind of stew, which was placed in front of her almost immediately.

"Eat up, Chloe," said a nun who didn't look much older than Charlotte. "You're eating for two now!"

Charlotte was trying hard to acclimatise herself both to her new name and the way everyone seemed to discuss her pregnancy openly.

The nun continued, "And, to be honest, Sister Mary Joseph is by far our best cook, so make the most of it. It's my turn to do the cooking next week, and that really is a penance for everyone."

Sister Mary smiled at the young nun. "Stop frightening the poor child, Sister Therese. We survive your cooking quite nicely, and pray daily for your improvement." A ripple of amusement ran round the table.

"We are not a silent order, as you can hear," continued Sister Mary, "but we do have times when speech is forbidden, so as not to distract us from our duty of prayer. But you will come to know these times if you are to stay with us for a while. Do you think you would like to do that, Chloe? Perhaps, at least, until your baby is born? That is what Greta is planning to do." And she nodded at the other girl, who smiled reassuringly at Charlotte. "No, Chloe dear, don't answer me now. You don't have to make up your mind yet. Wait until you are stronger, and have talked to Greta, or to Sister Therese, or indeed to any of us. We want you to understand that you are welcome here. God has sent you to us, and it is our privilege to offer you hospitality in his name. When you feel a little better, you might like to join us in the chapel occasionally, but only if you wish to do so."

After lunch, Greta and Charlotte helped to clear the dishes into the kitchen and wash up. When they had finished Charlotte was amazed at how tired she was. Greta looked at her with some concern. She was a tiny blonde girl with a broad cockney accent.

"You need to lie down. They said you were ever so poorly."

"Come and talk to me," invited Charlotte. The two girls made their way to Charlotte's room, where she gratefully sank on to the bed.

"So where's your mum and dad?" asked Greta. "Bet you ain't got no husband, like me. My dad threw me out. I thought my fella would stand by me but I didn't see him for dust after I told him 'bout the baby. Mum found me this place and said to come home when the baby's adopted. Sister Bernice says I can leave it here and they'll find a decent mum and dad for it. They're ever so good. There was a girl had a little boy soon after I got here and they helped her with the adoption and everything. She was really sad at parting with him, but what else can you do, really?"

Charlotte was stunned. Her baby had only just become real to her. The thought of giving it away was shocking.

"When are you due?" asked Greta.

Charlotte realised that she had never done the necessary arithmetic, and quickly did so now. "I think it must be in about three months," she said.

"Mine's due any minute. I'm a bit scared. Are you?"

"Not yet, but I think I will be when it gets nearer."

Greta leant toward her and lowered her voice.

"Look, I know this sounds a bit stupid. But do you know where it comes out? I mean, my mum always said she found me under a gooseberry bush and I know that's nonsense, but at school we reckoned it was through your belly button. There was this girl whose mum had seven and she said, well, she said they come out sort of, well, you know, down below. But I can't see how, and I don't like to ask the nuns."

For the first time in her life Charlotte was grateful for the pamphlets that Kitty had often left carelessly around the house, which she and Julian used to glance at and comment, "Ugh! Disgusting!" before turning them face down. She started to enlighten her new friend but before long they were both giggling and going, "Ugh, no".

Passing on her way to her own quarters, Sister Mary smiled to herself. "Bless them both," she thought. "Aren't they just a couple of children themselves?"

Two months later Charlotte was sitting in the garden of the convent, enjoying the early spring sunshine. High over her head, balanced precariously on a rather ancient ladder, Sister Bernice was painting a window-sill with dark brown paint. Her habit was hitched up into a large pair of workman's trousers which appeared to be about the same vintage as the ladder. These were secured around her waist with string. She had wound a tea-towel round her head to protect her headdress from paint spatters.

The rustle of heavy robes announced the approach of the more conventionally attired Sister Therese. Charlotte looked up and patted the bench beside her.

"I know you've been delegated to talk to me," she

said with a grin, "but I am not going to change my mind."

Sister Therese regarded her solemnly. "Chloe, how can you earn enough money to keep yourself and the child? The Sisters all understand how you feel, but might it not be better for the child if we were to find it a nice home with parents who can give it more than you can? And for you to start again, with a clean slate, so to speak?"

Charlotte looked at her affectionately. "I have come to love you all, and I admire what you do enormously. And I know that what you want me to do seems the best way to you all. But I don't think that I can do it, Sister Therese."

"Well, we are all in Our Lord's hands," said Sister Therese, rising to her feet. "And I am sure He will guide you when the time comes, Chloe."

Watching Sister Therese as she entered the little chapel for evensong, Charlotte felt a dull ache in her stomach. "Cramp," she thought and rose, preparing to walk it off. A minute later she was doubled up in pain. Sister Mary, also on her way to the chapel, glanced across as Charlotte fell gasping to her knees, clutching her belly. She ran across to her, shouting for Sister Bernice, who slid down her ladder in a most un-nun-like fashion.

Esther was born thirty six hours later, five weeks premature and weighing three and a half pounds. Charlotte lay in her bed, exhausted and frightened. "Please God, let my baby live and I'll do whatever you want me to," she promised.

1940

Charlotte often felt guilty for feeling so at peace when nearly the whole world was at war. Not that the war impinged much on the life of the convent. The evacuees billeted on them were the only infringement on their daily routine, and all the nuns were captivated by their young charges. It fell to Charlotte to supervise the children's morning ablutions and then to round them up into a crocodile for the march to the village school. Their twice daily journey had become a quite a feature of village life. Every morning the five children appeared scrubbed and shining with Charlotte at their head, wheeling Esther in her pram. The contrast with the five grubby urchins who fell out of school at a quarter-past-three was marked.

"How do they do it?" Charlotte asked Mrs Morris, the butcher's wife, as she struggled to relocate shirts back into trousers, straighten ties and pull up socks before the children arrived back at the convent.

"It's a talent, Chloe dear, and one that boys have from birth. You're lucky that they are not all boys." Mrs Morris had two boys herself and desperately hoped for a girl. "And how are you, my cherub?"

This was directed at six-year-old May, the only girl and the youngest of Charlotte's charges, who wriggled behind Charlotte, thumb in mouth, and peered round at her questioner from this safe haven.

"She is a real little beauty," smiled Mrs Morris. "And how is her little sister?" She peered into the pram.

"She's putting on weight wonderfully," replied Charlotte, looking with pride at the chubby, chortling infant and, as always, letting the misapprehension stand.

"She's lucky to have someone like you to look after her," said Mrs Morris.

"I enjoy it," answered Charlotte truthfully.

By the time Esther had become strong enough to be wheeled out, the evacuees had arrived and it had been assumed in the village that she was one of them. Charlotte sometimes thought that the war had been a godsend. It had enabled her to become an integral part of life in the convent, and she was happily aware that by caring for the children she was not a burden on the community, but considered to be a bonus.

She supposed that sooner or later she would have to find a way to keep herself and her daughter, but that was in the future. Charlotte had learnt to live in the present. The only cloud on her horizon was that she had no way of finding out how her family were. She knew that Percy had been a soldier in the Great War, and that her mother had done something as well, but she was very hazy as to what. If she thought about it at all, she imagined Kitty moving around the hospital wards smoothing the brows of the sick and looking glamorous in her sparklingly clean uniform as depicted in the movies that Charlotte had once so loved.

However, Charlotte did know that her Uncle Harry had died when he was not much older than Julian. She and Julian were just eighteen now. The nuns listened to the news on the Home Service every night and Charlotte realised that her twin had almost certainly joined up by now. Sometimes she lay awake at night thanking God for saving Esther, but asking Him to protect Julian. Given his adolescent passion for aircraft and ambitions to fly, she guessed that he would not wait for conscription, but was probably already in the R.A.F. She wished she knew how they all were, but thought that they must have forgotten her existence by now and believed that was for the best. There would come a time when she would begin to understand how dreadfully wrong she was.

In fact, Kitty was throwing herself into war work in order to take her mind off her daughter's death. After they had found Charlotte's note, she had been distraught. They had immediately alerted the police, and the nation-wide search that had commenced had eventually led their investigations to the railway station. The ticket clerk vaguely remembered a young girl taking a single fare to Hastings.

Alerted, a young Officer had remembered a suitcase that had been brought in, washed up with the tide some months before and assumed to have been lost overboard from some pleasure steamer. The contents were almost beyond recognition. But not quite. Kitty identified them as her daughter's. The search was called off. Sympathy was offered to the grieving family.

A million times a day, as Kitty doggedly pursued her work with the WRVS, the question hammered in her brain. "Why? How did I fail you? Why?" And her mind flew back to a hospital ward in 1915. A quarter of a century later, she found herself confessing to Percy about the young soldier who had begged to die. "This is my punishment," she wept. Percy's absolute refusal to believe in a God who would exact such terrible retribution for an act of charity, comforted but did not altogether erase her conviction of guilt.

Julian, just entering the air force, often mused upon

Charlotte's last intense farewell and wondered if he should have been more aware. But of what?

"I just think that I would know if she was really dead," he confided to his father.

Percy, struggling with his own desolation, pretended to agree.

And all the while, less than 50 miles away, Esther thrived.

1943

The telegraph boy did not often call at the convent but the appearance of his bicycle was enough to strike a chill into the hearts of the nuns at work in the vegetable garden. The last time he came it was to tell poor Sister Bernice that her brother had been killed. The nuns knew that he rarely, if ever, brought good news. Today was no exception.

At supper, they waited expectantly for Sister Mary, unusually late. She entered the refectory with a grave look on her face, and led the little community in saying grace. Charlotte sat with the nuns, her charges bedded down safely. The two oldest boys had gone back home the previous year, their mother having confided in Charlotte that she just missed them too much, and the other two brothers were being collected next month.

Charlotte was glad that Esther, a rather quiet and withdrawn child, would still have May for company. She worried about her daughter and thought she often seemed much older than her five years. Her great pleasure was music, and Charlotte, not especially musical herself, had been startled to find Esther entertaining the effervescent May by tinkling out recognisable tunes on the piano in the chapel.

Sister Mathilde said that she had natural ability and had undertaken to give both children formal lessons. May was a much more extrovert child and a natural performer. She had sung one of the solos at Midnight Mass on Christmas Eve at the convent. A lot of the villagers came to this and the purity of her voice had brought tears to many eyes. But Sister Mathilde, once a professional singer, insisted that it was Esther who was already showing signs of being the really extraordinary musician.

Sister Mary waited until the nuns had eaten. A pall of anxiety had begun to spread over the little community. This must be very serious. At last, she rose to her feet and began to address them. "Sisters, I have bad news indeed. Little May, the last one of our charges, is an orphan. I received news today that both her parents have been killed. Her grandmother was badly injured in the same raid and is not expected to live. We know of no other relations. We have to tell May, and we have to discuss what will become of her. I have telegraphed the Bishop, but, for the moment at least, she and her future seem to be our sole responsibility. Chloe, my dear, you are like another mother to her and have been for over three years. I know it is a lot to ask, but will you break the news to her?"

Charlotte nodded slowly. "Of course I will. She hasn't seen her parents for months, so I have no idea how she will react. She's only nine years old. I would rather tell her in the morning so that I can be with her all day if that is alright?"

"Certainly. We will begin a special novena for her, for her family, and for you, tonight. The Lord be with you, Chloe." And Sister Mary placed her hand on Charlotte's head and made the sign of the cross over her.

The following morning, leaving Esther practising scales with Sister Mathilde, Charlotte asked May to come for a walk with her. May was unusually silent until they were past the convent gardens and crossing the field beyond. Suddenly, the child stopped and turned to look at Charlotte.

"I saw the telegraph boy on his bike yesterday. When no-one said anything I sort of knew it was about me. My mum and dad got killed, didn't they?"

Charlotte's sharp intake of breath told the child everything she needed to know. Ignoring Charlotte's outstretched hand May ran into the field, her silent anguish worse than sobbing. Charlotte stumbled after her, half-blinded by her own unshed tears. Eventually she caught up. May was standing stock-still, looking at the horizon. Charlotte stood motionless beside her.

"The thing is, Chloe, like, the worse thing is that I can't really remember my other life. Last time I saw them, Mum said that I'd be home soon and everything would be back to normal. And I couldn't think what that meant. 'Cos this is where I live. With you and Esther and the Sisters. And I thought that I wanted to stay here. So I killed them, didn't I? 'Cos I didn't love them enough. It's like I wiped them out of my life and they were part of the bit I'd forgotten so when I couldn't remember properly they got killed. It's all my fault, Chloe. It's my fault that they're dead."

Charlotte gathered the girl's stiff form in her arms and, with the tears streaming down her own face, felt May relax into shuddering sobs. 'Please God help me to say the right thing,' she thought.

"Darling May," she said, "if only we had that much power, we could stop this wretched war right now. You know that really, don't you?" She knelt down beside the child. May lifted her tear stained face and, after a long pause, slowly nodded.

"Your mum told me herself how much it meant to them that you were safe and happy here. They loved you so much, May. They died knowing that you were here, out of harm's way. I am sure that was an enormous comfort to them."

"Can Mum see me?" demanded the child.

"I don't know," answered Charlotte with painful honesty. "But I do know that the nuns believe that she can, and that she will watch over you forever."

May's lower lip trembled again. "So she'll know how much I loved her? And my dad? 'Cos I did, Chloe. I really did."

"I think they will know that," said Charlotte, holding the child tightly in her arms. She absorbed May's spasmodic, gasping crying into her own body, her face buried in May's sweet-smelling dark hair.

They stayed like this for a long time, and then, hand in hand, they began the walk home.

Three weeks later Sister Mary Angelica called Charlotte into her study.

"Chloe, I have had a visit from Mr and Mrs Morris. They would like to adopt May."

Charlotte's face lit up. "Oh, Sister, that would be wonderful!"

Sister Mary held up a warning hand. "Wait, Chloe. That's not all. They also want to adopt Esther, who they have always believed to be May's sister."

Charlotte's hand flew to her mouth. "No, Sister. No! That is not possible."

The Sister looked at her compassionately. "Chloe, my dear. I want you to think carefully. This is a wonderful opportunity for Esther, as well as for May. The Morris's are quite well off, and would provide both girls with a good life and education. They are already talking about buying them a piano, and are proud of Esther's musical ability. Their two boys are both off soon, one to the army and the other to do an apprenticeship, but they have been party to their parent's wishes and thoroughly approve. Our girls would have a ready-made family to love and care for them. And they would be together. They think of themselves as sisters, they have grown up together and could hardly be closer."

"But they are not sisters. Esther is my daughter!"

"Yes, and we would have to tell the Morris's the truth. Not that you are their mother, that would not be necessary. Just that she came to us as a foundling."

Charlotte sat down abruptly. "A foundling? But she's not a foundling." Her voice quivered, and she was unable to check the tears that began to trickle down her cheeks.

"No, not strictly. But, Chloe, she is illegitimate, and the world is not kind to bastards. This must be your decision. I can only ask you to pray for guidance and the strength to do what is best for her. Think hard, my dear. Your daughter is showing signs of being exceptionally talented. How will you be able to nurture and foster that talent? The Bishop has already indicated that once the war is over, you cannot continue to stay here unless you become a member of our community. I admit I have sometimes thought, as I think you have yourself, that you might have a vocation to the religious life, but what then of Esther? That this might indeed be Our Lord taking a hand is something that I think you should consider. Mr and Mrs Morris are good people, my child."

Charlotte rose, her mind numb. "How long have I got?"

"I promised them an answer within the week."

Charlotte bowed her head, and left the room.

1945

Sister Mary Angelica gave a large sigh and looked over her tea cup at the Bishop. The two were old friends, having known each other since they were children in neighbouring streets in Liverpool.

"I believe that I made a terrible mistake, David. It seemed such a perfect answer. Mrs Morris wanted the girls so badly and she and her family love and care for them as if they were their own, as we knew they would. I was delighted when Chloe agreed to part with Esther. All the evacuees called her 'Auntie' and Esther had grown up doing the same, so the child didn't altogether realise that Chloe was her real mother, she was too young to question anything. We told Mr and Mrs Morris as much of the truth as they needed to know and I thought we had done the best for everybody."

"But obviously you no longer think that, Angie. So what has gone wrong?"

"As far as the children are concerned not very much, I think. Esther has always been a quiet child, and she still is, but May is such a strong and happy personality. Esther is never allowed too long in her own company and I think that benefits them both. Chalk and cheese in many ways, but bonded like real sisters, and they adore their adopted family. May, of course, was aware of the circumstances of the adoption. Esther had never known any family except for Chloe and us, so once she was assured that she would still see her beloved 'Auntie Chloe' regularly, and visit the convent on Sundays, she was happy. She was barely five years old at the time, remember."

The nun paused before putting down her tea cup and facing the Bishop squarely. "The problem is Chloe. When she told us that she thought she had a vocation, and wished to test it, we were delighted. Throughout the time she has been with us, and don't forget that is seven years now, we have watched her grow in so many ways. We don't know how old she is because we have never asked, any more than we know if Chloe is her real name. But she was little more than a child herself, when the fishermen brought her here, unconscious, half drowned and big with child."

The Sister sighed again. "We watched her turn into a young woman who cared devotedly not only for her own baby but then for the children sent to us. You see, if the war hadn't intervened, we would all, Chloe included, have been forced to confront the dilemma of her future, and that of little Esther. But as it was, it just seemed right that she should stay here and become the children's mainstay. She fitted so well. So when she became a postulant, it just felt like a natural progression. A gift from Our Lord to us all."

Again she fell silent. After a few moments the Bishop enquired gently, "And?"

Sister Mary had tears in her eyes. "It's tearing Chloe to pieces. She's as thin as a rake, we hear her sobbing herself to sleep, and she has been ill with glandular fever twice this winter. Idiotically, I thought that seeing Esther occasionally, being near her and watching her thrive, would be good for her. But it's not. It's like salt in an open wound. That wound is the knowledge that she cannot be the mother of her own child. At Christmas, both the girls sang solos at the Mass and afterwards they ran up to their 'Auntie Chloe' and hugged her. I watched her face as they ran back to their 'mother' and I hope never to see such a tortured soul again."

The Bishop reached over and patted her hand. "There, there, Angie, you did what you thought was right. So now we must try to think of a way to improve the situation. Obviously Chloe must move. Is her vocation genuine, do you think?"

Sister Mary shook her head. "I don't know, David. I'm sure she thought it was. But I would like you to talk to her yourself."

"Of course. Today?"

"I think so. This can't go on. I'll fetch her, she's in the chapel. It's where she spends most of her free time. I would find that admirable in other circumstances but in Chloe I think it is a mark of her wretchedness."

Left alone, the Bishop prayed for guidance. Although there were those in his diocese who thought him too interested in the whisky bottle, he was a good and caring man when faced with human misery. If he had a fault, it was that it was a long time since he had stirred himself to actively look for suffering in order that he might try to alleviate it.

Charlotte knocked quietly and entered, her cream postulants gown making a faint swishing noise as it just cleared the wooden floor. "Sister Mary said you wished to speak to me, Father?"

"Come and sit down, child. I think it is more that I wish you to speak to me. How would you feel about being moved to our convent in Norfolk? I think it is time you tested your vocation within a different community."

Charlotte went paper white; she half rose, then sank back in her chair. "No, no, I..." The rest of her words were lost as she fell forward into a deep faint.

1947

Michael had expected it to be bad. After all, everyone said that the majority of the country's mental hospitals were Dickensian. Heaven only knows, he had seen enough while he was training to make him realise that it was all pretty dire. He had still been convinced that he could make a difference. All the training, here and abroad, all the modern advances in psychiatry had engendered a crusading spirit in him. But right now he despised himself. Not for his original ideals but for the speed with which his zeal had been eroded.

He sat in his office trying to make sense of some of the case-notes in front of him. Sometimes he thought he would do better just to tear them all up and start again but he lacked the courage. When he had accepted the post of registrar his optimism was still intact. He had initiated several projects in his first year that had out worked well. The vegetable garden had proved to be therapeutic for several of the patients, but the space was limited and the staff required to oversee it unwilling to do so if the weather was less than perfect. He rose and crossed to the window, which overlooked the small area.

Old Tom was there, fastening his runner bean strings, and Polly was taking a break from hoeing her patch to shout encouragement at him. At least, he assumed that was what she was doing. Due to the cleft palate and hare lip with which she had been born, no-one had ever been able to understand her speech. Michael had painstakingly listened to her, however, and had begun to suspect that these disabilities, combined with a strong Birmingham accent, were all that was wrong with Polly and that her intelligence, though dulled by a lifetime in institutions, was miraculously still intact.

As he looked down on the two inmates, he felt a familiar sense of frustration and despair. How many of the four hundred and twenty patients in his charge should not be there, he wondered? And what in God's name was *he* doing here? His thoughts were interrupted by a knock on the door.

"Come in."

Michael turned with a smile to greet his caller. Nurse Williams was one of his few like-minded colleagues. Initially, he had been unaware how important such support would be. He was totally unprepared for the resentment that any change in procedure would inspire. The routine throwing of all the inmates' clothes into a basket in the middle of the ward each night, so that everyone was forced to scramble to find something that might cover them in the morning, had seemed to him obscene. His insistence that each person was fitted for two sets of clothes, and these marked with their name, had triggered considerable resistance.

Mercifully, there was a core of nurses who hated the various practices that contributed to the dehumanising of their charges and were prepared to absorb the extra work involved to combat these. Making the inmates wear ill-fitting and often soiled garments, was seen by them as a humiliating abuse, and their enthusiastic response to his proposal had enabled him to bring about this change. Their reward had been the restoration of comfort and self-respect to many of the patients. Unfortunately, the majority of the staff still endeavoured to block every innovation on the grounds that it would add to their work load. So he daily thanked whatever deity was in charge of such matters for Nurse Williams and the other more progressive members of staff.

"Guess what?" the nurse asked excitedly. This was obviously a rhetorical question as she gave him no chance to answer before continuing with her news. "I've found us a hairdresser!"

Iris Williams was a small Welsh woman whose husband had returned from a Japanese POW camp broken in body and spirit and who had hanged himself three months after returning home. His widow, already a trained nurse, had decided that the only way for her to make sense of his death was to throw herself into working with the mentally afflicted. She refused to use the term 'insane'.

It was her idea that it would be good for the morale of the patients to have proper haircuts. At the moment the staff cut everyone's hair, as no inmate was allowed a sharp instrument. This meant that every woman either had their hair dragged back into a bun, or sported the same ragged 'pudding basin' cut, while all the men had their hair cut close to the head. Combined with their institutional clothes, this meant that virtually all individuality was erased.

"I've found a woman and her daughter who are prepared to come up here for a whole day every week and help us. I've told them we have hardly any money, but they are still happy to come."

Michael felt his spirits lift. "Nurse, you are an amazing woman! Who shall we start with?"

"Ward Nine, I think. Some interesting cases there. What do we know about the convent girl? Chloe. She never speaks, and she's so pale. But she's a pretty woman for all that. Was she a nun?"

Michael rifled through the notes on his desk. "I was looking at her case notes earlier. We know very little about her, actually. She collapsed after a long period of various physical illnesses. She lived and worked at the convent throughout the war, let me see, yes, here we are, she helped to look after the evacuees. No note on where she came from, or even how old she is. The convent was very vague about that. The order she was with has undergone some changes; it seems the church felt a certain laxness had crept in and there is now a more disciplined regime in charge. Chloe had been in the infirmary there for some months, but, after the death of the Bishop from a heart attack, the new prelate felt she should be moved into a secular environment. Due to her inability, or unwillingness, to speak, she was sent to …oh, my goodness!"

He passed the paper to Nurse Williams, who looked

at it glumly, "One of our most famous – or should I say infamous? – institutions. Poor girl. A thousand patients. What chance for her there? I've been watching her, Michael. She is deeply depressed, but I think she knows everything that is going on. She just doesn't care anymore. But I feel quite sure that she did once."

Michael was still looking at the notes. "They gave her insulin coma therapy and electroplexy. They were going to do a pre-frontal leucotomy, but mercifully, they decided to send her here instead."

He looked up with a grin. Nurse Williams noticed that it made him look ten years younger.

"Right then, Iris, everything else has failed, so let's see what a hair-cut will do."

In fact, although Janet and her daughter Veronica sometimes wondered what they had let themselves in for, it soon became apparent that their hairdressing skills did indeed make a difference. Many of the male patients asked to have their beards trimmed and tidied as well, showing a care for their appearance that had been totally absent until now. They all sported some kind of beard as the task of shaving them was beyond the limited resources of the staff, and there was no question of the men having razors.

But it was the effect of their skills on the morale of the female patients that was the real reward of the two volunteers. Within a few weeks there were so many requests for their services that Michael took the unprecedented step of asking the Board to consider employing the women for two more days a week, as their voluntary and therefore unpaid time was hopelessly insufficient.

"What kind of chance do you think we have of them saying 'yes'?" asked Iris of her boss.

"Not a lot, I'm afraid," answered Michael. "In spite of all the modern research, this kind of therapy is still not high on their agenda. Three representatives are going to talk to us about it when they do the usual inspection next week. We just might be in luck, though. There is a new, Government appointed, health inspector attached to the Board and I believe she's quite forward thinking."

"Mrs Bradshaw? Yes, I've heard good things about her on the grapevine. And at least she is a qualified nurse. I'm told she's been a bit of a rebel in her time."

"I think we should definitely let her meet Chloe. She's our star, really. We still don't know a lot about her but she's actually helping on the ward now. Yesterday she washed and dressed dear old Edith on her own. The ward sister says Edith is so much calmer when Chloe is with her. Who would have thought..?"

He tailed off but both of them were remembering the same scene. Chloe, sitting impassively as always, while Veronica cut and shaped her hair. Hair that was silver gray in spite of her obvious youth. Veronica chattering on, as she always did, regardless of whether she received any reaction or not.

"There now, Chloe, I'm going to do away with this straggly old bun, goodness, it makes you look about a hundred, and I doubt you're as old as me. Here, we're going to wash it, and cut it really short so that it curls round your face, there's people would give a fortune to have such curly hair and in such an unusual colour." And so on, with no response from the figure in the chair as she worked her magic with the scissors. Then, finished, she stood back and looked at the girl for a long moment before fetching the only mirror on the ward and holding it in front of her.

There was a silence. Iris had left her work to watch as had another nurse. The transformation of Chloe from a possibly pretty young woman to a stunning beauty was extraordinary. Chloe raised her eyes to the mirror. She lifted her hand and touched her hair, watching her reflection. An expression of disbelief flitted across her face. Her voice, husky from disuse, asked, "Is that really me?"

Veronica laughed though, like the nurses, she had tears in her eyes, "Yes, my lovely, that is really you."

It had been an astonishing turning point. Within days Chloe was communicating with the other patients and starting to listen to the wireless when it was on in the ward. Her accent had startled them, somehow they had not expected it to be that of an educated woman, which it undoubtedly was. But although Michael had conducted two lengthy interviews with her, he was no nearer to finding out her background, or indeed anything else about her. He and Iris were both increasingly sure that Chloe was suffering from some form of amnesia and that she genuinely had no inkling of what had happened to her or who she really was.

"At least she seems to care now, though," said Iris. "I think she really would like to know about herself. Veronica gave her back some sense of identity, I suppose. Good old-fashioned self-respect."

"I wonder if she was caught in a bombing raid. People saw their whole families wiped out before their eyes. Something like that might conceivably have caused such a trauma," said Michael. "I wish we had more information from that convent. It might help us to find a way into her memory."

"Well, anyway, let's hope the account of her progress will encourage this Mrs Bradshaw to allocate us some money for prettying up our patients," replied Iris.

The day of the inspection found the staff in the usual state of tension that always preceded official visits. So often the necessary disruption to the daily routine affected the patients and even the calmer ones could become difficult and temperamental. Michael met the members of the Board at the main door and served them coffee in his office. There he explained the success of various innovations, such as the vegetable plots, and the calming effect that some music had been found to have on the patients. He talked at length of the struggle involved in making progress within a budget that meant the hospital often had to rely on voluntary donations of equipment such as wirelesses. He told how the gift of a gramophone and some dance records had resulted in the patients having their own 'tea dance' once a month, and how he would have liked to have held this weekly but for staffing difficulties.

He felt almost immediately that Mrs Bradshaw was on his side. When one of the older members of the Board asked rather churlishly what was being achieved by such 'new fangled methods' it was she who met Michaels eyes whilst answering the question coolly but firmly, "Possibly rehabilitation eventually, I should think, but certainly a more humane way of living," and, turning to face Michael's interlocutor, she had added, "Both of which are things we must all surely strive for, don't you agree, Mr Brown?"

The question had cornered Mr Brown into a somewhat surly assent, Michael noted with amusement. He and Iris had planned the ward inspection in such a way that Ward Nine and Chloe would be the last stop. "A sort of grand finale, with luck," he confided in Iris, who understood perfectly.

It was therefore well into the afternoon before the group arrived at Ward Nine. Chloe was sitting reading one of the books that Iris had begun to bring in for her from her own collection. Michael noticed that it was a book of poetry. He wondered if he dared ask her to read from it, but then decided that even to impress the Board, he would not ask his charges to perform for them like precocious children.

Mrs Bradshaw took in the calm atmosphere of the ward, and the gramophone playing music softly in the background. "Is it always so quiet?" she smiled.

"No," Michael replied. "But we have a patient on the ward who helps to choose the music and sometimes reads to some of the others."

"Ah, yes. The famous Chloe. Nurse Williams was telling me about her improvement. Amazing. Might I meet her?"

Michael gestured to the figure under the window, the late sunlight falling on her silver hair.

"Oh, I thought she was young," whispered Mrs Bradshaw.

Michael put a finger to his lips. "She is. Go and speak to her, she knows we have visitors today."

Kitty Bradshaw crossed and gently touched the girl on the shoulder. Chloe looked up and met her eyes questioningly. Michael heard the sharp intake of breath from his visitor. Behind them, he sensed Mrs Bradshaw control herself as she asked about the book Chloe was reading and listened to her answers. Then bending, she kissed the girl's brow before walking rapidly from the ward, leaving Michael and the other Board members staring after her.

At a glance from Michael, Iris hurried after the Health Visitor. She found her in the corridor, shaking uncontrollably with silent tears running down her face. "Mrs Bradshaw," began Iris, but Kitty Bradshaw stopped her with a gesture.

Taking a deep breath and fighting for control she gasped, "That is my daughter, Charlotte. My daughter Charlotte. They told us she was dead. And now I have found her, and she doesn't even know who I am."

But in that instant, the ward door was thrown open, and followed closely by Michael, Chloe appeared. She stood, framed in the doorway, her beautiful face suddenly animated but with such anguish that Nurse Williams caught her breath.

"Mummy. Oh Mummy. I am so sorry. How can you ever forgive me?"

And Kitty took Charlotte in her arms and held her as if she would never let go again.

1948

Percy regarded his wife gravely. "Kitty, darling, I am as excited as you are that Charlotte is coming to stay. But the hospital, and Michael in particular, have made it very clear that we should try not to make too much of it. 'Try to be casual and matter of fact' is what Michael said. We still have no idea what happened to her, and it has taken her a long time to be ready for this. If it goes well, she might soon be ready to take her place in the world again, but we both know that she could run like a frightened rabbit back to the hospital if we don't get it right."

"But we've got no rules, no guidelines," replied Kitty with barely concealed distress. "I feel so frustrated, so… so..," she searched for words, "so *rudderless*. Should I try to make her room look as it was ten years ago? Or will that send her back into some dark, secret world that we are not party to? Why won't she talk, Percy? Why won't she tell us why she ran away?"

"When we understand that, darling, perhaps we will have some inkling of how to help her. Possibly she will feel able talk to Julian, if she can't to us."

He paused, trying to find a way to comfort his wife. They had never been able to really share the feelings of guilt that had gnawed away at both of them for so many years. Charlotte had, after all, run away from *them*, and both were privately convinced that they must have done something dreadfully wrong, albeit unwittingly.

Percy had been conscious of the questioning glances thrown his way when his daughter's supposed suicide had been headlined in the newspapers. It had made him cautious about discussing how much he loved his daughter. Sometimes the thought even crossed his mind that perhaps he had been prey to thoughts that were less than fatherly toward her but even as his cheeks burned with shame he knew that this was nonsense. His love for his daughter had been straightforward and paternal, but the need to castigate himself for failing her, as he must have done, was always with him.

Kitty had always blamed herself, remaining convinced that she was being punished for her long ago act of compassion. This guilt was compounded by remembering how much of her life had been devoted to her profession. She told herself that she had driven her daughter away. Night after night she lay awake thinking that if she had devoted herself to her family, been a storybook, exemplary mother, she would have known that there was something badly wrong in Charlotte's life. Only Elizabeth's sound commonsense had acted as a salve for these two troubled souls.

"You are good people and loving, caring parents," she stated repeatedly and firmly to each of them. "Whatever drove Charlotte to such extremities, it was not either of you."

And it was Elizabeth, now in her seventieth year and an iconic figure at the hospital, where she still lectured students twice weekly, who was adding her voice to Michael's. "Don't rush her. Give her time. Whatever she does, it must be her own initiative. Be patient."

Percy put his arms round his wife. "Julian is coming tomorrow. He's decided to come on his own. He phoned earlier and said he felt that seeing him would be a bit of a shock for her, and he thought it would be easier this way. Penny agrees. She can meet Charlotte when that particular hurdle is crossed. And now come along, sweetheart. She'll be here in a minute. Her room is clean and tidy and so are you. Give me a kiss and I'll go and put the kettle on in readiness for our daughter."

Before Kitty had a chance to comply, a ring at the doorbell caused them both to jump. "Come on," said

Kitty. "Let's go together."

Charlotte, dressed in the green wool suit that Kitty had bought her, stood on the doorstep holding a small case. She was looking up at the windows of the house with a worried expression. "I thought it was bigger," she said, before putting the suitcase down on the step. Then, "Oh Mummy, oh Daddy," and she was hugging them both at once with a ferocity that took them by surprise and filled them with joy.

Kitty led her daughter up the hallway with Percy coming behind with her case. In the sitting room, Charlotte looked round her with an air of wonder. "You've got new curtains, these are lovely. The old ones were brown, weren't they?"

Kitty nodded. "They fell to pieces in the war. The windows kept being blown in. After the war, when we got everything back together again, we found we wanted something more cheerful. So there are lots of gold and reds everywhere. I do hope you like it."

Charlotte smiled slowly. "It feels a bit like that film. You know, *The Wizard of Oz*. Nurse Williams took me to see it. Everything changes from black and white to Technicolor. That's what this feels like. It makes me realise how little colour there has been in my life for so long. I suppose the convent was a bit monochrome really."

An unfathomable expression crossed her face, and Percy, quick to sense her sudden tension, took her hand, "Come and help me make the tea. There have been some changes in the kitchen, too, and for the better, I hope. You can see how modern we've become."

Left setting out the teacups, Kitty thought that already Charlotte had told them more about the last, lost, ten years than ever before. Although Michael had told them of Charlotte's years in the convent, he knew almost no details, and this was the first time she had mentioned it to anybody as far as they knew. "Please God, let it be a good sign," she prayed.

The following day Julian arrived before Charlotte was up. "How goes it?" he asked his father before he was through the door.

"O.K., I think," replied Percy when they were safely in the sitting-room with the door shut. "She wanted to know when you were coming. We haven't told her anything. She hasn't asked so we haven't said."

"Well, let's hope I'm not too much of a shock, then," said Julian.

Percy patted his son reassuringly. "Don't be daft, old man. But I expect your Aunt Elizabeth's advice holds good for us all. Give her time to adjust. It's been ten years and the whole world has changed, not just you. Sometimes it's almost as if the war has passed your sister by, she never mentions it."

"Well, that can't be all bad," grinned Julian.

Kitty's head came round the door. "Charlotte's up, lads. Are you sure that you want to meet her alone, Julian?"

Julian nodded. "I think so. Shall I go up?"

He paused for breath at the top of the stairs and realised that he was, if not nervous, at least apprehensive. Crossing to Charlotte's room he knocked on the door and, instinctively using the terminology and silly voice that had bound their mutual childhood, he said, "Charlie twin, let Juli-in, this is where our day begin!"

A gurgle of surprise and delight came from the

other side of the door. In a trice Charlotte was in his arms and giggling like the sixteen-year-old she had been when he last saw her. Then, as she stepped away, still laughing, to hold him at arm's length the laughter died on her lips to be replaced by a look of dismay.

"Julian, your face! What happened?"

"You should have seen me before Archie MacIndoe got hold of me! No face at all to speak of, twin. But, although I must admit that you are now easily the most beautiful of the two of us, I can boast, as you see, of nose, eyes and mouth, and even a certain success with the ladies. So watch what you say!" With the last sentence he planted an affectionate kiss on her forehead.

She ran her fingers over his face, lightly tracing his scars. "When did it happen... how..? Of course, the war. Oh, Juli, I have been so incredibly selfish. I should have tried to find out, at very least, how you all were. I guessed you would be in the Forces. I thought of you often, but I just sort of assumed you would be OK."

"And so I am. As you can see. It *was* the war, of course. I was a fighter pilot. Bought it very near the start of the good old B of B. Mum, Dad and the baby brothers were wonderful. Couldn't move for days. Done up like a mummy, swathed from head to foot. Very boring. Then along came Archie and his merry men. The rest is history, Sis. Except that I got lucky and persuaded one of the nurses at East Grinstead to marry me. Penny. She's coming tomorrow if you'd like to meet her. With my daughter. She's three months old. I'm hoping you'll be around for the christening."

Charlotte held his gaze for what seemed to be a century. Then she sat heavily on the bed. "You might not want me."

Barely daring to breathe, Julian sat down beside her. "Try me, Charlie twin."

And at first hesitatingly, then with increasing fluency, Charlotte began to speak, "It's knowing where to begin really. But I suppose, in a way, it all started with Mrs Battersley." Charlotte registered Julian's look of utter bewilderment. "I'm sorry. I forgot that you were away at school. Oh, Julian, if only…"

Seeing that Charlotte was on the verge of tears, Julian took her hands in his, "Charlie-twin, you don't have to tell me anything. But you might feel better if you do. I won't ever tell anyone anything you tell me, unless you ask me to. But who, in God's name, is Mrs Battersley?"

"She was Clara's grandmother. Do you remember Clara? She was my best friend. Mrs Battersley offered to escort me on the voyage out to see Aunt Hyacinth. Mummy and Daddy weren't going to let me go."

Charlotte lapsed into silence once more as her ebullient fifteen-year-old self danced across her memory. The bitter-sweet reminiscence threatened the still delicate balance of her reason. His parents had warned Julian that Michael had instructed them not to force Charlotte into confronting her past. 'It must be in her own time and in her own way,' he had cautioned them.

Sensing that she was about to sink into a pit of depression that he might not be able to penetrate, Julian instinctively guided her away from the edge. "Charlie-twin, why not start at the end and go backwards? What is this terrible thing that you have done that makes you believe that I would not want you, of all people, at my

Francesca's christening?"

Charlotte looked up at him. "Francesca? Oh, Juli, that's lovely." She rose from the bed and crossed to look out of the window. He watched her silhouette straighten in a way that had once been familiar to him. He remembered her pulling back her shoulders and raising her head in just such a manner when they had confessed various childhood misdemeanours to their parents. He found that he was holding his breath.

In what was barely more than a whisper, he just managed to hear his sister say, "My daughter's name is Esther. It was her tenth birthday last week."

The next moment she was in his arms, her body racked by sobs, and Julian whispered into her hair, "Oh, my poor darling girl. Why, where…?"

It was as if the floodgates were opened. Charlotte had confessed the worst and now no secret, barring one, mattered anymore. She told him of her agony at seeing Esther every day, and hearing her call someone else 'mother'. She explained how she believed, then as now, that she had done the best thing for her daughter, and also for May, who had become her surrogate child. However, what she had not understood was that she would be incapable of coping with the anguish of Esther's proximity.

"The nuns thought it would work, too, and with my head I knew it was the perfect answer," she explained defensively.

"But not with your heart," he responded compassionately.

She nodded mutely, deeply moved by his instant understanding. He held her to him and, as the years between them fell away, she remembered how they had always possessed the power to soothe and comfort each other. Later, when she was calmer, he asked her why she had not told them. Why she had let them believe that she was dead? She looked at him in amazement.

"But, Juli, how could you all have survived my shame? We were always being told about girls who were 'no better than they should have been'. I couldn't possibly have put you all through that terrible disgrace. I thought it was so much better for everyone if I just disappeared. Later, I thought it would be better for everyone if I was dead, but then, when it came to it, I couldn't do it. When I heard, months later, that I had actually been presumed dead, it felt like a miracle. You had been spared the humiliation, the dishonour that I would have brought on the whole family."

Even as he stroked her hair soothingly, Julian thought that Charlotte must never know the years of bewilderment and hell her 'miracle' had put them all through. Out loud, he murmured, "Of course, you were only fifteen. And the chap, Esther's father, how old was he? Did he know? Tell me what you can bear to, Charlie-twin?"

"Oh Julian, I was so ignorant. I didn't even realise that was how babies were conceived. I'm not sure that he did, either. No, I never saw him again after we got back home. I think we were both thoroughly embarrassed and ashamed of ourselves. I didn't realise for ages that I was going to have a baby."

She turned to face him. "I keep wondering if it might have been easier when I couldn't remember. I was existing in a kind of twilight world. Then when Mummy came it all flooded back. How am I going to get through the rest of my life without my little girl?"

And she began to weep again.

It was another three hours before Julian finally came down to sit with Kitty and Percy. He had persuaded Charlotte to a mug of cocoa and some toast, and finally tucked her up in bed. She had asked him to tell their parents the whole story. They listened to him with increasing bewilderment. When he had finally finished, Percy stood up and began to pace the floor. Kitty's head was in her hands, her face covered.

"How did we fail her so completely? She really believed that we'd rather she was dead?" This from Percy.

Julian nodded.

Kitty looked up. "But, Percy, how *would* we have reacted? I know that we would have stood by her, but would we have understood immediately? Perhaps we would have done what the Watsons did."

"Who the devil are the Watsons?"

"They lived down the road. Their daughter Maria was sent away to the country in mysterious circumstances. She came back much thinner six months later, and cried all the time. I remember Charlotte saying that she didn't go back to school. The family moved in the end, but rumours abounded that her older sister's addition to the family was actually Maria's baby. There was an awful lot of unpleasant gossip and Mr Watson gave up a really important post in the Government when they moved away."

"But we wouldn't have been like that," exclaimed Percy.

"Like what?" replied Kitty. "They did their best. You know as well as I do that some families won't have anything to do with a daughter who gets pregnant, and we middle classes are as harsh and judgemental as anyone. With us it's not just money, one of the more valid excuses of the working classes, it's a consciousness of what the neighbours might say. And it's always the girl's fault, of course. Would we have been brave enough to let her have the baby and bring it up here, Percy, and not care what the world thought? It's all very well to say what we would have done, with hindsight, but it would have taken even more courage ten years ago, before the war. I think we would have done what everyone else does. We would have tried to persuade her to give the baby away, whilst convincing ourselves it was the best thing for her."

Percy sat down heavily. "As always, darling, you are probably right. But the fact remains that our granddaughter *has* been adopted, and is living, apparently happily, with someone else in spite of everything that has happened. So now our job is to try and help Charlotte to come to terms with this."

He turned to Julian. "What about the boy? The father? Do we know who it is?"

Julian shook his head. "No, Charlotte says that he never knew and she never saw him again once she was home. Probably some young sailor on board the ship, I should think."

"So," said Kitty. "Do we have any way of seeing our granddaughter?"

Again, Julian shook his head. "No. I don't think you should attempt to. I have no doubt that the adoption was valid and Charlotte is probably right in thinking that she was doing the best thing for her child. It was seeing Esther every day, and knowing that the child believed that someone else was her mother, that Charlotte couldn't cope with. If she wants to talk about Esther I'm sure we should encourage her, but I think anything more might put her back into what she described as 'the twilight world'. She's very fragile. We must talk to Michael, but I think he'll agree that our main job is to help Charlotte to find her place in the world again. Whatever and wherever that may be."

"Please God," said Kitty, "Let us be more successful at that. Don't let us fail her this time.

1952

Charlotte was laughing as she was tugged across the playground by several small children. "No, Avril," she remonstrated with a golden haired and very sticky-faced child, "I am not going to join in the skipping, though I will happily help you count."

Reluctantly Avril let go of Charlotte's hand and waited patiently for her turn with the rope. "Salt, mustard, vinegar, pepper," the chant began.

Charlotte, standing in the sun and counting the revolutions, was filled with a sense of well-being. She loved the little primary school where she taught, and she prized the mixed bag of children who attended. This was her second summer term and she felt a slight pang of regret that some of these pupils would move on to secondary schools in a few weeks, but this was tempered by the excitement of getting to know the new arrivals.

And excitement was what she felt. Every morning she arose with a feeling of gratitude to whatever deity there might be. She was constantly aware that she was that comparatively rare being, a round peg in a round hole. She loved teaching with a passion. She found something in even the most recalcitrant and deprived child to admire and cultivate, and consequently her reputation for connecting with her charges and being able to inspire them was growing apace amongst her colleagues.

She had been surprised and delighted to find that she possessed the multi-faceted talents that went into making a good primary school teacher. Her inclination toward music and the arts was balanced by a great curiosity regarding the workings of science which she was able to share with her charges, thereby making their voyages of discovery mutual. This morning she had been told by her head-master that the school had achieved the highest ever number of children gaining grammar school places, and he believed that was owed in no small measure to the enthusiasm and dedication of his staff. She did not think she had imagined the unsaid accolade that was directed her way.

Charlotte looked forward to telling Julian. She was to dine with him and Penny that evening, always a great pleasure and a chance to spoil her goddaughter, Francesca. The previous day she had bought her a miniature doll, dressed in a beautiful crocheted pink and blue dress and bonnet. It would look wonderful gracing Francesca's beloved doll's house and she intended to give it to her tonight.

Francesca was delighted with her present. "I shall call her Polly," the four-year-old announced, "because she is going to stand in the kitchen putting the kettle on. Come and help me, Auntie Charlotte."

"Go on, Charlotte," called Penny from her rather larger kitchen, "Supper is running a bit late tonight because Julian is bringing a friend home."

"I hope he's not trying to marry me off again," laughed Charlotte, with an oblique reference to a friend of Julian's who had developed a totally unrequited passion for her the previous year, to Julian's declared embarrassment.

"No, this is an old friend whose been working up North since the war. In the police force, I think Julian said. He hasn't seen him in ages. I've never met him. Go and keep Franny quiet for me while I finish making this sauce, there's a love."

Once Polly was established perpetually putting her kettle on, Charlotte took Francesca upstairs to bath her. Donning Penny's wraparound apron to save her clothes, she readied her goddaughter for bed. As she buttoned up Francesca's pyjamas she allowed herself her daily ration of what she had come to call 'Esther thoughts'. She wondered what her fourteen-year-old daughter was doing, with her 'sister' May. In her role of 'Aunt Chloe' she had re-established contact with Mr and Mrs Morris since her recovery, but an annual note on a Christmas card had been the extent of their intimacy. Charlotte, grateful just to know that the children were thriving, understood that this was probably best for them all, but she still cherished her secret 'Esther time'. Readied for bed, Francesca demanded a story before her mother came to kiss her goodnight. Précising Beatrice Potter unashamedly in view of the time, Charlotte went downstairs to fetch Penny.

"Julian is home, Charlie," smiled her sister-in-law. "They are in the sitting room. Be an angel and tell them that I'll be down in a moment, will you?"

Divesting herself of the pinafore and running her

hands through her hair, Charlotte entered the sitting room. Julian rose to kiss her. A tall and rather good-looking man rose to his feet behind him.

"Charlotte, darling, I'm sure you two must have met before. Let me introduce your old school friend Clara's brother, Leonard."

Charlotte felt the world grind to a halt. "How do you do," she stammered, holding out her hand.

1953

Charlotte regarded the handsome young man on his knees before her with a mixture of amusement and frustration. "Leonard, please get up, you are making us both ridiculous."

It was true that the other diners in the restaurant were beginning to look their way and that the background hum of voices was petering out. Thank God it wasn't full, thought Charlotte. Leonard glanced over his shoulder and then reluctantly resumed his seat. Mercifully, their fellow diners immediately lost interest.

"But I mean it, Charlotte. You know that I want to marry you more than anything on earth. I never forgot you. When I heard that you had..." he broke off.

Charlotte took pity on him. "When you heard that I had killed myself, is that what you mean, Leonard? Yes, now there's something we never have discussed. What did you think?"

"I never believed it. Clara said it must have been something you were doing for a bet or something like that and it had just gone wrong. She said you were always up to stuff at school and it made more sense than thinking you had done it on purpose. Of course, I never told her about us."

"But there wasn't really an 'us', was there, Leonard?"

"Well, I suppose it was really just a shipboard romance, but, you know, it meant so much to me, Charlotte. I always hoped that it did for you as well. In a funny sort of way, I realise now that I never met another girl who lived up to my memories of you."

Charlotte laughed out loud. "Oh, Leonard. Julian tells me you brought a different girl into the mess every week during the war. We only knew each other for two weeks."

"But those two weeks changed my life. I can see that it didn't have the same effect on you, though." This last was said ruefully but with some humour. Charlotte refrained from commenting.

During the last few months Charlotte sometimes felt that she had stepped through the looking glass. After the first shock of meeting Leonard she had grown fond of him, but she was determined never to share the little bit of Esther that still belonged to her, the tiny bit that no one could take away from her, with him. She realised that if their relationship persisted, she would have to tell him about their daughter. The idea was ludicrous to her. That some juvenile fumbling had produced Esther was extraordinary enough, but she had reached a plateau where she could rest contentedly, and she knew that fragile contentment could be destroyed by him. With hindsight, she wished she had not allowed their friendship to develop at all, but her curiosity had undermined her better judgement.

The problem now was that Leonard declared himself in love with her. The irony of the situation did not escape her. She wondered if, under different circumstances, she could have loved him, but was unable to contemplate this possibility. There was too much at stake for her now. Last summer Mr and Mrs Morris had invited her to attend a concert at Esther and May's school. She had talked over the invitation with Michael and they had agreed that she was strong enough to see her daughter again. She had taken Julian with her.

They had arrived with just enough time to greet Mr and Mrs Morris before the concert began. Charlotte had introduced her brother and Mrs Morris had told them both how excited the girls were at seeing 'Auntie Chloe' again.

"It's been a long time, my dear," she had commented.

Indeed. Charlotte nodded her agreement. Julian squeezed her arm and Charlotte smiled to him to show how well she was coping. As she was.

The girls were due to perform just before the interval, though Charlotte glimpsed them both in two of the choral numbers and was able to point them out to Julian. Esther reminded her of someone, but she was unable to identify who it was. May was the real revelation. The child had grown into a young woman and, although she was not as tall as her younger sibling, her dark good looks and innate vivacity made her stand out from the crowd. Charlotte felt immense pride in, and love for, them both.

When their turn came, Esther, dressed in a calf-length, demure powder-blue dress with a peplum round the hips, entered first. She curtsied to the audience who cheered loudly. It was obvious she was popular. Then she sat at the piano and began to play.

Charlotte and Julian listened enraptured as Esther launched into Greig's *Morning* from his *Peer Gynt Suite*. Charlotte was no musician but as she listened she found herself caught up into Grieg's haunting world. Esther finished to tumultuous applause and then played some of The *Hall of the Mountain Kings* from the same suite, to the great approval of her younger listeners who stamped their feet enthusiastically.

As she rose to acknowledge the acclaim, her headmistress came onto the stage and held up a hand for silence. "Esther's parents have given me permission to announce this evening that Esther will be leaving this term, as will her sister. Although only fifteen, Esther has been accepted by the Guildhall School of Music as one of their youngest ever students. We shall miss her, of course, but we hope she will not forget her friends here when she is rich and famous."

Checking the laughter and applause that followed this announcement, the headmistress continued, "And now, most of you know already that May Morris has been offered a contract with the J Arthur Rank Film School, and her parents have today signed on her behalf. So it is with enormous delight and our very best wishes for their future that I introduce for the last time as pupils here, May and Esther Morris."

At this May entered, dressed in brilliant jade-green dress that showed her dark looks to perfection. Julian noticed with amusement that there was a definite quickening of interest amongst the men in the audience. Esther seated herself back at the piano and the two girls began a medley of folk songs. Charlotte reflected that May had a very good range and looked wonderful.

At the end of the medley, during rapturous applause, May left the side of the piano where she had been standing and stepped to the centre of the stage. She waited for the ovation to die down and then threw a mischievous glance at her accompanist. At a note from Esther, May's voice suddenly turned to liquid gold, and the schoolgirl became a wounded, knowing adult. '*Fish gotta swim, birds gotta fly,*' the words and melody washed around the room. The song reached out and grabbed the hearts and minds of the audience. At the end there was a stunned silence. Charlotte found herself on her feet and clapping until her hands hurt along with everyone else in the room.

Julian whispered, "That is definitely what they call star quality!" and she nodded, finding that she was choked with tears.

After the concert the two girls had come and hugged her enthusiastically. She had struggled for words to express her pride in them and they had all ended up laughing at their own mild embarrassment. For Charlotte it had been a wonderfully happy moment. She introduced Esther and May to Julian, conscious that his presence and support had contributed to her own ease with the situation.

Julian shook both girls by the hand, saying with a grin, "I know that Chloe and I don't look much like twins nowadays, but I used to be the pretty one, you know!"

May stood back and examined him. "You're still not so bad," she concluded cheerfully, "In fact, half the girls here have already been sorry to hear you are married."

Mrs Morris came and touched her arm, "May, you

are so cheeky. Behave yourself." But she was smiling broadly. Turning to Julian she asked, "Could you cope with these two young madams for a minute while Chloe and I have a quiet word?"

"With great pleasure," replied Julian. "Come along, girls, introduce me to your father and brothers." Holding a girl on each arm he escorted them with exaggerated gallantry across the hall. May's infectious laugh could be heard echoing round the hall.

Outside, Mrs Morris led Charlotte away from the school building to a bench under a tree. "I often wondered, Chloe, but tonight I watched you and I knew. She is so like you. You are Esther's real mother, aren't you?"

Charlotte could only stare and nod. No words came.

"Does your brother know?" asked Mrs Morris. Charlotte nodded again. "Don't tell her until she's grown up, Chloe. She doesn't need to know yet."

"Oh, but I wouldn't..." Charlotte began but the other woman interrupted.

"I know you don't intend to, or you would have done it by now, but don't let it slip out, or show when you see more of her. As you will when she moves to London. She's not as mature as she looks and she is very sensitive. When she is older it will be good for her to know, but it would be disruptive at the moment. The girls talk about being adopted, and they know we love them as if they were born to us. But she is not ready to cope with anything more yet."

"Will you mind?" asked Charlotte.

"No, I don't think so. I'll always be their mother in one way. Nothing can alter that. But you see, Chloe, I had a child before I was married. My parents made me give her away. There is a not a day of my life when I don't wonder where she is. That's our secret. My husband knows, but no one else, until now. But I wanted you to understand that I will not try to stand between you and Esther when the time is right. There is room for both of us in her life. And, my dear," she took Charlotte's hands in hers, "I owe you so much. I know what it must have cost you. I hope you approve of her."

"Oh, I do, I do," whispered Charlotte. "Thank you. Thank you so much. For everything."

All this happened just after Leonard had re-entered her life. If this was fiction, thought Charlotte, I'd fall into his arms and we'd live happily ever after. I expect Esther and May would come and live with us and the sun would shine every day. But this is real life and I have a career that I love and find fulfilling, as well as a cherished place in Esther's life. One day I will tell her that I am her mother, when the time is right for her to know. All that telling Leonard about her now would achieve are complications that none of us need.

A small voice somewhere at the back of her mind was asking if Esther might not have the right to know who her father was, when Charlotte finally told her the truth about herself, but she pushed it aside. It may never happen, she told herself firmly, and I am not going to risk everyone's happiness at this stage of all our lives. Charlotte looked across the restaurant table at Leonard, grateful that he showed no further inclination to sink to his knees.

"Leonard, I am very fond of you. But, though it may be hard for you to accept, I don't need you. In fact, I don't need marriage. No, please don't interrupt me.

Marriage seems to me to be based on mutual need. Financial, social, physical," (she realised that she had nearly said 'sexual', goodness, I am turning into one of these modern women, she thought) "all sorts of needs that I find I just don't have. I like my life as it is. Thank you, but no thank you. Now, I should like this rather sumptuous looking rum baba thing for pudding, please. Will you call the waiter, or shall I?"

Several weeks later Kitty asked Julian if he knew whether Leonard had proposed to Charlotte. "He was so obviously smitten, and yet he seems to have completely disappeared from the scene," she said.

Julian replied that he gathered that Charlotte had turned him down.

"Oh, what a pity. Do you know," said Charlotte's mother, "I sometimes think she may be waiting for that sailor chap to appear again. Wouldn't that be wonderful? Everything to turn out right after all these years?"

"Perhaps," replied Julian.

Part Six: Esther

1959

"Esther, you can't possibly mean it. I just don't believe that you've thought about this at all."

"Oh, but I have. In fact, I've thought about nothing else for days. I'm fed up with all the touring, May. I don't want to spend the rest of my life smiling inanely at newspaper men and signing autographs for people I don't know."

"But your music, Esther. What about your music?"

Esther smiled at her sister's consternation. "That's the point. It will be *my* music. Not something I have to do for everyone else. I'm not going to give up music, only public performing. Thomas says that no wife of his is going to have to earn her own living."

May sat down heavily in the chair by the window. She loved her top floor flat in London's unfashionable Islington, loved looking over the rooftops to the hustle and bustle of an increasingly cosmopolitan London. In fact, she loved everything about her life and frequently thanked her lucky stars that both she and her beloved sister had been able to pursue their ambitions.

May had opted out of the Rank charm school after two months, to the relief of all parties. "I just wasn't ladylike enough," she had told Esther. "It was the rule about wearing a hat and white gloves whenever we were in public that first made me think I might have made a terrible mistake. I thought they were joking. But they weren't. It was downhill all the way after that."

Due to the enormous interest in Mr Rank's 'starlets', her departure had made headlines in several newspapers, and as a result of the publicity May had landed a job in the most prestigious night club in the West End. Initially appearing in the small hours, after the male crooner and the illusionist, to say nothing of the line of long-legged chorus girls, she quickly cornered her own fan base.

Now it was she, billed as 'May Morris, London's very own torch singer', who topped the framed poster at the entrance to the club. And she was enjoying every minute of her success. She was earning very good money doing what she did best, as well as flirting outrageously with a succession of stage door Johnnies. Once in a while she reflected thankfully how differently things could have turned out for her, the orphaned cockney kid.

She had thought that Esther felt the same. Esther's career as a concert pianist had been spectacular. She had made a sensational solo debut at the Albert Hall when only seventeen and subsequently had been feted all over Europe. Now there was talk of an American tour. So the bombshell that she had just dropped had taken May completely by surprise.

She turned to Esther, "But if Thomas loves you, surely he wants you to continue with your career. Goodness only knows, if he feels so strongly about the money, give it away. Though I would hardly have thought that was practical. He can't earn anything like the money that you do."

Thomas, who May privately thought was the most dull of all the boring young men that Esther had been out with, worked in a bank as a rather lowly clerk. Esther looked at May with a mixture of affection and amusement.

"You don't understand. It's what I want, too. I want to be a full time wife. Thomas's wife. With our own home. I don't want to be forever traipsing around, leaving Thomas behind, worrying that I haven't practised enough, or that my dress will be all creased when I stand up. Always wondering whether the conductor and the orchestra will like me. It's awful when you feel they don't. I get even more tense than usual."

May burst out laughing. "Esther, everyone loves you. What *are* you talking about?"

Esther's face was set in the resolute expression that May knew only too well. "Anyway, I've told Patti. No more bookings, no more tours. I might do some recordings next year. Thomas says he won't mind that. So it's a bridesmaids dress for you, Sis. My last contract expires in November and we've set the date for two weeks later."

May sighed, but she recognised when she was beaten. "I think you are quite mad, but I suppose you know what you are doing. What did Patti say?"

"More or less the same as you, really, but then, she'll lose her ten per cent of me, won't she, so that was to be expected."

"Esther, you know she's much more than your agent. She's in awe of your talent. I think she'll be devastated, as a lot of people will be."

May was right. When the news that Esther was retiring at the age of twenty-one to get married became public knowledge, there was almost a sense of grief amongst her many admirers. But there were also a great many articles in the plethora of women's magazines of the day applauding her decision. One headline that read '*A woman's place*' held Esther up as a shining example of womanhood. A woman who was prepared to give up what was described as sparkling career, to assume the mantle of housewifery for the man she loved, was lauded for her courage and generosity.

Much was made of the many 'show biz' marriages that barely lasted beyond the plighting of troths. May was fascinated to read that this was almost always perceived as the fault of the still performing wife. As one pundit put it didactically, 'these men would never have strayed if their wives had stayed at home to make sure that all was right with their lives.'

To Esther's delight, she and Thomas had found a flat not far from May. May was conscious that Thomas had some reservations regarding their proximity. The two of them circled round each other warily, determined not to become enemies but equally both believing that they knew what was best for Esther. Certainly, they had little in common except Esther. Her life-long physical fragility made almost everyone she came into contact with feel protective toward her. Thomas was no exception. To May's horror, he had taken to calling Esther 'my little wifey to be' and Esther appeared to think this was endearing.

"I'd kill him," she muttered to Charlotte. Charlotte's place in the girls' lives had finally been revealed just before Esther's twenty first birthday, and with their adoptive mother's help had been accepted almost seamlessly.

"Actually," May had informed them at the family meeting where a nervous Charlotte had told Esther that she was her 'birth' mother, "we worked it out ages ago, didn't we, Essie?"

Mrs Morris smiled at her daughters and then at Charlotte. "We had a feeling you might have done, didn't we?" Charlotte had felt a quite overwhelming surge of gratitude toward this amazingly generous woman.

Now Charlotte looked across at May, sprawling elegantly on the sofa in her flat and giggled. "I do know what you mean, darling. 'Wifey' indeed! But it's her choice. She's twenty-one and determined to do this, so we can only back her up and hope she's right. And I do think that they adore each other, you know."

"Let's just hope that's enough then," replied May.

The previous week, May, suspecting that Esther's grasp of physical intimacy was limited, had tried to explain the rudiments of contraception to her.

"Have you slept with him yet?" she asked her sister.

Esther's eyes widened. "No, of course not!" she replied. "How could you even ask, May?" Then, enlightenment dawning, she exclaimed, "May! Have you..? Oh my goodness, May, you don't mean that you..?"

May sometimes wondered how Esther could be so sure she was in love.

"Dear innocent Essie, I thought as much. Just listen and learn and don't ask any questions."

The day of the wedding dawned, surprisingly sunny for November. Esther was to be married in the convent chapel. Charlotte had worried that she might find it difficult to be back there, as it would inevitably revive so many bad memories. However, in the event, surrounded by both her family and her daughter's adoptive family, she found the familiarity of the building reassuring.

May, accompanied by the current man in her life, had been persuaded to wear what she described as a 'pink meringue' for her role as bridesmaid, but she somehow still managed to look astonishingly sophisticated. Her dark good looks provided the perfect counter balance to Esther's ethereal fairness. As the girls approached the altar, Thomas, tall, dark and handsome, turned to greet his bride with a smile. They certainly do look right together, thought May, hoping that this was a good omen.

The ceremony passed smoothly enough, and as Esther came back down the aisle on Thomas's arm, radiant in a fairy-tale princess dress, Kitty squeezed Charlotte's hand tightly. "My granddaughter is so beautiful," she murmured to her, and Charlotte smiled at her mother in agreement. Esther did indeed look ravishing.

The reception was in the village hall and the whole village had turned out to wish the happy couple well. Finally, everyone waved them off in the small Hillman Minx that Thomas, refusing to let Esther contribute, had bought on the 'never-never'.

Later in the day, Esther was embarrassed when confetti fell out their clothes in their honeymoon hotel in Bournemouth. "All the staff will know we are just married," she complained, trying ineffectually to sweep it up in her cupped hands.

Thomas pulled her upright. "Good. I want the whole world to know how lucky I am," he said, smothering her protests with a kiss.

The next day May was startled to see pictures of the wedding splashed all over the front page of the national newspapers. "I suppose we should have been prepared, Mum," she said to Mrs Morris. "There's been so much interest in Esther giving up performing. I mean, we knew the newspaper people were there, but I didn't expect all this, and I'm sure Esther and Thomas didn't either. I expect the papers will soon move on to something else and leave her alone. Have you heard from her?"

"Yes, I had a postcard, came second post today. She sounds very happy. May," Mrs Morris paused, looking for words. She often found herself slightly daunted by her vibrant and self-confident elder daughter. "May, I know you think she's wrong to give up her piano. But she's so sure, and well, you know, your dad and I have been married for over thirty years, and we've had a good life together. It's the kind of life that I'd like you and Esther to have, and I think perhaps that's what she wants. And probably what is right for her. She's not like you, dear. She's a home-maker, like me. It's what most women want. A home, with babies, when they come."

Mrs Morris blushed, and May realised that it was the longest speech she had ever heard her mother make. Impulsively she hugged her, smelling the familiar soapy smell on her mother's only slightly greying hair.

"How lucky we both are to have you and Dad. Two little orphans of the storm, rescued and loved and nurtured. And you're still trying to save me from myself. Or at least, save Esther from me." She laughed. "You're probably right, Mum. I promise not to nag her."

Mrs Morris kissed her fondly. "I know you wouldn't do that. But support her when she needs it, May. You've always been the strong one."

May recalled this conversation vividly the following week when Esther, home from her honeymoon, invited her round to their flat. It was on the second floor of a three story Victorian terrace which had suffered some bomb damage and, although repaired, was still rather creaky. May had not been allowed to visit in the weeks preceding the wedding, as Thomas and Esther had been, in Thomas's words, 'getting everything shipshape.' The invitation was to supper, and Charlotte was also coming. They met at May's flat and walked through the streets together.

"I feel as if I'm going to one of Esther's 'first nights'," said Charlotte. "She sounded quite nervous on the phone."

"I'm just glad she insisted on *having* a phone," said May. "Thomas thought it was a waste of money, you know. But, for once, Esther insisted – after all, it was her money she wanted to use."

"I think tonight is important to her, though," said Charlotte thoughtfully. "Like she feels she has to prove something."

"Not to us, surely?" asked May. Charlotte shrugged, and the two women walked in companionable silence through the dusk until they arrived at the flat.

They heard the bell ringing throughout the house, followed almost instantly by the sound of footsteps, and Thomas appeared to let them in.

"Do be careful," he warned. "We are trying to persuade the landlord to have a light put in over the stairs but we can't get an answer out of him."

The stairs were indeed dark and there was a damp smell about the building. Esther had done so much touring in the last few years that, when home, she had divided her time between Charlotte, May, and her parents, never seeming to want a permanent base of her own. May found herself hoping that this rather depressing building would turn out to be only a temporary residence.

But once they had reached the flat, Thomas threw open the door with a flourish and the hallway was suffused with light. "Darling, they're here," he called, somewhat unnecessarily as Esther was already through the room like a whirlwind and hugging them both.

"Thomas, you take their coats and I'll show them the flat," she said. Obediently Thomas collected hats, coats, scarves and gloves and disappeared through the bedroom door pretending to stagger under the burden.

"Something smells wonderful," said Charlotte.

"Oh, I do hope so," giggled Esther. "I think I should have learnt to cook instead of thumping a piano. But, you know, reading a recipe is like reading music really, as long as you follow the instructions it begins to come to life in your hands."

"Is it as rewarding?" asked May before she stop herself. Charlotte threw her a warning look.

Esther, however, was unconcerned. "I don't know yet. You're my guinea pigs. Though I should warn you that Thomas won't let me invite his parents until I've had a bit more practice. But never mind that, I want to show you the flat. The grand tour starts here."

Thomas re-appeared from the bedroom. "Off you go then. I'll keep an eye on the gravy, shall I?"

Esther's hand flew to her mouth. "Oh goodness, I'd forgotten it! Please, darling."

The tour of the flat did not take long, but May was pleased to admit that that she was impressed with the décor. Everywhere was bright and light, and although the main room was not large it managed to hold quite comfortably a dining table and four chairs as well as a dark green three piece suite covered in uncut moquette. A small fire glowed in the grate, so that room felt quite warm, but May noticed that the bedroom was freezing.

Esther saw her shiver and laughed. "We've got loads of blankets and a thick candlewick bed-spread as well as an eiderdown. And, of course, we've got each other," and she blushed, making May laugh affectionately at her.

The other bedroom was no more than a large cupboard. There was just room for Esther's piano. May looked askance at Esther.

"Well, I play during the day. When Thomas is out. He says we don't want to annoy the neighbours in the evening. Anyway," said Esther defensively, "we listen to the radio mostly, and Thomas thinks we might get a television when he gets his next rise. Actually," she moved closer and whispered conspiratorially to May, "I am going to buy him one for Christmas, but I don't want him to know."

Thomas was chatting with Charlotte in the tiny kitchen. The estate agent had described it as a 'kitchenette' which May felt was a fair comment as Charlotte and Thomas had to exit to make room for Esther and her to go in.

"Well, at least I don't have to walk miles to get things," said Esther, seeing her sister's face.

"You've made it all so pretty," said May quickly, and, she realised with relief, truthfully. "Where's the bathroom? Through there?" She pointed to a door.

"Oh no," giggled Esther, "that's just a cupboard. The bathroom is on the landing. We all share it."

May looked at her in consternation. "What, you have to go downstairs to use the lavatory in this cold old house? Oh, Esther, what are you thinking of? You could easily have found a place with your own bathroom."

Esther looked away. "Thomas won't use my money. We're going to put it in trust for when our children get to twenty-one. He says it wouldn't be proper for us to live on my money and I agree."

"Look, Essie, I'm sure that's very laudable but is he happy for you to catch pneumonia bathing down there? This house is freezing outside the sitting room. You've always managed to get colds and stuff at the drop of a hat."

"May, I am very happy. Thomas only wants what is best for me. Now, go and sit with the others. If you want to be useful, go and set the table."

Thus dismissed, May did as she was told. Later that evening, as she and Charlotte walked home, Charlotte suddenly said, "I'm sure they'll be alright. They obviously really care for each other. And they've made the flat nice."

May nodded. She was remembering the view from the sitting-room window, glimpsed before the daylight finally drained away. I hope it's not a bad omen that it overlooks a bombsite, she thought.

But she didn't say it out loud.

1961

Esther was hot. So hot that she could feel the perspiration running down her back. She wondered if the pink nylon blouse that Thomas had bought her after she weaned Jacqueline was making her hotter, but she knew he liked to see her wearing it. They hardly ever went out together nowadays so she wanted him to be pleased. It had been difficult enough to find a baby-sitter. Thank heavens Mrs Burt from downstairs had rented the flat after that strange couple had moved on. Esther had confided to Thomas that she didn't know for ages whether they were two women, two men, or one of each.

"Better you don't, little wifey," he had said, kissing her forehead and blowing a kiss to Jacqueline, who was very sticky at the time. Esther had pondered briefly on this but then she forgot about the ambiguously named Chris and Jo, as nice Mr and Mrs Burt had moved in. It was the first time she had left Jacqueline with anyone who wasn't 'family', but although May was an adoring godmother, she was not often available as a baby-sitter due to her own working hours. As luck would have it, Charlotte's school had a parents' evening tonight, and as she was now the headmistress she could hardly not attend.

Thomas was insistent that someone must be found, as his wife's presence at his side on this occasion was important. "One of the big brass from Head Office is coming down, Esther. My promotion could depend on how well you and I come over. He's taking us to a really swish night club with the two other chaps who are in the running for the job, and their wives are invited, too. We all know that we are on trial, but we have to pretend it's just a social occasion. I have a good chance, because apparently he used to be a fan of yours and he's looking forward to meeting you."

She pushed the hair back from her forehead but then remembered that Thomas liked it falling gently round her face. She had hoped to have a bath, but by the time she had persuaded Jacqueline to have her after-dinner nap it was nearly five o'clock and someone else was in the bathroom. She didn't really like to leave Jacqueline alone even for those few minutes, anyway, so she had resorted to a strip wash in the kitchen. She had just run a powder puff over her face to try and tone down her flushed cheeks and applied the soft pink lipstick that was the only make up Thomas liked to see her wear, when he came bounding up the stairs.

Barely stopping to brush her cheek with his lips, he rushed into the bedroom. Five minutes later he came out wearing his best brown suit. "The firm's car will be here in ten minutes," he said. "I do like your outfit, Essie. You look very pretty."

A knock on the door heralded the arrival of Mrs Burt. Esther showed her the sleeping baby, cocooned in the bedside cot. "I think she may not wake before we are back. She's been awake all day, little monkey."

"Don't you worry, my dear," replied Mrs Burt. "You have a lovely time, you deserve an evening out."

At that moment a car horn was heard tooting outside the house and drawing back the net curtain Thomas waved down to the chauffeur. "Come on, Esther, we mustn't keep him waiting."

Esther blew her daughter a last kiss and, thanking Mrs Burt, descended the stairs with Thomas, being careful to hold her skirt so that it did not brush the damp walls. She was aware that Thomas was tense. Squeezing his hand in the car she said, "Come on, sweetheart, stop worrying. Let's just have a good time."

Thomas shook off her hand impatiently. "Esther, you don't understand. A lot depends on this evening. This could be my chance to get you and Jacqueline out of the flat and into our own house. With a big enough pay rise we'd be able to get a mortgage through the bank."

Esther sat back and looked out of the window. They were approaching the West End and she found herself cheered by the kaleidoscope of coloured lights they were driving through. She reflected that she had enough money to buy a small house in the suburbs outright, but Thomas was adamant about not using her money, though they had not yet got round to setting up a trust for Jacqueline. Two years ago she had admired Thomas's determination to support her, but now she was beginning to wonder if it was not some strange kind of male pride. The flat was really no longer suitable for them now that they had Jacqueline.

The Jaguar drew up smoothly outside a brightly lit club and Esther recognised it as the one where May sang. She had been to it many times in the past, but not since Jacqueline was born. It came as a very pleasant surprise to recognise the pictures of May illuminated outside.

"Did you know we were coming here?" she asked Thomas, who shook his head.

"But I bet it's not coincidence" he murmured, "If the big white chief is a fan of yours he'll have done his homework."

He was right. As they entered the club, the grandly attired gentleman on the door who basked in the title of 'major-domo' greeted Esther with something akin to reverence, and ushered them to the table where the rest of their party were already waiting.

Thomas's 'big white chief' stepped forward eagerly to greet them. "Mr and Mrs Brown, or may I call you Thomas and Esther?"

They laughingly gave assent and Esther realised that the picture of a grey-suited elderly man she had formed could not be further from the truth. Paul, as he insisted they call him, was in his early thirties, with a charming transatlantic accent. He was very handsome and reminded Esther of President Kennedy, whose picture was constantly in the British papers. He was obviously delighted to meet Esther 'in the flesh' as he put it.

"Esther, I cannot tell you how exciting this is for me," he said, "I shall drop your name like crazy when I get back home."

Laughing, Esther found herself relaxing and enjoying the evening in spite of being conscious that Thomas was not really joining in the conversation. The two other couples were easy company and Paul forbade any talk of the bank, which suited them all well. The talk was of their families, and their holidays, although Thomas and Esther had to admit they hadn't been away since their honeymoon. One of the couples had been to a Butlins holiday camp with their two children and the other (childless as yet) had been cycling in Norfolk. Privately, Esther thought that she would rather have stayed at home than undergone either of these holidays, but she could see that Thomas felt that he had failed in some competition. Fortunately, they were soon distracted by the food.

"My goodness," said Paul, "Things are really looking up over here at last. A choice of either prawns or scampi for hors d'oeuvres! Last time I was over from the States I asked for caviar and was told there was smoked cod's roe or nothing. This is quite an interesting menu."

"Don't be patronising, young man," said a voice behind him.

Paul jumped to his feet in some confusion, but the lights had gone down to signal the start of the cabaret. Through the gloom Esther made out the figure of May, resplendent in a full-length red and purple dress with a glorious ruby tiara on her dark hair. She sprang up to give her sister a hug.

May put a finger to her lips, and continued in a whisper, "Couldn't resist coming and saying hallo. You must be the boss man?" Paul made a mock bow. "Have to go," hissed May as the four musicians on the small round stage went into the Jerome Kern song that had become her signature tune, "See you after the show."

Leaving Paul with his jaw dropping, she quickly positioned herself at the top of the adjoining staircase where the spotlight found her. Her accompanist glanced up, found her, and started to play. May slowly and gracefully descended the stairs to the stage as she began to sing softly into the hush that had greeted her appearance, *"Fish gotta swim..."*

Paul remained on his feet and Esther, watching him, realised with quiet amusement that he was mesmerised by her sister. 'Be gentle with him, May,' she thought to herself. May sang for twenty minutes, and then vacated the stage to tumultuous applause and with a promise to return.

Esther was aware that Thomas was increasingly uncomfortable in this environment. He was as restless as she had ever seen him, constantly running his finger round his collar and fiddling with his tie. She found herself unobtrusively guiding him through the menu, much of which was in French. For the first time she understood that her career, and the experiences that had resulted from it, had given her a greater sophistication than Thomas. Her naturally introverted personality had fooled them both. 'It doesn't matter,' she thought, almost in a panic, 'I love him. It doesn't matter at all.' But as she glanced across the table at him, instead of finding reassurance, he suddenly seemed like a stranger.

The moment was erased by May's re-appearance. Esther realised that she had only the haziest awareness of the subsidiary acts that had filled the bill. May held the stage for a magic moment, now dressed in gold and ivory. As the applause died down she began the haunting, *Summertime*. Esther let herself be absorbed into the song, and the other blues numbers that followed. What an artiste her sister had become, she thought proudly as she joined the audience who were on their feet applauding.

May held up her hand and the cheering gradually subsided. With what Esther recognised as a mischievous glance in her direction, May said, "I have a request of my own to make tonight." With a mixture of horror and amusement Esther suddenly knew what was coming next.

May glanced up at their table, in the gallery over the

little stage, her face suffused with merriment. "Ladies and Gentlemen, I wonder if we can persuade my sister Esther to play for us?"

The spotlight picked up a blushing Esther, laughing at her sister's audacity. She was about to decline with as much grace as possible in spite of the increasing clamour from the audience, when she heard Thomas say, "Certainly not, of course you're not going to do any such thing. Come along, Esther, we are leaving." And, standing abruptly, he reached over and made as if to take her arm. Esther turned to look at him, evading his touch. Then she slowly got to her feet.

Without stopping to analyse her response, Esther walked past her husband and went to meet May, who was by now halfway up the staircase, holding out her hands in delight. The audience was on their feet again. Esther was suddenly conscious of her blouse and skirt, a far cry from her glamorous days. She mentally shrugged, amazed at her rush of confidence.

May led her to the piano, vacated by her accompanist who was himself clapping madly as he stepped out of the spotlight. Esther seated herself and ran her fingers experimentally over the keys. The audience fell quiet in anticipation. May leaned over her and asked quietly, "What will you play, Essie?"

"Anything I can do without the music," replied Esther. "Some Chopin, I think. Do you want to pass me the mike?"

"With very great pleasure," replied May. Handing it to Esther, she went to sit at the edge of the small semi-circular stage.

Esther turned to her audience. "I should like to play *The Minute Waltz*". Another storm of clapping. Esther continued, "It always amuses me that Chopin's original title for this piece was *The Little Dog*. He was trying to paint a picture of a man chasing a small dog, and it is a great favourite of mine. I hope you will enjoy it, too."

May smiled to herself as Esther began the charming, humorous piece that Sister Mathilde had taught the two girls so many years ago. When her sister had finished, May crossed to her, "You're going to have to do an encore, Sis."

Esther looked up at her and laughed. She had forgotten the thrill, the exhilaration, of inhabiting music and interpreting her vision of it for an eager public. Without further ado she launched into Puccini's *One fine day*, beckoning May to join her. The two girls had performed the song together so many times in the past that the impromptu performance swept their listeners along.

When it was over May blew a kiss to her sister and went back to sit on the edge of the stage. The club rang with cries of, 'More, bravo, encore,' and Esther light-heartedly indicated that she would play one more piece. Her medley from Bizet's *Carmen* had the audience on their feet again, but she laughingly closed the piano and made her way back to her table.

"You are wonderful! I can hardly believe that I've been fortunate enough to hear you play," enthused Paul, and the rest of their table joined in with congratulations with the notable exception of Thomas, whose expression was thunderous. At the moment Esther didn't care. She was high on the music and the acclaim, and conscious that she had been wrong two years before. She was a performer, just like her sister, and perform she must.

Returning home soon after, she was glad of the glass panel that screened them from the driver. Thomas turned to her immediately the car drew away from the crowd of waving well wishers who had followed Esther out.

"How could you do that?" he demanded. "You have made an exhibition of us both."

Esther turned to him in astonishment. "Thomas, I played the piano. I was, no, I think that perhaps I am still, a concert pianist. How have I made an exhibition of either of us?"

"The whole world will now think that I am unable to support my wife. She has to go out banging on a piano to keep us."

Esther looked at him coldly. It was as if the events of the evening had conspired to smash her rose-coloured spectacles. She had realised tonight that his refusal to contemplate her continuing her career, which had seemed so chivalrous and caring, was an aberration. An aberration in which she had conspired.

But he was her husband, the father of her daughter, and they loved each other, she told herself. Neither of them were quite themselves this evening. It must be to do with the unaccustomed wine they had both drunk and perhaps they would feel differently in the morning. She would tackle the subject when she had time to think, and time to explain properly how she had felt this evening. She squeezed Thomas's hand affectionately; ignoring his stony profile as he resolutely gazed ahead, and decided to keep her own counsel for the time being. She was aware, though, that she was still alight with the reception her performance had received, and that an invisible milestone in their marriage had just been passed.

When they arrived home she preceded Thomas up the stairs hoping Jacqueline had been good, and suddenly anxious to see her. She was surprised to find the door to their flat was locked.

"Mrs Burt," she called as loudly as she dared, in case Jacqueline was asleep. "We're home, Mrs Burt. Can you let us in, please?"

There was no answer. Esther's mind began to race and panic grabbed at her.

"I've got my key," Thomas's voice was behind her. She stood back to let him unlock the door, and then pushed past him into the uncannily quiet flat. She rushed into the bedroom. There was no-one there. And Jacqueline's cot had gone.

"Mrs Burt must have taken her downstairs," said Thomas. They turned in unison and ran down the stairs, "Esther, don't worry I'm sure she's ..."

But the door to the Burts' flat was open. The flat was empty. There was a note on the table. Esther picked it up with trembling hands.

Then she began to scream.

The police were kind. They responded to Thomas's 999 call in minutes, but Esther had already run into the road, more or less straight into the arms of their local beat policeman. By the time his fellow officers had arrived he had taken Esther back upstairs, told Thomas to go and put the kettle on, and was reading the note.

"Don't pick it up again," he ordered. "We can test it for fingerprints, and see if these people have a criminal record."

The note was simple.

She will be better off with us. Sorry.

That was all it said. Very soon the two flats were crawling with police.

"They've no more idea what to do than us," thought Esther.

Thomas came and stood by her. "We shouldn't have left her."

Esther remained silent. There was no answer to that. No answers to anything anymore, she thought wildly. "I'm going to phone May," she said and without waiting for a response she went out into the hall.

May had just arrived home, flushed with pleasure from the events of the evening, and accompanied, apparently, by Paul. "May, please come," Esther stammered out and then was unable to go on.

The beat officer, whose name was George, took the phone and quickly explained.

"Oh, my God," said May. "Tell her I'm on my way. She's to hold on."

Esther went back into the crowded little sitting room. "May's coming," she said.

Thomas came and put an arm round her shoulders. "They'll find her, won't they?" he asked. "They'll find our baby?"

Esther put her arms round him. "Yes," she said firmly. Inside her head she was screaming, "This is the wrong way round! You keep telling me that you are the strong one. Please, please be strong for me now."

Minutes later May arrived with Paul. "I think you should both come home with me."

"Can't leave," replied Esther, through visibly dry lips, "something might happen. They might find my baby. There might be a message…"

May took Thomas aside. "For heaven's sake ring your doctor, Thomas. Esther needs a sedative or something. She is very shocked. She's going to pass out any minute."

Thomas glanced across to where Paul was sitting holding Esther's hand. "Yes, yes, of course. I should have thought of that."

Yes, you should have, thought May to herself.

The doctor arrived and ordered Esther to bed. Too exhausted to argue she allowed May to help her into the bedroom and undress. She barely felt the prick in her arm as the doctor administered a strong tranquiliser.

"She'll be out cold till morning," he informed May.

May saw him out, and then went to speak to Thomas. He was slumped in an armchair beside a full ashtray.

Paul was sitting beside him silently. "How is she?" he asked quietly, as both men looked up.

"Asleep," replied May. Kneeling beside Thomas, she asked him, "Shall I stay here tonight? And, Thomas, we must let the family know what has happened. Someone may have already told the papers and we can't have Mum and Dad and Charlotte finding out that way."

Thomas looked at her blankly. "Do whatever you like," he said, rising and going into the kitchen.

For the first time, May realised the extent of his dislike of her. But she brushed the thought away. He was in shock, as they all were. Then the police officer who appeared to be in charge of operations asked if he could speak to them all and Paul fetched Thomas back.

"I'm leaving George on duty here in case the kidnappers call you. He will be replaced by another officer in the morning, who will accompany you to the station to see if we can identify this couple. In the meantime, I will be alerting every force in the country of the situation. These people won't get far."

But they all knew that Jacqueline's abductors had a good five hours start on them. May subdued the panic that kept threatening to submerge her.

The officer continued, "I should like to inform the press. All and any publicity must be helpful." They nodded agreement. "May I take this?" He indicated a photograph of Jacqueline taken at her baptism the previous month. Thomas slipped it out of the silver frame that Charlotte had given them as a christening present and passed it to him.

The officer touched him on the shoulder. "I'll take good care of it," he promised.

"More than I managed with my daughter," blurted Thomas, stumbling from the room. With a glance at May, Paul went after him.

The departing officer had a quiet word with George in the hall. "Keep an eye. Dig a bit. See if there is anything more they know about this couple. They don't seem to, but something might have been said that they've forgotten about. We both know that people don't always identify what's important."

George went back into the sitting room. "Do you want to contact your family?" he asked May.

She nodded. "I'll ring Charlotte. I'll have to go and see our parents tomorrow. They are not on the phone. But I'll go early and get there before the papers come out. Will it be in the papers by tomorrow, do you think?"

George nodded. "The DI was going straight off to

make a statement. He wants to make sure it gets in before they go to press."

May poked her head into the kitchen but retreated silently at a sign from Paul. Thomas was slumped in front of the window, his head in his hands. She left Paul to cope in whatever way he could. How strange, she thought, I only met him a few hours ago. But disaster put a different perspective on so many things and she was grateful for his presence. He seemed to possess the happy knack of being helpful without being intrusive. Glancing at the time as she went into the hall, she saw that it was nearly three o'clock in the morning. She dialled Charlotte's number. She let it ring for a long time, and eventually a sleepy voice said, "Hallo?"

"Charlotte, this is May."

An audible intake of breath. "May, darling, what is the matter? Are you alright?"

"Yes, sort of. But, Charlotte, something dreadful has happened." May paused, then decided that there was no easy way of breaking the news, "Charlotte, Jacqueline has been kidnapped."

"No! Oh my God, May, where, who..?"

May interrupted, "Charlotte, I need you to come and be with Esther so that I can go and tell Mum and Dad and the family before they see the papers."

May was conscious that Charlotte was struggling for control. Then, "Of course, I'm on my way. I'll be with you in about half an hour. You can tell me everything then."

May thanked God, not for the first time in her life, for Charlotte. As she replaced the phone she became aware that her whole body was shaking. She went back into the sitting room to find Paul and George waiting for her.

"Thomas has gone to lie down in the spare room. He doesn't want to disturb Esther. I gave him some whisky," Paul indicated a hip flask in his pocket, "and he's gone out like a light. Is your friend coming?"

May contemplated trying to explain the complicated relationship that existed between her and Charlotte but decided that 'friend' was more than adequate. She nodded. "Charlotte will be here soon."

Paul got to his feet. "Then I'll go and make a large jug of coffee for us all. I'm sure George will be glad of some too."

"You have been such a tower of strength. Thank you," said May simply.

Paul crossed and put his hands on her shoulders. Looking down at her he replied, "I think you are the tower of strength, May. I am just glad to be useful in any way that I can. Like making the coffee." He brushed her forehead with the lightest of kisses before disappearing into the kitchen.

As she peeped into the bedroom to make sure that Esther was sleeping soundly, May could hear a muffled sound coming from the spare bedroom. She knocked on the door gently. "Thomas, would you like some coffee?" Silence. Then movement. Thomas opened the door. He looked so lost and so ... *unanchored* was the word that came into her head. Instinctively she stepped forward and put her arms round him. She felt a tremor run through him and realised it was the effort of not sobbing out loud. Gently, she led him back to the bed and sat beside him.

"Thomas, try to get some sleep. Esther will need you tomorrow. Whatever happens, you must be strong for her."

Thomas held her hands tightly. She could see the tears glistening on his cheeks and realised that she had never seen a man cry before.

"I can't be strong. Not in the right way. Can't you see, that's the problem? This is all my fault. I should have taken better care of them, but I don't know how. And she knows that I don't. It's been becoming more and more obvious. I love her so much, May. And my baby, oh, God, my baby, my Jacqueline. But I should have loved Esther enough to understand what she was. What you both are. I wanted her to be like my mother. I fell in love with her because she was talented and special and brilliant, and then I tried to stop her being like that. If I'd let her be herself we could have lived somewhere decent and then none of this would have happened. But no, I had to be the breadwinner, just like my father. My parents consider it shameful for a woman to go out to work, and I tried to impose that on Esther without even thinking about how it might affect her. I made everything about *me*, instead of about *us*. And now I've lost them both."

May shook her head. "Thomas, it wasn't just your choice. It was Esther's decision, too. She knew how you felt and she embraced that. She told me that she was happy to retire, that she was ready to turn her back on being a performer. But," she paused, wondering if this was the right conversation for them to be having at such a time, "I don't think either of you took on board how much she would miss it. She *is* a strong person, Thomas. Stronger perhaps than either of you realised. So treasure that. You will never need each other more than you do at the moment. Support her while asking for her support. You both seem to be stuck in some ancient culture where wives are not supposed to have brains and husbands are not supposed to have feelings."

Thomas nodded slowly. "Thank you, May. We haven't really got to know each other, have we? I always knew you thought that I was the wrong man for her, and I was so jealous of your closeness. It seems that I have been wrong about so many things. But," he stood up, "I think I should start by making sure I am in the same bed as her when Esther wakes up, don't you?"

As she went back into the sitting room to join Paul and George, May heard Charlotte's voice.

"Oh, Charlotte," she exclaimed throwing herself into the other woman's embrace," Thank you for coming so quickly. I can't tell you how pleased I am to see you."

Charlotte, looking pale and strained, asked, "Is Esther still asleep?"

"Mercifully, yes. The sedative really knocked her out."

"These gentlemen have been filling me in, and I think I might be able to help," said Charlotte, "Chris and Jo, who had the flat before this couple, are friends with my Head of Art at school. They probably saw quite a lot of this Mr and Mrs Burt before the move, and I believe Jo is an artist herself. I wonder if she could sketch them for us? It would give the police a bit more to go on than just Thomas and Esther's descriptions. I never saw them, did you?"

May shook her head. "No, Esther just mentioned that they were happy to baby-sit. I didn't even know their names till yesterday. Let's face it, people living in the same house, who would ever suspect..?" she tailed off miserably.

George rose as they heard a gentle tap at the front door. Coming back into the room with his fellow officer, May was about to ask if there was any news when Charlotte stepped forward. "Leonard! What are you doing here?"

"Charlotte! I have only just been transferred to this part of the world. I had hoped to meet up with you again, but in happier circumstances than these. Is the baby a relation? I am the DS in charge of finding her. I'm afraid we have no news yet, but the papers are alerted and will be blazoning the story on their front pages in a couple of hour's time."

"She's my granddaughter," replied Charlotte numbly. "Leonard, I…"

Leonard stared at her.

"Miss Bradshaw thinks she might know someone who could do a sketch of the Burts, sir," interrupted George.

"Oh, yes. Yes, I do." Charlotte was relieved to have this to focus on. "In fact, I'll try to get hold of Jo now. But I'll have to go back home to get her address and see if she is on the phone."

"I'll drive you," said Leonard. "Are the baby's parents asleep?"

May nodded.

"We won't be long," and he ushered Charlotte out.

May caught Paul's questioning glance and shrugged her shoulders. "I don't know any more than you. But they're obviously old friends."

As they drew away from the curb, Leonard said, "Charlotte, what were you going to tell me just now?"

Charlotte hesitated. She thought of the

complications that would ensue if she blurted out the truth after so many years. Not for the first time she wondered if she had made the right decision.

"I'm sorry, Leonard, this is not the time or the place for personal revelations. Its eight years since we last met. Julian told me that you had married. I am so happy for you."

"Don't be too happy, Charlotte. Debbie left me three years ago. She lives in Australia now with her new husband and my sons. It's a long way to go. And expensive. I haven't seen my boys for two years."

"I'm so sorry. That must be so hard for you."

He glanced at her. "Yes. I don't even know whether I am right to interfere in their lives. Perhaps that just messes up their relationship with their new father."

Charlotte gazed down at her hands. I don't believe this is happening, she thought. Between us, his wife and I have stolen all his children.

Leonard glanced at her quizzically. "So is Esther your daughter, or Thomas your son? I had no idea the baby was your granddaughter."

"Esther is my daughter. She and May were adopted by a wonderful couple during the war. May's parents were killed in the Blitz. The two girls grew up together. Until they were adult Esther thought I was her unofficial aunt, as I was to May."

Leonard fell silent. "But obviously she knows the truth now?"

"Yes," replied Charlotte, ending the conversation abruptly as they drew up outside her tiny Victorian terraced cottage.

"Is this where you live?" asked Leonard.

She murmured assent, and led the way up the short

path to a scarlet front door, glowing in the moonlight. The door opened directly into a sitting room that was larger than Leonard expected. As Charlotte rummaged in a small Maplewood bureau that stood against the wall, Leonard looked round the room and realised that an entrance hall had been incorporated into the space. The result was cosy without being remotely claustrophobic.

Charlotte found her address book and went straight to the phone. It was obviously picked up immediately and she explained the situation briefly and succinctly to Jo, the break in her voice when she spoke Jacqueline's name being the only indication of the strain she was feeling. She replaced the instrument and turned to face him.

"She remembers them well, especially Mrs Burt. She's going to do a sketch of her and bring it round to Esther's flat. And she says that they had a mini-van, pale green, a bit battered, that they used to park just round the corner from the flat."

"May I use your phone?" Leonard had pushed past her and was already dialling. As he alerted his officers and gave orders for the description of the van to go out on an all points bulletin, Charlotte waited by the front door. They drove back to the flat in silence, only broken when they turned into Esther's road.

"She's mine, isn't she?"

Charlotte shuddered, though whether from cold or the anticipation of having to answer this was not clear. "Yes," she said, adding, without stopping to analyse why, "I'm sorry."

"I think," said Leonard, "that I should be the one apologising. Oh, my God, Charlotte, why..? No, don't answer, I think I can guess."

"Please, don't tell her. Not now. She mustn't have anything else to cope with."

The car drew smoothly alongside the curb. "What kind of a monster do you think I am, Charlotte? The only thing that that matters at the moment is finding the baby. And find her we will, I promise you."

I believe him, thought Charlotte. But will it be in time? Dawn was breaking by the time they arrived back.

Esther answered the door to them. "Have you found her? Where is my baby?"

Charlotte was relieved to see Thomas was at his wife's side. He drew her back soothingly to allow them in. Leonard gently explained where they had been and that they were waiting for Jo's drawing.

Esther asked the question that was at the back of all their minds. "Why haven't they phoned and asked us for money? For a ransom? Isn't that what kidnappers do? It's been hours now. She must be so hungry…and so scared…" her voice broke and she pushed her fist into her mouth to stop the screams welling up inside her.

"Esther, we are doing our best. All the train stations and the sea and airports have been alerted. Believe me, we shall find her soon." Leonard held Esther's gaze.

After a moment spent searching his face, she said, "You really do care, don't you? More than just doing a job."

"Yes," he replied.

Yes, indeed, thought Charlotte, watching them both.

George appeared behind them. "Sir, there's a message." He indicated the phone. "Can you contact the station?"

Two minutes later Leonard was on his way out again. "They've found a van that might be theirs. Abandoned somewhere near Eastbourne. I'll keep you informed."

Charlotte ran down the stairs with him. "Why do they think it might be the one?"

He paused. "There's a dismantled cot in the back of it. Yellow, like the description of Jacqueline's."

Charlotte paled. "Where in Eastbourne? Tell me, Leonard."

He gripped her hands. "Beachy Head. Don't tell her." And he was gone.

An hour later Jo arrived with the drawings, having, according to Thomas, reproduced an uncanny likeness of Mrs Burt. Mr Burt was a more shadowy figure as Jo had not seen so much of him, but he was a definite 'type' with his rangy body and bald head and wire-rimmed glasses. George's relief had arrived, so George took possession of the sketches and departed back to the station.

Mr and Mrs Morris arrived by mid-morning in May's little car. Mrs Morris had obviously been crying, and Esther found herself paradoxically growing stronger as she comforted her mother. Mr Morris and Thomas busied themselves making tea for their women. Charlotte and May left them in charge with promises to return in the afternoon.

"What is happening?" asked May, as they walked down the road together. Charlotte told her about the van.

"Oh, my God," said May. Then, "But surely if they wanted to kill themselves they would have driven it over the cliff? Isn't that what people go to Beachy Head to do?"

Charlotte shook her head, "I wish I knew, darling. Perhaps it is some kind of a diversion. To stop the police working out where they really are. Let's hope someone recognises them from Jo's sketch. It'll be in the evening papers."

By the time the evening papers were out, George was back with them. "Asked specially if I could be here," he told Thomas, "Didn't think your lady wife needed any more strangers tramping around."

The phone rang at about six o'clock. The Burts had been recognised. By Mrs Burt's sister. She was at her local police station in Watford making a statement now. Leonard arrived soon after. The statement had been wired to him.

"It's not what we thought," he told Esther. "I think you can be sure that this couple won't hurt Jacqueline. Apparently Mrs Burt can't have children of her own. She had some kind of breakdown last year. They were hoping to adopt but recently were told that they were too old. This is not about money."

"No," said Esther, "it's about madness, isn't it?"

"A kind of madness," agreed Leonard. "But the madness of despair, I think. Not the madness of malice. I think Jacqueline's life will be as precious to her as it is to you, Esther. Try to hang on to that."

Charlotte wondered how she could ever have thought this man superficial. Leonard left them soon after.

Esther sent their parents home with May. "Mummy, Daddy, you can't do anything here. Go home. May will take you." With a ghastly attempt at light-heartedness she added, "This flat is too small for us all, I'll only be worrying about where to put you."

They recognised the truth behind the brave declaration and left, May insisting that she would return later. After all, the entire country understood why she would not be singing at the club tonight.

George tactfully withdrew to the hall, "So as to be nearer the phone."

Charlotte went off to see Kitty and Percy, who she knew would be frantic with worry by now, having had the briefest of phone calls from her the previous evening.

Esther and Thomas were finally alone for the first time since Jacqueline's disappearance. For a moment they stood in silence. Then Esther blurted out, "What if we don't ever see her again, Thomas?"

"We will," he replied stalwartly. "Soon. I know it." He paused. "Esther, I've made a lot of mistakes. No," he put a finger to her lips as she started to protest, "no, not now. But when our baby comes back then we are going to get everything right for her. And for us, if it's not too late. Now, come and sit beside me and let's see if we can get this television to work. Leonard said they were putting an appeal out tonight."

The television had been Esther's present to Thomas a couple of Christmas's ago. A small screen encased in an enormous wooden box, it stood on the floor in one corner of the sitting room, rarely watched because the reception was so bad. Tonight, however, through the flickering black and white images, they were able to watch the BBC news.

Jacqueline's picture was flashed on just as the phone rang. They heard George pick it up at the same moment as Peter Haig's voice said: 'We have just heard that the couple police wish to interview regarding the disappearance of Baby Jacqueline have been apprehended at a boarding house in Margate. As yet, we have no information regarding the whereabouts of Jacqueline.'

Before the shocked parents had time to register what they had just heard, George came bursting through the door. His wide smile illuminated the room.

1965

"That's my Mummy!" Jacqueline's voice echoed round the beautiful room.

Momentarily embarrassed, Thomas 'shushed' his daughter. A head turned slightly in front of him and he caught a familiar smile. Then everyone's attention was focused on Esther, as she moved toward the seated figure. Wearing a simple black gown, she made a faultless curtsey before seating herself at the piano. Only Thomas knew how many hours had gone into practising that curtsy. The request to perform at Windsor Castle had taken them both by surprise. Esther had written back asking if they might possibly bring Jacqueline and had been delighted when the Queen Mother's equerry had replied positively.

Invited to take dinner with the family, Thomas and Esther had been met by a lady who took them along to the Royal Nursery. Catching Esther's sudden look of panic, she smiled reassuringly, "Don't worry, my dear. She'll be safer here than anywhere on earth."

Esther knew she was right. It was the first time that they had handed their daughter over to strangers since

Jacqueline's kidnapping four years earlier, but a glimpse of the small boy who introduced himself gravely to Jacqueline with a hand-shake was totally reassuring.

"I don't think that even I can be too worried when she's having her supper with Prince Andrew," she murmured to Thomas.

Accompanied by one of the Castle's many footmen, Thomas had collected his daughter in time for Esther's recital. Thoughtfully seated at the end of the row behind the family, Jacqueline had a full view of the piano. Thomas had little doubt that his daughter would listen and watch quietly until she fell asleep in his arms. The day had been exhausting for a not yet five-year-old. The highlight of her day had been meeting the Queen's dogs and Thomas doubted if that treat would be bettered.

But she loved it when she was allowed to go to one of Esther's performances, and due to her parents' reluctance to leave her behind, was already a veteran of the concert circuit. Settling back as the music drifted over them, Thomas felt, rather than saw, her thumb locate her mouth and within minutes she grew heavier in his arms. He relaxed and let Esther's playing engulf him.

Even Thomas's parents had been impressed by the invitation. He admitted ruefully to himself that they weren't impressed by much that he did nowadays. When he had told them that he was giving up work to look after Jacqueline while Esther continued her career he seriously thought that his father was going to have a heart attack. His mother had been mortified when an article had appeared in one of the more popular papers describing Thomas as a 'house husband'.

"I shall never go to the Townswomen's Guild again. Whatever will people think?" she had wailed into the phone that evening. However, she was just beginning to discover that some of her female acquaintances thought it was a very sensible idea and admired the couple's courage.

"Wish my Sandra's Billy would stay at home and look after the kids," commented one of her close friends, "She's a teacher; she could earn ever so much more than him. But no, he's got to be the breadwinner. Or his mates might tease him. So they'll probably be stuck in that council flat twelve floors up forever, as far as I can see. Your Thomas and his wife have got the right idea."

Thomas was aware that his mother was slowly coming round to accepting what would once have been unthinkable to her. As it would indeed have been to him.

No-one, certainly not Esther, he thought, would ever know how much courage it had taken for him to leave the bank. It had been hard to ignore the barely concealed contempt of some of his older colleagues when he told them of his decision to swap roles with his wife. The puzzled and sometimes ribald comments from his peers had hurt, even though he pretended to take them in his stride.

It had required all his determination to steel himself against the barrage of derisory looks the first time he had pushed his daughter's pram out on his own. In fact, he was quite wrong to believe that Esther had not known. She had quietly watched and applauded his battle. She sometimes thought that was when she really fell in love with him. Their decision had been based on the practical consideration of her greater earning capacity and the impossibility for both of them of trusting their daughter with anyone else after everything that had happened. And their mutual, if latent, realisation that Esther's talent was a gift that should not be cast aside lightly.

Subsequently, as they had hoped, Esther's career had blossomed again. As well as a diary full of concert appearances, she had become a favourite with television audiences, appearing the previous Christmas with a well-loved comedian on his immensely popular annual spectacular. Sending herself up with great charm, she flew straight into the hearts of many members of the public who would never have dreamt of attending a classical concert.

There was now talk of Esther and May having their own show. "But I don't think we'll hold our breath," said the irrepressible May. "These things have a habit of falling through, and, anyway, the BBC are terrible payers!" Both girls were keeping their fingers crossed though. They still worked as well and as instinctively together as they always had.

Four years on from the trauma of Jacqueline's kidnapping, Thomas and Esther were buying a house in Chislehurst with a large garden, and life felt good to them both. Their second child was expected before the end of the year and Jacqueline was due to start school in a few months time. Thomas had achieved minor fame – or notoriety as he humorously claimed – as the most famous 'house husband' in the country. He had recently accepted an offer from a weekly woman's magazine to write regularly for them 'from the father's point of view'. He was surprised by his aptitude for, as well as his enjoyment of, the task. He had also been amazed at the letters he had received from men and women all over the country, applauding his position. His finest accolade, however, had been hearing his column praised on the wireless and himself described as a 'trendsetter'. Although he and Esther giggled together at the concept, secretly both were delighted.

The week following the successful Windsor concert, Jacqueline had another big day coming up. She was to be a bridesmaid at her Granny Charlotte's wedding. The marriage of Charlotte to her handsome police officer, Leonard, had come as no surprise to anyone. They had been 'an item' for several years. What *had* come as a shock to Esther had been Charlotte's smiling admittance to her that she also was pregnant.

Charlotte had sworn her to secrecy with the laughing words, "Swinging London has not penetrated the educational establishment yet, and I like my job."

Esther was forced to confront the possibility that she was a bit of a prude. She knew that Charlotte had given birth to her out of wedlock. She also had come to understand the extent of Charlotte's love for her, and the sacrifices that she had made on her behalf. Kitty had told her how nearly Charlotte had lost her sanity when she thought she had lost Esther forever, and her 'real' parents, as Esther thought of Mr and Mrs Morris, had always made clear their love and respect for Charlotte.

So why did Esther feel that this pregnancy was a betrayal? Why was she not overjoyed for Charlotte? Had she been able to discuss it with Thomas or May, she might have hit on the truth. But as it was, she forced it to the back of her mind, telling herself that it was merely that she was worried that at forty-three, Charlotte was too old to be giving birth. That she, Esther, might be fearing displacement in Charlotte's affections simply never crossed her mind.

Leonard and Charlotte's wedding was a comparatively low-key affair. Julian's daughter, Francesca, just into her teens, was the other bridesmaid, keeping a watchful eye on Jacqueline as they walked up the aisle behind Charlotte and Percy. Kitty surreptitiously wiped a tear from her eye. She did not know whether it was from the sight of her still handsome husband escorting their daughter with such pride or from sheer relief at seeing Charlotte so happy, and she didn't care. Probably both, she thought.

After the ceremony, they adjourned to the local hotel for the wedding breakfast. When, in the inevitable wedding speeches, Leonard announced that they had sold both their houses and were moving to a larger one within the month, only Esther understood the reason for their haste. She was in the cloakroom applying some restorative therapy to her make-up when Charlotte came in. Her mother grasped her hand.

"Esther, darling. We are going away for a few days, then coming back to my house till we get sorted. I've just asked May and Paul if they will baby-sit Jacqueline so that you and Thomas can come to supper."

Esther started to shake her head, but Charlotte stopped her, "You know Jacqueline will be safe. May worships her. You have to let go a little bit, Esther. And Leonard and I need to speak to you both about something important."

Two weeks later Esther and Thomas arrived

clutching a bottle of wine. "An end to speculation," said Thomas, as they rang the front door bell. "We shall finally find out what new revelation Charlotte is about to stun us with."

"I wish I hadn't told you what she said now," replied Esther affectionately," they've probably become vegetarians, or something like that."

"Oh, that would be a letdown," replied Thomas with a laugh, "I'm expecting something much more exciting than that."

Leonard threw open the door with a flourish and ushered them in. The round table was already set in the middle of the room, which was lit by many candles. The quivering flames from these and the open fire in the small hearth were combining to make dancing shadows on the walls.

"Oh, how lovely it all looks!" cried Esther. "My goodness, this must have taken you ages."

"And we're going to start with champagne tonight," said Leonard, taking their bottle from them. "Come and sit down."

The champagne and glasses were already on a tray on a side table, Esther noticed.

Charlotte emerged from the kitchen and gave them both enormous hugs. Thomas and Esther sat together on the sofa, while Leonard hovered by the door. Charlotte held out her hand to him and he crossed to her.

Esther thought that Charlotte looked strangely nervous in the flickering light. "Come on, you two," she said with a smile, "What this important thing you have to tell us? Champagne, indeed! And all these wonderful candles! Are we allowed to know what we are celebrating?"

Charlotte took a deep breath. "Esther. I hope you will forgive me for not telling you this before. I suppose, in extenuation, I have to say that I think I would have done if you had asked but you never did. But Esther, dearest daughter, this baby that I am expecting. It will not be your half-sister or brother. It will truly be your sibling."

There was a silence as Esther and Thomas mulled this statement over. Then, her eyes widening in shock, Esther asked, "Charlotte, are you telling me that Leonard is my father?"

Charlotte nodded. "He didn't know about you. Not till Jacqueline's kidnapping. Then I asked him to wait till things had settled down for you again. Please, try to understand…"

But before she could finish Esther was on her feet and in Leonard's arms. "I never dreamt… oh I am so relieved…"

"Relieved?" questioned Charlotte, taken aback.

"I never asked because I was so frightened of what you might tell me. I thought that my father must be a murderer or a rapist or something dreadful. I thought that I would just rather not know. And all the time…" she lifted her face to Leonard, who took it gently between his hands and kissed her forehead.

Then he held a hand out to Thomas, who, grinning from ear to ear, shook it enthusiastically. "Hello, Father-in-law, fancy meeting you," he said, deliberately rupturing the almost unbearable emotion in the room.

They all laughed, but then Charlotte caught her breath and burst into tears. "Can you forgive me? I've been so frightened of telling you."

"With all my heart," replied her daughter, crossing

to Charlotte, and folding her in her arms. "With all my heart," she repeated, her own joyful tears mingling with those of her mother.

Epilogue

1966

"But you know that I have always loved Christmas. You're turning into a crotchety old man, I really don't know how I put up with you." Elizabeth's smile belied her words.

From the arm-chair on the other side of the fire, John grinned back at her. "O.K. I know when I'm beaten. How did I dare even voice a protest? I shall abandon all my fantasies of a quiet yuletide. And it will certainly be splendid to have Hyacinth and Toby here with us again. I confess that I could no more face another trip across the Atlantic Ocean than climb Everest and I am absolutely, definitely, not flying any more. So I imagine our only hope of seeing them is when they can find a hole in their busy schedule to visit their ancient parents."

Elizabeth laughed out loud. "Oh, John, darling, you are such a poseur! You and Hyacinth have been a mutual admiration society since the day she was born, and, as neglected parents go, you don't even reach the starting block. We are very lucky that they still want to spend so much time with us. It's only two months since they were last here. The children won't be coming with them this time..." She stopped abruptly as she caught the expression on her husband's face.

"Children?" he asked mildly, unable, however, to completely subdue the smile beginning to curve his lips. "Do you know, I thought that Jeff and Linda were in their thirties, and have been relatively prolific themselves. Little American great-grandchildren all over the place. Was it seven at the last count, or did I imagine that?"

Elizabeth regarded him affectionately. "You know perfectly well how many it is. It was you who made that collage of pictures of them, on the wall behind you. So stop pretending and behave yourself!"

Having, as always, managed to have the last word, she got down to business. "The thing is, as you know, Kitty and Percy want us all to get together on Christmas day for the first time in years and I think that would be lovely. And so do you, only you won't admit it. After all, I don't suppose there will be that many more opportunities. But we have to get the logistics sorted out so that no-one is landed with all the work."

John nodded. "Do you think being octogenarians will enable us to rest on our laurels and let them all rush round after us? How many of us will there be?"

"The answer to your first question is 'probably', I should think. You're allowed to be a bit indolent at our age. And as to the second one, I really don't know. I keep trying to add us all up but I make it different every time. Kitty is popping in later so we'll get down to it then."

"You mean that asking me for my opinion was just a formality? It's all been decided already?"

Elizabeth twinkled at her husband. Sixty-two years of marriage gave you certain privileges. "Of course it has, darling," she replied.

It was one of those magical Christmas days, dry and crisp. The children had prayed for snow but to the relief of the adults their exhortations had been ignored.

Hyacinth and Toby had insisted on hiring a suite of rooms at the Savoy. Hyacinth, on an echoing transatlantic telephone line, had been adamant.

"Mummy, we're as rich as Croesus. For heaven's sake let us do something. Believe me, it's a drop in the ocean. Anyway, we've already made the reservations. It'll be fun."

Contemplating the view over London's theatre land from the luxurious sitting-room that was part of the Savoy suite, Elizabeth had to agree. It *was* fun. She turned as Hyacinth entered the room.

"Good morning, darling," she said, kissing her daughter before standing back to admire her. "You look gorgeous. But you always do. Love the dress. Green was always your colour. I wanted to get here early so we had a chance to catch up on our own. I've been watching the world go by, my goodness, some of these skirts are shorter than the ones you wanted to wear forty years ago! The others should arrive soon. Daddy's talking shop with Toby. 20th Century Fox are interested in that screen play he wrote ages ago based on the life of your grandmother, Mary, but he'd much rather you two had it if you want it."

"Isn't it strange the repercussions things have? If Daddy hadn't written that play all those years ago for Toby, our lives might have been very different," commented Hyacinth, joining Elizabeth at the window. "It not only started Daddy off on another career, but it gave Toby the part that first put him in the public eye, and I suppose that led to everything else that happened."

As so often over the years, Elizabeth was conscious of a frisson of unease. She regarded her famous daughter with a measure of concern. Hyacinth looked wonderful. Her youthful looks gave no clue to her approaching 60th birthday. And yet there were times when Elizabeth felt that she no more understood her than the millions of film fans who knew Hyacinth only from one of the very occasional interviews she gave to the papers, or her even more rare appearances on the television when Hytobe's latest production needed publicity.

She heard herself say, "Are you happy, Hyacinth?"

Hyacinth looked at her with surprise. "Don't I look it?" she replied with a smile.

Elizabeth regarded her steadily. "I'm asking the questions, darling. Well?"

Hyacinth sank into one of the enormous arm-chairs and looked up at her mother. "I didn't know it was going to be soul searching stuff. But, yes, I think I am. I have a terrific career, wonderful kids and when I have time I enjoy my grandchildren. What more can any woman ask for?"

As the question hung in the air between them, they heard the sound of the lift disgorging the first guests into the hallway and Toby's laughter as he greeted them.

Hyacinth rose and gave Elizabeth a quick hug. "And I have wonderful parents, of course."

She hurried into the hall, leaving Elizabeth to follow more slowly. She was horribly aware that Toby hadn't figured on Hyacinth's list of positives. Her handsome son-in-law was still playing romantic leads in Hollywood, always 'getting the girl' even though the female lead was sometimes forty years younger than him. But the length of their marriage was legendary in a town where the divorce could follow the wedding before the confetti was swept away.

There had been rumours, of course. Never about other women, which was unusual enough in their profession, though Elizabeth thought her daughter would not have countenanced that humiliation. There were, however, persistent whispers that Toby had links to the Mafia, and that his continuing success was largely dependent on that. Elizabeth had thought these allusions in the press absurd. Toby was a middle-class Englishman, for heaven's sake. And Hyacinth and Hytobe had produced some wonderful films, almost all of them managing to be box office hits as well as being thoughtful and often downright crusading. No mean achievement in a world that sometimes felt increasingly superficial.

There were a great many minority groups on both sides of the Atlantic who spoke of Hyacinth with something approaching reverence. Elizabeth suddenly wondered when her daughter had become a campaigner. Hyacinth had always had such a privileged and, indeed, charmed life. Untouched by violence or tragedy.

Then Elizabeth smiled to herself. 'What a question for me, of all people, to ask. She comes from a long line of reformers, after all. I'm too old,' she thought, 'I'm seeing problems where there aren't any.'

A minute later Julian's daughter, Francesca, came hurtling through the doorway and she was enveloped in a bear hug. "Aunt Elizabeth, we haven't seen you for ages, I've missed you! Uncle John says it's your fault, you've turned into an old stay-at-home!"

"Does he indeed?" laughed Elizabeth. "Wait till I

get him home! Seriously, Franny, we neither of us drive anymore and it's made us lazy. I promise we'll make more of an effort when the weather is warmer."

Another voice intervened, "I should think so. You're in danger of becoming a couple of hermits. Franny, let Aunt Elizabeth breathe, you're squashing her. Go and distract Jacqueline for a minute, there's a good girl." Kitty's amused tones rose above the mêlée of greetings that were beginning to reverberate through the suite.

Released from Franny's embrace, Elizabeth collapsed into the nearest chair.

"Kitty, you are so clever. You were right, it is wonderful to have everyone here together. I was just summoning up enough strength to enter the fray."

Kitty settled comfortably next to her. "It was Charlotte's wedding last year that made me realise how all our lives have been so interlinked. We're not family, yet in a way we've been closer than any family. I grew up knowing about your mother, and everything she did. Her courage influenced us all. My mother never stopped missing her really. When we were all Suffragettes together, if I wanted to go to a rally and Mum wasn't sure, Dad used to say, 'Now, Violet, what do you think Mary would do?'"

"Dear Harold," murmured Elizabeth. "He was such a stalwart, your father. Always there to support us all. Granny once told me that my mother was quite upset when Violet got engaged to him, and Violet told her very firmly that all men were not like Daniel. I find it so strange to think that Daniel was my father, you know. He must have been a dreadful man. I'm quite glad that I never knew him, after what he did to Mother and me. My poor mother didn't have a lot of luck, did she?"

"Except in her friends, I suppose," replied Kitty. "But she changed a lot of lives. Some people can use their own misfortune positively, and Mary was one of them. Why, without her and her travelling soup kitchens, Valerie would probably have died on the streets of London. Then where would I be? Percy would never have been born!"

The two women smiled at each other.

"I wish Rosalie could have been here. I still miss her, even though it's more than ten years now. And I know Percy does," said Kitty. "That's the worst bit about getting older. So many friends and relations gone. So many people to miss."

"I know. And time sort of telescopes. It doesn't seem two minutes since Alice died. I actually catch myself thinking occasionally, 'Oh, I'll ask Alice what she thinks'. Isn't that absurd? She and Anthony were wonderful to me when my mother was killed. They virtually brought me up. With Granny's help, of course."

"My goodness, Granny was a feisty lady," rejoined Kitty "I was only what they call a 'teenager' nowadays when she died but I remember her well. Mind you, I'm quite glad she didn't live long enough to know about Edward's death."

"So am I, though she'd have coped, as she always did. Come through it all somehow. That was a dreadful time. So many lives wasted. And for what? But in the end the only choice is to go on or go under. Well, *you* know all about that, Kitty."

The silence that fell between them was full of

mutual memories. Then Kitty broke the mood and grinned at her friend, suddenly looking much younger than her seventy-two years.

"But we've so much to be grateful for, Lizzie. We've had some high old times as well as the bad ones. How about when you all went together to vote for the first time? I couldn't vote because I was only twenty-five, but I went and stood outside and I was so proud. We'd done it! Women had the vote. At last. And we've seen such changes in our lifetime, cars, aeroplanes, telephones, films, oh, I could go on forever. But, best of all, I reckon is that we're allowed to wear sensible clothes nowadays. Goodness, do you remember the corsets!? Or 'stays' as Granny used to call them?"

The two women went into paroxysms of laughter, just as John's face appeared round the door.

"So what's all this merriment? Can anyone join in? You two are holding up proceedings, sitting there reminiscing when the rest of us are ready to have the first mince pies. It just won't do, I'm afraid. Jacqueline has sent me to round you up. I can tell you that she will brook no arguments. She's a very demanding young lady and becoming more and more impatient."

Kitty rose. "Right. I shall go and sort out my great-granddaughter immediately. You two come when you are ready. Don't be too long, though."

"We won't be two minutes," replied Elizabeth, "I just want a word with this husband of mine."

John seated himself in Kitty's chair and reached for his wife's hands. "What?" he demanded.

Elizabeth smiled at him. "Merry Christmas, darling. And I think I would like to say thank you, my love. It seems like a good moment."

"Whatever for?"

"For a lifetime of love. For letting me share your mother when I lost mine. For being my brother when Alice became my mother. For being my lover. For taking on a woman who was busy taking on the world. For all the years we've had together."

"Stuff and nonsense," replied her husband. "The pleasure, as they say, has been all mine." He leant forward to kiss her.

The strains of *Oh, come all ye faithful* filtered into the room as the door opened once more. Jacqueline appeared, exuding somewhat precocious authority

"Aunt Elizabeth and Uncle John, what *are* you doing? We want to start Christmas, you know. Please come. Everybody is waiting for you."

John rose and offered Elizabeth his arm. "We're coming, sweetheart. It's all your Aunt's fault. I'm afraid she is one of those women who has never known her place."

Chuckling, they followed Jacqueline into the dining-room.

The End

Made in the USA
Charleston, SC
02 January 2017